Dark

IN THE STRANGE labyrinth of pipes on the planet called Dark, things are falling apart. Dun doesn't want to be a hero, he just wants to find an answer to the terrifying dreams he's been having. But the answers, the real answers, are going to take him places he's never imagined and tear him from the only home he's ever known.

With only a half-made map from his missing father, he'll need all the help he can get. With an old friend, a new friend and the mysterious Myrch to guide him, he journeys through parts of his world he's never imagined.

Are his dreams real foretellings? Who can he trust to be who they say there are? What are the strange forces that seem to be literally pulling their world apart? As he travels through a world that is much bigger than he thought it was, he learns more about himself than he ever knew there was to know.

PAUL ARVIDSON is a forty-something ex lighting designer who lives in rural Somerset. He juggles his non-author time bringing up his children and fighting against being sucked into his wife's chicken breeding business. The Dark Trilogy is his first series.

Dark

Dark

a novel by

Paul L Arvidson

ISBN-13: 978-1535486682
ISBN-10: 1535486686

Ed. Lauren Schmeltz from Write Divas and cover by betibup33 from thebookcoverdesigner.com, both with grateful thanks.
Printed with CreateSpace
Available online from paularvidson.co.uk and real-life bookshops.

© Copyright Paul L Arvidson 2016

For Cheryl, Leah, and Nenna

Dark

Contents

Chapter One 13
Chapter Two 17
Chapter Three 27
Chapter Four 33
Chapter Five 37
Chapter Six 45
Chapter Seven 53
Chapter Eight 55
Chapter Nine 59
Chapter Ten 65
Chapter Eleven 71
Chapter Twelve 79
Chapter Thirteen 87
Chapter Fourteen 93
Chapter Fifteen 99
Chapter Sixteen 105
Chapter Seventeen 111
Chapter Eighteen 115
Chapter Nineteen 123
Chapter Twenty 131
Chapter Twenty-One 137
Chapter Twenty-Two 143
Chapter Twenty-Three 147
Chapter Twenty-Four 153
Chapter Twenty-Five 159
Chapter Twenty-Six 163
Chapter Twenty-Seven 169
Chapter Twenty-Eight 173
Chapter Twenty-Nine 179
Chapter Thirty 187
Chapter Thirty-One 193
Chapter Thirty-Two 197
Chapter Thirty-Three 201
Chapter Thirty-Four 205
Chapter Thirty-Five 213
Chapter Thirty-Six 223
Chapter Thirty-Seven 227
Chapter Thirty-Eight 231

Chapter Thirty-Nine 235
Chapter Forty 243
Chapter Forty-One 247
Chapter Forty-Two 253
Chapter Forty-Three 259
Chapter Forty-Four 265
Chapter Forty-Five 275
Chapter Forty-Six 279
Chapter Forty-Seven 287
Chapter Forty-Eight 295
Chapter Forty-Nine 301
Chapter Fifty 307
Chapter Fifty-One 315
Chapter Fifty-Two 323
Chapter Fifty-Three 327
Chapter Fifty-Four 333
Chapter Fifty-Five 339
Chapter Fifty-One 343
Chapter Fifty-Seven 349
Chapter Fifty-Eight 355
Chapter Fifty-Nine 359
Chapter Sixty 367
Next... Darker 369
Newsletter 377
Thank you 379

Dark

Dark

"This is Lt. Myrch Weston, service number NXBF-105345-GDT. Not that that matters overmuch now. I'm the last of the mission to Deepspace Colony Sirius 4, though the natives here call it Dark."

Excerpts from <Distress Beacon SN-1853001>.
Found by E.S.V Vixen Terradate: 26102225.

Dark

Chapter One

Dun sat bolt upright in the darkness. Eyes open. Heart battering. He could still feel it coming.

Churning cold metallic water, spray everywhere, his sinews twanged tight, heart banging, ears singing. At least that's blocking out the sound of... What? What is it? What in the Gods is it? It's coming, still coming. It's like it's, it's a hunger. Driven. Want and hate. Blood and bone. Closer. Closer and ... He inhaled a final struggling breath and shoved the horror in his head away.

He could hear his brothers and sisters making small stirring noises not far from him. He hoped he hadn't woken Mother too; he'd never hear the end of it. Since Father had disappeared, Mother had changed. Not close to him. Not warm. He'd become the man of the family and that was that. He still felt too young but what could he do? Someone had to hunt and forage while Mother cared for the little ones and he was the eldest. And now he was waking everyone more nights than not with these blasted dreams.

All that was familiar trickled into his brain: his bed of reeds underneath him, the drone of the fans, and the warm mammalian smell of his family. A new span in the Dark; time to wake up. The nightmares took longer to shake off. He dreamed of something pursuing him through tunnels, his calves deep in water. It was something horrible hunting him down. He ran and ran until his lungs felt like rags. Then, of course, as it got to him, he'd wake up. Every time he tried to get back to sleep, there it would be again, waiting.

He sighed. There was no telling Mother about his dreams. One day Father had gone out and had never come back. Just like that. It was like he'd ceased to exist. Once Father's smell had faded from their home, it grew harder and harder to remember he had ever been there.

Thinking about Father always made him feel a sharp sadness, even though it had happened two ages ago. Mother had pined, of course. Crying at night once she knew the babies were asleep. Hearing her weep in the darkness, Dun knew he'd be growing up faster than his friends. He couldn't talk to most of them about his concerns, except Padg. The others were busy playing and chasing each other as if nothing had happened; for them nothing had.

Padg, though, he had his own responsibilities. Being the son of the Shaman could do that. They'd known each other since they'd been the two youngest pups in the village. Padg had always been the most worldly of all their group, not averse to getting into trouble with the rest of them, but certainly averse to getting caught. He'd saved them all from many a beating. Now with Father gone, it felt to Dun like Padg was the only one he could talk to. Odd. The sense of responsibility Dun felt he'd had thrust upon him, Padg had been born with.

***

After breakfast and helping Mother feed the little ones, Dun went out, slamming the rush door behind him. He walked to the wooden span across the massive river pipe; the crossing that gave the Bridge-folk their name. From there, it was easy to follow the rope path to the village. He needed to reach the Shaman's compound on the opposite side of the village if he wanted to talk to Padg about why he'd been feeling so odd.

Out of the burrow, he was enveloped by the hum of smell and noise from the village. Some kind of auction of a new piece of found tech seemed to be taking place in the market. He heard raised voices, oddly (usually trading in Bridge-town was a good-natured affair). He couldn't process any of it today. It was all he could do to follow the rope guides underfoot without walking into anything. His head buzzed. He was relieved to finally reach the woven gate and the wisps of incense and worked wood told him he'd reached his destination.

"Dunno..." was all his friend could muster after Dun retold his dream.

"Well, thanks for that; great help."

"I mean, it might be something, it might be nothing."

"Somehow, none of today is working out how I'd planned," Dun sighed.

A breeze outside stirred the wooden wind chimes beside the lean-to shed Padg used as his workshop. Dun stretched out his arm to feel along the rack that held his friend's work in progress. He felt twisted bamboo staves that would be made into sword-spears, preferred weapon among the Bridge-folk. A shup-shup-shup sound indicated Padg had resumed work with sanding the sword-spear at his bench. The sword was made out of the extremely hard, woody stem of one of the larger fungi growing in the depths; it didn't stay sharp for very long, but long enough. The hunters usually carried two or three strapped to their backs for good measure. Padg carved particularly well; he was especially good at forming the helical twist in the shaft of the weapon that made it fly true when thrown.

"Padg? Hello?"

"Hush, I'm sanding."

"Oh."

The rhythm of the sanding was a reassuring odd kind of tune with the wooden, just musical, clunking of the chimes.

"Padg?"

"Sanding? Tricky. Needs concentration."

"Sorry, it's just..."

The sanding block clattered to the floor.

"Right! I give up," Padg said. "Grab a rod from the rack; there's some scraps in the bucket. You need something to occupy your hands."

Fishing was always Padg's go-to in a crisis. They left through the back flap of Padg's workshop and headed to his favorite spot: a rusted through hole at the top of the massive pipe. They scrambled up the side using massive bolt heads in the metal surface of the pipe as a makeshift ladder. Once at the top they gathered their kit, baited the long lines necessary to get down far enough and let each one fall through the hole with a satisfying 'plop'.

They fished for a while in companionable silence. A lazy breeze, scented faintly with vinegar, drifted up through the hole.

"Detail!" Padg cried suddenly.

"Eh?" Dun cocked his head, bewildered.

"Detail, my friend. That's what was bothering me."

"Good, I'm glad. Care to tell me why?"

"Your dream. Most peoples' dreams are vague, full of confused smells, feelings, sometimes sounds. You know, the I was there with my friend but it was really my sister and then the tunnel became my house, kind of thing. Yours felt like you were there."

"You can say that again," Dun said.

"Maybe you were."

"What do you mean?"

"Just what I said. Maybe you were there. Or at least maybe you will be."

"You're talking in riddles."

"Might be I'm not explaining it right. Listen, Dad talks about this kind of stuff all the time. You sit around and hear enough of it, and you kind of get a feel for it. Let's go back and find him; I think he'll be able to help. Besides, the fishing's rubbish today."

Chapter Two

"Do you know what foretelling is, Dun?" The voice of Barg the Shaman was deep and reassuring. Dun guessed that came with the job.

"No."

Dun, Padg, and his father enjoyed the warmth of the small air vent in the hut. Many of the shared buildings and all homes had a vent somewhere. They all came out of the ground or walls and delivered air in varying temperatures and smells, ending usually in a metal grill or mesh. The vent in Barg's floor had the unusual combination of a warm air flow and no smell other than a slight tinge of metal. This allowed Barg to place bags of herbs on the grill, which warmed by the air flow, would permeate the hut. Dun felt wrapped in perfume: the sweet and the spicy, the nutty and the resinous; too enveloped and overwhelmed to work out one smell from the next. It was a warm blanket of aroma, comforting and welcoming.

"Have you been sleeping well, Dun?"

"Well...er...no. Not really."

The Shaman didn't reply. Dun felt he had to fill the void, but his brain skittered to work out exactly what to say, without sounding foolish.

"I've been dreaming quite a bit. Every rest. Usually several times each rest."

"And you've been remembering them all, in great detail?"

"Yes. How did you..."

"Getting more compelling, more vital?"

"Yes."

Somewhere in the depths of the vent Dun could hear the ping of metal expanding. The Shaman made a non-committal humming sound.

"When they first started, they were weird. On the inside of my head. Noises and scents but really vivid, quite random. Then there was this odd sensation... Like tingling or prickling, waves of something, blankets maybe but not, sometimes filling the whole of the inside of my head and hurting. I'm not describing this very well."

"Those are called extra-sensory factors."

"Oh?"

"Things that you can't describe in sounds, touch, smell, taste or air-sense. It takes a while to get used to those, but you will. They're something that you won't really make a lot of, unfortunately. We don't know what they mean. They come in different types; some foretellers have called them flavors; it helps to categorize them, but ultimately it's hard to tell what they might mean. Historically, foretellers tend to ignore them, to be honest."

Dun was so lost in his own thoughts in the effort to take everything in. Barg filled the gap this time.

"Have the dreams been getting more consistent? Recurring?"

"I've been having one dream that has, yes."

"What happens?"

"I'm running along one of the rivers, in a tunnel and I'm being chased by something. A horrible something. It's hunting me. It won't give up and it's gaining on me. But I can't smell it or air-sense it; I just know it's coming. Almost, but not quite like, I know what it's thinking... A horrible 'other' thing."

"The same every time?"

"Yes, well, starting the same every time, but it seems like there's some more each time. Like a story?" Dun had intended his tone to be rhetorical, but Barg answered.

"Yes, like a story. Except this one may be real. And you may be in it."

"Hey, I said that," Padg chipped in.

"Thank you, Padg," his father replied. "You have been listening all these years. It is a shame, though, that you've never had the foretelling gift."

Dark

"Curse, more like."

"Padg!" The Shaman could crack his voice like a whip.

"Sorry, Father."

"What do you mean, 'curse?'" Dun asked, worried.

"Some people find the responsibility that comes with the gift of foretelling too much for them."

"That's the folk it doesn't drive bats!"

"Padg! That's quite enough. This is a serious discussion of a very serious matter. If you can't listen seriously then go outside. Young Dun here has the gift of foretelling whether he wants it or not. What matters now is that he understands it and what he does with it."

"Sorry."

"Hmm."

A distant clang echoed up the air vent with a sigh of acrid air.

"So is it the future then? I'm experiencing the future?"

"No. Not exactly. Sometimes it may be the future, sometimes it can be the past, sometimes it is a foretelling from far away. Neither your future or your past."

"So what use is that to me? Or to anyone?"

"That is for you to decide," Berg said. "That is what makes the difference between a good Foreteller and Mad-folk. That is the riddle that is foretelling."

"So you can't tell me what my dream meant?"

"No. Only you can know that. All I can say is that you do have the gift."

"But this dream," he corrected himself, "foretelling seemed so real. And it's not happened to me yet, so it must be my future, mustn't it?"

"Each foretelling appears from the mind of someone there, sometimes many minds. All of that appears in *your* mind. It seems like it's come from you. This is a lot to take in for one day, my young friend. Go home and think about it. Return to me after the next rest, and we'll talk some more."

Dun left the hut in a daze, foretelling, multiple futures, madness, extra-sensory-whatever-the-hells-they-were. He already had way more responsibility than ever he felt ready for, and now this. It was a long while before Dun realized Padg was still there walking alongside him, and to be honest with himself, Dun hadn't the first idea where he was going. He let his legs and the noisy current of folk carry him, while his conscious brain wasn't occupied with the task of directing him. The smell of Dodg's sweet-food stall on the market hit him just before he hit it.

"Dun!" Padg laughed.

"Sorry—in another world there."

Feeling guilty for dragging his friend halfway across the village, Dun felt in his shoulder bag for some trade strips he knew still carried some credit. He could smell the Sweetcrackle dried mushrooms on the stand. He asked for two handfuls and handed over the wooden trade strip. The sound of a few brief scratches followed as Dodg made tallies on it, before handing it back to Dun.

"Thanks."

The friends walked on munching side by side for a while. They tried to give the bowl in the center of the village, where auctions usually took place, a wide berth. The rowdy market that Dun had heard earlier seemed to have descended into a full-blown row. The raised voices of Bridge-folk seemed to be interspersed with the nasal shrieks of a group of River-folk traders.

"You don't think that'll happen to me do you?" Dun said.

"What?" Padg said. "Foretelling? Sounds like it already has."

"No, not the foretelling or whatever it's called; the going mad."

"Don't know. Probably not."

Probably. That was reassuring. Well, he'd have to settle for that for now, while he worked out what exactly was going on inside his head. Until then, he was supposed to do chores. Mother would need him by now. It would be chaos there, though; the pups fighting, Mother shouting. It wasn't much better staying here, whatever the hells was going on today. He needed time alone to think. He said good-bye to Padg. Maybe another go at some fish?

***

Dun crept back through the rush door of the family home at River-hole. It was eerily quiet. Maybe Mother had taken the little ones to crêche in the village; it was about that time. He searched for his hunting bag. His mother had made it for his father, and Dun felt awkward using it. The bag was a traditional folk woven one from reeds, as opposed to the recent trends of making bags out of materials from found-things. Dun didn't have much to do with found-things. Not particularly because of the inherent danger or because of any traditionalist streak in him, but mostly because they were usually so damned expensive. The market traders and traveling visitors from the Machine-folk who collected and sold found-things made plenty of trade tallies to offset the risks they took, but on the whole, Dun didn't get it. For most problems, there was a folk generated solution available, cheaper or free, and that suited him fine. He swung the bag over his shoulder and made for the passage that led from the family room down to the river. The texture of the bag in his hands was strangely comforting today.

He could feel the cloud of fresh moisture many strides before he reached the river. The sensation was something he took for granted. It permeated the whole tribe's life, his family's especially since of all the tribe, they lived closest to it, their home called "River-hole" due to a convenient tunnel to the bank. The noise of the water rose and fell with the seemingly random levels of the river, quieter today as it happened, but it was always there. He walked down to the edge of the water; there was the walkway along the edge of the river. He walked the familiar route to his favorite fishing place, underfoot the textured metal mesh lightly crunching with rust. Stopping at his usual place, just after the air grill on the wall, he lay down on his belly, arm in the water, to wait.

Patience was one of his strong points. He was always able to distract himself in one part of his brain, working out what he'd do next, planning ahead, while another part of him lay in wait, wired and sprung to pounce. A swish in the water and a fish would be caught, stunned and in his bag. That is, if a fish came along. He twitched his fingers. Funny, it seemed like he was having to reach farther down today, to even reach the water. Ah well, everything today seemed like more effort. Maybe, it was his attitude he should be focussing on...

"Aaaaaaaang!"

In the water, the blood, his hand, the pain. Something churning in the water. Angry, cold, alien. He snatched his hand out, sure to feel blood dripping down his arm but no. His hand was fine, wet with water, but fine. He wiggled his fingers. What the hell was going on? His pulse hammered. The dreaming, foretelling, again? While he was awake? He could scarcely cope with it every night. Would it be every night? Gods, he hoped not. He forced his breath slowly through his teeth.

Whether or not he could stand it, he was starting to understand the folk who couldn't. When he was very young, there was someone from the village who had started behaving oddly. Beng? Or was it Teng? Dun couldn't recall, but he could remember that the poor unfortunate became more and more strange and disassociated, talking to himself, arguing with absent demons. Eventually, you couldn't smell him in the village and no one talked about him anymore. Now Dun knew why. He was beginning to imagine how this new "gift" could easily crack someone. The sleeplessness alone was enough to fray him at the edges.

He slowly clenched and unclenched his hand. He had the gift, want it or not, and he was just going to have to cope. There was no one else.

A cramp in his shoulder told Dun how long he'd been there. It never normally took this much effort to find a catch. He moved his spot to somewhere farther upstream, a spot he liked less but nearer the village bridge where the pipe turned. It was busier there. Dun didn't like the disturbance, people going into the village, the noise of the market more obvious, but it was a sure place to catch something. He waited again. Slowly a chilling feeling crept up his insides; he carried on fishing, trying to quell it, but in the end, he had to let the obvious overwhelm him. No fish. There were no fish.

Dark

There had always been fish. How could there not be? He sat back on his haunches, head in his hands trying to think. The family would be fine—there were mushrooms he could find if he wanted—but that wasn't the point. They'd be fine for now. All the Bridge-folk would be fine for now. But fish were an important part of what everyone had to eat. And then there was trade, although the woven weed bags that the Bridge-folk produced were very fine, by far the most important trade good was the fish. And there was something else he couldn't put his finger on. A tickling in the back of his mind. Something important. He had all the fragments, but he couldn't make them into one piece. Something was terribly wrong. One of the Elders in the village needed to know. Now.

He went straight to the Shaman's hut. All he heard when he got in earshot was the snick-snick of Padg whittling. Dun could tell the noise of Padg's carving from twenty or thirty strides away.

"Padg!"

"Hey! What's wrong? You're panting."

"Where's your father?"

"Some meeting of the elders in the Moot-hall. Why?"

Dun grabbed Padg by his shoulder and pulled him up to standing. The sword-spear he was working on fell to the floor with a clatter.

"Hells! Do you know how long those things take to sharpen?"

Dun kept pulling. "Come on, we've got to go there. Now!"

Padg stopped resisting and fell into an easy lope, alongside Dun. "Why?"

"Fish!" Dun shouted.

"Eh?"

"There's no fish. In the river. None."

"Gods!"

They slowed only as they reached the Moot-hall, a long low building built like the rest of the village hut dwellings from reeds and mud, but this was the largest building in the village and had the added feature of double-skinned walls, stuffed on the inside with fur to damp down noise from inside and out. However, no amount of auditory dampening or protection was going to hide the raised voices heard when the friends arrived.

"...care how important this is. He's too young!"

Padg grabbed Dun and pulled him down into a crouch, just around the edge of the Moot-hall from its door.

"He's wise for his years."

"But not many of those!"

"He's perfectly capable."

"Enough!" The voice of Ardg, the village Alpha, was heard loudly, and then more quietly he said, "We have no choice."

"But we would be sending him to certain... danger. Why can we not send a fully grown band of hunters?"

"You know why, Greng. We and only we of the Elders-moot know of the other threat that faces us. We must act with that in mind."

"How goes the discussion with our River-folk 'guest?'" Dun made out the odd, deep tones of Myrch, the Alpha's most recent advisor.

"He still won't tell us what he was searching for." A female voice was Swych's, the head of the Hunter's Guild.

"Though clearly up to no good, poking through the Bibliotheca. All of our records and maps?" Myrch said.

"We have nothing to hide," Ardg said.

"You say that like it's a good thing," Myrch said.

Both Padg and Dun were lifted off their feet swiftly and silently, gripped by the scruff from behind.

"People who listen at doors, get bent noses."

Dark

The quiet, precise voice carried almost no scent. It could only be Swych, head of the hunter's guild and tutor to both Padg and Dun in fighting and tracking and stalking food.

Dun and Padg, in mid-air, were still too stunned to reply. She had come out of nowhere, like a wraith, without even disturbing the air.

"Now what should we do with a pair of ear-flapping vagabonds, eh?" Swych said, hauling them up effortlessly. "I think we'll let Ardg decide what punishment is fitting."

With that, she swirled them around the corner and kicked the door to the Moot-hall deftly, so it swung inward.

"Friends, Elders, our meeting is adjourned. I have found some skulkers at the door jamb. What punishment do we deem fit?"

"Ah," the Alpha said when the scent of Dun and Padg quickly followed them into the hut. "I suspect what we have to say to these young rogues may be punishment enough."

Chapter Three

"But the fish?" Dun tried not to stutter.

"Pardon?"

"Fish." Facing the Alpha it was all Dun could muster. So far his day had not worked out at all how he'd planned.

"I think for all concerned here, you'll need to be just a little clearer."

"Gone. They're all gone."

"The fish?"

Ardg, despite winning his role as village Alpha in combat, had spent many years in his position perfecting his diplomacy and forbearance against, what some would consider, extreme odds.

"Yes."

"Ah."

The low muttering next to Ardg was Myrch, the advisor, but it was too quiet for Dun to hear.

"That is worrying. We will investigate the matter of the fish in due course. We're glad you came, Dun; we wanted to talk to you. About another matter." He paused. "There's something you can do for us, for everyone."

"Me?"

"Yes," Ardg replied simply. "It has come to our attention that some old neighbors of ours, the Machine-folk, have gone very quiet. They are not near neighbors—they live far upstream—but we have not had a whisker-twitch of them for some time."

Dun and Padg listened intently but still weren't sure where they might come into it themselves. After all, they were the first to realize that in terms of the tribe, they were very small reeds in a very big basket.

"We usually meet them once a cycle at the tribes-moot fair," the Alpha continued. "They have occasionally missed a cycle; some tribes do sometimes; it isn't unusual. However, they send traders here all the time but no one has bumped into any of them for nearly an eon and now, pieces of found-tech are making their way here, brought by River-folk. That is troubling."

Dun twitched. From his tone, what the Alpha said was true, but equally, there was something he wasn't saying. He tried to think of what he knew of the Machine-folk. They came to the tribes-moots, of course, bringing some kind of clever mechanical toy or more often beautiful and useful pieces of rare metal. There were rumors about them being the custodians of wonderful machines. They could predict the future, could read your mind, that kind of thing and more. Dun was starting to realize that most of what he knew was conjecture and rumor; that was going to be of little help to him. Dun furrowed his brow. Not enough to go on.

"The tribe needs to send a small hunting party to check that all is well. We have chosen you, Dun, to fulfill this task, and you must choose who will go with you. Also, you must decide what provisions and equipment you need to fulfill your task. This will be provided by the tribe. Consider this wisely. Tonight there is feasting for Old Gryr; he has hung up his hunting spear this cycle, and it is time to celebrate his victories. Tomorrow we will talk again. Until then you must speak of this to no one."

"But, why choose me? There are plenty of older, smarter, tougher folk than me," Dun said

"There are. It is you we have chosen, nonetheless." Again, there was more that Ardg wasn't saying, but his tone brooked no argument.

"Mother and the little ones? Who will take care of them? Since Father..."

"The tribe will keep your people safe, rest assured, young Dun."

"May I go and think about it? It's ... a lot."

"We would expect no less."

***

"It's a lot..." He didn't finish his sentence in the tent. He didn't finish it as he stumbled outside. He couldn't finish it later, as he wandered through the village. There was just "a lot". A lot in his head. A lot of fear about what he was getting into. A lot he didn't know, and that frightened him most of all. There were many, many pieces to this puzzle, and he only had one or two. He felt like he was walking straight into the jaws of some horrible cave hunting predator. Something that sat with its jaws wide open and waited. Waited till someone was right on its tongue and then...

A pain seared through Dun's leg. Padg was laughing.

"Ow! What was that for?"

"Well, you've been such great company today, I had to entertain myself somehow."

"Ow," Dun said again, more quietly this time. He sat and rubbed his shin.

"So," Padg said. Half-question, half-statement.

"So?"

Padg left a gap in the conversation that a cart could've been pulled through. Then, as Dun was drawing breath to reply, he said as quickly as he could, "So are you going to take me with you on this stupid errand or what?"

"Oh. That."

"Oh! Yes of course that. What have you been brooding but not talking to me about, for gods' know how long?"

"Sorry," Dun said, back-footed. "I didn't know if you'd want to."

"Hmm...the biggest adventure of either of our lives and you're not sure if I'd want to? Did it ever occur to you that you need to take someone to prevent you getting your miserable hide eaten or lost?"

"Well, yes."

"And so?"

"So?"

Dark

"You still haven't asked me!"

"Oh. Sorry. Will you come with me?"

"I might be busy..."

Dun sprung on Padg shouting "ratbag!" and they rolled over the ground, crashing into a fence and earning a stern "hey!" from its owner. The play fight lasted some time, until Padg got the better of his old friend and sat astride his neck. Dun tapped his leg in a gesture of defeat. They sat on the ground panting.

"You know it's going to be really dangerous?" Dun said.

"Yes?" Padg replied.

"No, I mean *really* dangerous."

"Come on," Padg said. "Let's work while we talk. I know a secret Myconid-folk cave a good walk from here. No one goes there; there are good pickings, and it means you're not going back empty-handed to your mother if there's no fish."

"Ever the practical one, eh?"

"I just know your mother. She scares me."

So the friends walked and talked, keeping air-senses open for anyone else near, but Padg's cave, just as he'd said, was some way from the village. The passage was accessed by squeezing through a damaged grating at floor level, just large enough for the two friends. Padg was right; a full-grown adult would not fit. Sometime after all sound of the village and the river had died away, Dun began again.

"I don't think I'm explaining this well. By dangerous I mean, endangering-the-whole-tribe dangerous. More, if that were possible."

"How do you know? The dreams?"

"Not the dreams exactly. At least, not what's in them. It's just a feeling I get when I'm in the dream. And now, when I'm awake too."

"What kind of dangerous? You know, I wouldn't let you go alone. Death doesn't bother me; I've been trained as a hunter. So have you."

"Not death, at least not just death. Worse than that, somehow. It's really not that clear in the dreams."

"Great. Already I'm not enjoying the role of 'Foreseer's companion'. You get to scare the hairs off me and then say, 'Oh, it's really not that clear. Just worse than death.' Great."

"Listen, I'm not very good at this yet. I'm just saying I hope you know what you're agreeing to before you get too far in."

"You haven't really agreed yourself yet, from what I remember in the Moot-hall," Padg reminded Dun.

"True. But I think I have to. You've got a choice."

"Not if you're going."

And so it was decided.

***

The first two members of the party to hunt and find the Machine-folk sat in the warmth of the Moot-hall and listened to the village skald, Ebun, sing the Ballad of Yarra and Jaris. No one knew how old the song was, but it was old indeed. They'd heard its strains scores of times since being small; it was a favorite at festivals and feasts, but somehow this time there was a new romance to it; a frisson of knowing that they were on the verge of the kind of journey that was worthy of a song.

Ballad of Yarra and Jaris

In the place of long ago, outside the egg upon its back
Yarra looked upon the deep—and her shimmered hair was black
Resplendent in the void and deep—and her shimmered hair was black.

Jaris came and warmed her heart—he came to her along the track
Came from the deep and warmed her heart—he came to her along the track.

Dark

*They loved as one an eons breadth—and half was
warm and half was black
They loved as none before or since—and half was
warm and half was black.*

*And then a one came in between—she felt her heart
begin to crack
The darkest face came in between—she felt her heart
begin to crack.*

*Then he was gone and never seen—and none was
warm and all was black
He faded went and never seen—and none was warm
and all was black.*

*Then we climbed back inside the egg—how long to wait
till he came back
Returned ourselves inside the egg—how long to wait
till he came back?*

      Dun heard no more of the ballad that night as the strain overtook him and he slept. Padg hadn't the heart to wake him.

Chapter Four

Dun's family had always been unusual in that they didn't live in a hut. "River-hole" comprised two dirt-floored rooms near a short tunnel which led to the pipe and the river. Why they had wound up there Dun didn't know. He supposed there might have been a story if he pestered his mother, but he couldn't bring himself to. She still seemed lost in her own world.

Living there certainly had its perks. Besides the obvious benefit of being so close to the river, something the family had always made the most of, there were odd storage compartments on the walls and nooks and crannies for the children to play in. The floor beneath them was always strangely warm but without an air vent. Not a huge difference, but noticeable when you went outside. Beneath a covering of packed soil in their rooms, the base floor was a metal; Dun had dug down in a corner one day as a child.

Mother and Father must have moved earth in from elsewhere to make things more comfortable. Thinking about it now, their home had so many advantages, it was strange that an Elder didn't live there. They must have done something to be allowed to live there? Dun started to think life was turning out like the floor in their house; scratch the surface a little and something odd laid not that far below.

"Oi! Dozy!" Padg shouted at the rush door, rattling the door in its frame.

"Oh sorry," Dun said.

"Rough sleep?"

"No, not too bad..." Dun began absently

"Good. Let's go back to our hut," Padg said. "Father's not in. He's off having another Elders' meeting. We need to plan."

Dun grabbed his bag and off they went.

On the way through the village, passing the edge of the market stalls, Padg piped up, "If I'm providing the venue, you're providing the provisions."

Dark

"Sounds fair."

Dun dug out his tally sticks and bought two cups of burnt-smelling, bitter-dry Racta in wooden cups from one vendor and two handfuls of sweet crackle from Dodg. The middle of the village was oddly quiet. A hiatus after something? He was clearly thinking too hard. Dun shook his head, and they went back to the hut. Padg sat Dun down on a log, then rustled off into distant corners, searching for who knew what. After a few moments and a grunt of satisfaction, he returned to the log and prodded a stylus and a bark-roll into Dun's hands.

"What's this?" Dun said.

"List," Padg replied, with that tone of certainty that previous times even Dun had found annoying. Oddly, this time, Dun found it comforting. More than that, he had a creeping suspicion the traits in question could just save their lives.

"Check these off."

"Go ahead."

"Firstly, weapons: me." The low scraping of stylus on bark filled the tent.

"You?" Dun asked, slightly too surprised.

"Yes," Padg returned. "Even Orsn the Maker said my stuff is really good now. I can carve a sword-spear that flies true, make pipe darts, knives, bolas. I've been collecting stuff."

"Stockpiling? Whatever for?"

"I was going to start trading them, but it seems like they've got a different fate now. I've got knives and a stack of sword-spears that I'm really pleased with. I spent ages foraging the plants for them but I found this odd group of plants way out toward where the Myconid-folk live. Took me ages to get them but they're rock hard and sharpen up really well. There's a bit more weight to them too so they fly really good."

"Wow," Dun said. "What's next here? Food."

"Food: We've got to guess this, but say, twelve spans there and twelve back; allows six spans to explore."

Thirty spans; that was a whole cycle. The scale of this whole undertaking was slowly sinking in for Dun, and it was one of the many things he wasn't comfortable with.

Padg continued his train of thought. "We probably want something we can eat easily; something we don't have to cook and that doesn't weigh much. Dried mushrooms, caked fish—that kind of thing. We might find fresh stuff on the way, but we can't count on that."

"And there's no fish," Dun reminded.

"Okay, true. Next: bed-rolls," Dun said. "I can get us some from home. We've always got spares. Mother weaves them when she's bored."

"Add some packs with shoulder straps," Padg said. "All this stuff won't carry in just bags; there'll be too much. Plus it keeps our hands free should we need to fight."

"Who in the gods would we fight?" Dun tried to hide the rising tension in his voice.

"Dunno. Bandits maybe? It has been known. There are supposed to be big arachnoids in the deepest caves, not that I know anyone who's met one. And then there's whatever the hells that thing in your dream is. That hardly seems friendly, does it?"

"No." Dun swallowed. "I don't suppose it is."

After a pause, Padg pushed on. "What else? Rope? We'll need to go to the weavers for that. Is your Aunt Danya still the weavers' guild leader?"

"Yes, she'll recommend us something good. She may have backpacks too."

"Clicker-beetle and grubs for timekeeping; got those back here somewhere," Padg said. There was a scratch as Dun ticked the scroll.

"Healing stuff from the midwives?

"We should probably pay them a visit. There may be things we've not thought of."

"Padg?"

"What?"

"There's been something bothering me this morning," Dun began hesitantly.

"Well, if it's about supplies or equipment, I thought we were going out now to collect the last bits we need and then sleep on any final 'forgets' and pick them up before we leave next span?"

"No it's not that; I think we're on top of most things and between us, I think we know what we need later. No, I had another dream last night."

"Oh good, more doom. I was beginning to miss that."

"No, not doom this time. More a feeling."

"Go on."

"Well, this is going to sound odd, but we were in a particularly dull part of our journey, sometime soon, plodding along. I wasn't sure exactly where we were, or even what our surroundings were..."

"Sounds like one of your foretellings; I'm beginning to enjoy their particular non-specific, not-all-that-helpful nature."

Dun ignored the jibe and continued, "But one thing I *was* sure of. There weren't just the two of us."

"What? We were being followed? Didn't you cover that part of the foretelling in the bit about the slavering monster?"

"No, it wasn't that at all. There was someone else in our party. Someone with us. Padg, I think we need to find someone else."

"Oh," Padg said, a bit floored. "I know Father's already said this to you or something like, but you know not to take all of this too seriously, right? I mean, some of the things you dream might not be our future, or yours. Some of the possibilities don't come true because of your choices—all that kind of thing. Because if you do take it too seriously, pretty soon you can't take a pee without having dreamed about it first."

"No, I know." Dun giggled, the tension released. "I was just saying, is all. I guess it just feels like an unanswered question."

"Hmm. Come on, let's go find some questions we can answer—to the midwives," Padg said.

Chapter Five

Midwives in the tribes were respected, and a prestigious, high-status path to take that males and females sought to pursue it in equal measure. Along with the expected duties of delivering the young and caring for the mothers of the tribe, the role in the tribe had spread to cover all of the healing too, except where the spiritual requirements overlapped the Shaman's work. The swirling smells of the garden made detecting people outside almost impossible, and varying levels of noise in the large series of huts that made up the infirmary meant listening wasn't always an option, so there was a bell hung from the door of the nearest hut to the village. It was a large piece of metal, beaten by the village maker into an instrument that would "bong" satisfactorily when hit with the mushroom-wood beater that hung below it.

Padg stepped up and bonged. The two stood and waited for the last harmonics to die away before the hut door creaked open. They heard someone puffing behind it; an apprentice, presumably.

"Sari is very busy today, supervising making salves. What do you want?" the apprentice said in a too proud manner.

Padg had recognized Porf from the puffing before the door opened. Although worst in all their classes at fighting or hunting, Porf had shown a gift for the healer's arts, and he knew it.

"What we want," Padg started, deliberately, "is to be taken to your guild leader, Porf. We've got tribe business, and you'd do well to be quick about it."

"Wait here then," Porf said stiffly, "I'll go and get her."

"He asked for that," Dun said, once Porf had puffed off out of earshot.

"He's been asking for it for a long, long while."

"Are you all right?" Dun asked.

"I'm fine; just have my head filled up with details, and I want to get going now."

"Yes, I know how you feel. I want to be on our way already, but I don't want to miss anything out..."

"That might potentially kill us," Padg finished.

"I wasn't going to be that blunt," Dun said.

'Ah, but that's why you've got me along."

"Dun and Padg, I presume?" The voice of Sari, head of the midwives-guild, cut through their merriment, along with a waft of something floral and astringent smelling, which clung to her robes. Whatever it was she was supervising the making of, it smelled like powerful stuff. "I heard from Ardg that you might be visiting. What can I do for you?"

"We need you to send us off with... err... with everything we should be taking on a journey," Dun said.

His answer from Sari was a bell-peal of laughter.

"If I sent you out with everything possible, you'd hardly be able to walk."

"It's just- I've never really done this before," Dun began in explanation.

"Don't worry, Dun," Sari said in a warm but gently mocking voice. "We'll sort you out with an emergency kit. We make them quite often for travelers and traders. It should have most things in that you'll need. I think we have one ready made up here somewhere."

She clapped her hands twice, sharply. From somewhere nearby, the apprentice shuffled into the room.

"Good. Porf, go back to the workshop and under my bench, there should be an emergency kit already. If there is, bring it here. Hurry now."

And off he scuttled, returning with a rustling bundle that Sari unrolled on the floor in front of Dun and Padg inviting them to sit and get acquainted with what was in the bundle.

"These are vials of wound-heal," she began, passing the small stoppered bottles to Dun and Padg in turn. "Please, open them, smell, get familiar with the texture."

They did and it answered the question about what it was that clung to her robes.

"I must ask you to try and return all the empty bottles to us. They are found-things, you know, and so hard to come by. This powder"—she passed them a bag as she talked—"is a fever-cure. It does not work on all diseases, but it does help your own body fight off many things." She paused, searching out her next item. "These leaves, from river-thistle, help stave off sleep. These, from jad-in-the-wall, help promote it. And the paste in this bag is a blood cleanser. If you become poisoned or bitten by something unclean, this will slow the poison and allow you a chance to heal."

She waited while their quickest of lessons sank in. "You understand what you have? There are bandages and pads in there too."

"Er- yes," Dun said. "Thank you."

"You're both welcome. I wish you a good journey and my best hope is that you need none of it."

"Ours too," Padg said.

"Oh, one more thing, if we may?" Dun asked.

"Yes?"

"You wouldn't, by any chance, have someone that wants to come along with us? Would you?"

Again that laugh from Sari. "It would be an interesting outing for an apprentice, I think. Sadly we have no one to spare. You might try the Alchemists' guild; you may have more luck there," Sari said and went back inside.

"Right," Padg said. "Alchemists then."

The Alchemist's guild was as far upstream of the village as it was possible to go. Dun and Padg could tell their proximity to it by two signs: Firstly the sulfur and carbon smell was unmistakable, and secondly, there was a high earth bank all the way around. The only entrance through this protective levee was riverside, down a small path.

Dark

They could hear a classroom style recitation, the echoes of call and response drifting out to them through the door of the large building.

"... metal, earth, air, and blood..."

As was traditional, on the right-hand side of the front door was an announcing post. The alchemists' front door was no different. It usually featured a symbol of the house, hung, carved or in relief, and some kind of noise-making device. Dun felt for a string and found a complicated six-pointed star, tied to a long piece of river string. Dun tweaked the string. A loud glassy tinkling noise came from farther up the post; the string, it seemed, was tied to some of those glass tubes the alchemists seemed so fond of using.

"...metal, earth, air, and blood..."

The door creaked open with a whiff of sulfur and a sniffling noise.

"Hello, can I help you?" the small voice attached to the sniffle enquired.

Dun formulated a reply carefully in his head; he knew Tali and quite liked her.

"Only, if you could hurry?" Tali said. "I've kind of left a beaker on the heater and... it's a bit finely balanced...and...y'know..."

There was a faint tinkle from inside.

"Oh..."

Then a "crump", felt more than heard.

"Oh shreds..."

The whoomph that followed ripped the door off its post and threw it. Dun caught the door full in the face and Padg caught Tali.

They lay on the floor in that hiatus that follows an explosion. Dust, debris, and the alchemist's door chimes fell all around them.

"Nice," Padg said, coughing.

"Yeah," Tali said. "Can you... er...? You're leaning on my..."

"Oh, sorry," Padg said. Tali stood, brushing off debris.

Dun rolled himself out from under the door. "I... er... don't suppose your Master is in, is he?"

"Oh gods," Tali said. "You know I kind of thought I might avoid him for a span or two."

"Avoid whom?" came a deep voice. From Dun's air-sense he could tell that the person speaking virtually filled the doorway, in each direction. The smell of rust and sulfur hung with the question.

"We need to talk to him now," Padg hissed to Tali. "Dun here has something important to ask him."

"Okay," Tali said.

"There'd better be a good excuse for this. A very good excuse," Gatryn said in a voice not used to contradiction.

"Can we borrow an alchemist?" Padg said cheerfully.

"Borrow?" Gatryn said sternly. "An alchemist is not a piece of laboratory equipment, an alembic to be returned once washed!"

"Rather," Dun backtracked, "can we ask your permission to let someone come with us on-" He stopped, not sure how to carry on without saying too much.

"That is, we've been asked by the Alpha to go..."

"... exploring," Padg butted in. "We've got the village map to update."

"How interesting," Gatryn said suspiciously. "And you need an Alchemist why?"

"Well... for... making..." Dun struggled.

"Paper!" Padg said. "Spare... y'know. Paper..."

The sound of dragging furniture and sweeping of glass came from within.

"Can you take this one?" Gatryn said.

"This?"

"Alchemist. Despite Tali falling behind in her studies by trotting off on some 'scribe's errand' that could equally well be done by traders, she might learn something at that. And we might all appreciate the calm around here for a while. You'd like to go?"

"Great!" she said, a little too brightly, then a little more levelly, "with your permission, Master Gatryn, I'd like to go."

"Well, if that's all the disturbance, for now, I've got a class to finish. I'm sure you three have much to discuss."

"Thank you, Master Gatryn," Tali said.

Then as he left, over his shoulder, he added, "Oh and do try and bring Tali back in one piece. She is a handful, but we've all gotten used to her around here." He sighed. "Although I don't suppose it's any more dangerous out there than it is in here, is it?"

As if to punctuate his sentence there was another low frequency "oumph", then a faint whiff of rotted fish.

"Nice," Padg said.

"Ahh," Gatryn sighed, "duty calls. Good luck on your journey."

When Gatryn was out of earshot, Tali said, "I think you've just saved me from having to clean the drains and the sludge-pit for the rest of my natural life."

"You're... welcome?" Dun said.

"I've got stuff to get from here," Tali said. "Meet you by the bridge in a thousand clicks or so?"

"Great, we'll pick up food and a pack for you," Padg said. "What about weapons?"

"Don't really need any; I'm an alchemist!" Tali laughed. "Find me a good knife, if you like. Smell you later."

She headed inside, leaving the friends standing there. Dun stood the door up next to the frame and they turned back toward the village, giggling.

***

"Do you think she means it?" Dun said as they headed back to the market.

"Means what?"

"All that stuff about not needing weapons to fight."

"I don't know," Padg said. "Gatryn seems impressed with her, and he's a cantankerous old stick and, I gather, quite hard to impress."

Dun and Padg knew of Tali's reputation, although the duties of an apprentice, especially one to the alchemists' guild, meant that she didn't get out a lot from her studies. She was the youngest apprentice to have been selected by the guild for many an age, chosen for her brains and ability to pick things up quickly. However, those things were often ones she'd dropped herself. That they wanted her to come with them was a simple acknowledgment between Dun and Padg. They knew it was right. But they had a couple of formalities to sort out.

They stuffed the rations of fish-mush in the extra pack that Padg had bartered from the Makers. Dun noticed the fine texture on the outside of the newly-made sack. Its straps felt sturdy and well attached to the main body of the pack. It was a physical reminder of why Dun preferred folk-made goods to the more popular modified found materials. He knew what he was getting with a folk-made thing: exactly what it would do, how it would perform, and how long it would last. It was a view influenced by his father but shared by few of Dun's contemporaries. But for this expedition, Dun was in charge, and for all his friendship for Padg, he knew his position; all their carrying kit was folk-made, all their weapons crafted by Padg—all ultimately reliable. Dun knew that the trip on which they were about to embark was going to have many unpredictable aspects. He didn't want their kit to be one of those aspects. In a way, that all informed his question about Tali. The whole idea of alchemy, experimentation; that unpredictability made him uneasy. He knew in a way that it was a failing in himself. He always took longer to adapt than Padg, who of course mocked him mercilessly for it, but that didn't change Dun's feelings. On their way to the bridge, Dun realized that at the same time, his unease was sitting alongside a feeling they had the right team. The chaos that Tali brought was right. He thought about it, hearing her singing en route to the rendezvous point at the bridge. Whatever she was carrying in her bags clinked in time.

"As sure as the river flows in the tunnel. As sure as the fish swim free. As sure as the water runs in the runnel... oh. Hi."

"Hey," Padg said.

"So," Dun said, "we're going on a journey, far from here, far upriver, maybe where no folk have ever been."

There was a long silence.

"It may be dangerous," Padg chipped in.

"Great! When do we start?" Tali asked cheerfully.

They sat on the low curved earth wall at the village side of the bridge. They heard a hoarse male pant as a someone sped to the bridge. He stopped. The accompanying cloud of dust smelled of dust and the village runner, Macky.

"Alpha... wants you... back in the Moot-hall. Now, he says."

Chapter Six

"Dun, this is your father's map," Ardg said. "It is one of the Bridge-folk's greatest treasures. Take good care of it."

They sat in the Moot-hall in a rough circle, gathered around a low table that had been brought in. They all leaned in close, heads down, and reached out to touch a large roll of gossamer-thin bark, weighed down by a stone at one end, and an odd metal found-thing at the other. Dun could still pick up traces of his father's scent. He swallowed. The entire surface of the scroll was inscribed in a complex and extremely skillful fashion. Dun, Padg, Ardg, the tribe leader, Barg, Swych, Myrch, and even Ebun the village Skald was there, in his capacity of historian for the tribe. The intensity in the hut was almost palpable.

"So where are we again, relative to the river?" Padg asked. Map reading was never his strong point.

'Feel! Here!' Swych guided Padg's hand to the place on the map representing the village. She much preferred teaching Padg fighting. That, at least, he had some aptitude for.

Dun was lost in thought. First, in fascination at the detail and craft that had gone into the map's making, then in an effort to try and absorb the details necessary for their journey. His fingertips traced the beautiful details: his father had an artist's touch. All of the world as the Bridge-folk knew it was on here. The river stretching off up the map, territories of their nearest neighbors: River-folk, Myconid-folk, Wind-folk, Stone-folk; arrows and symbols off the map indicating where, at the best guess, other tribes lived. The mysterious trading Deep-folk with all their wonderful found things, the odd distant and uncommunicative Tunnel-folk and their home, the Pipe Forest, the fabled Fire-folk far upstream, and then farthest upstream, just an arrow and a label for the Machine-folk. Slowly but surely, it was sinking into place and for Dun, this was something for which he had an aptitude.

There was one more thing about the map, though. It was a piece of his father. The writing, the phrasing of jotted comments and notes.

"The village is near-bank, here."

Everything on the village side of the river was always referred to as "near-bank", everything across the bridge, the side Dun's house was on, was called "far-bank".

Dun carried on. "And the map is aligned downstream at the bottom and upstream at the top. The map maker has drawn a symbol in the river, like an arrowhead to show the water flow. It's really clever, really."

"You know no one likes a smartass, right?" Padg shot back.

"You'll get it," Dun said, trying not to sound patronizing.

"I've got a feeling I might not ever really get it, but as long as you do..." He lifted his head up to address the whole group. "So, not to be rude, but moving along from examining the map, what do we need to know about what's on it?"

Short, thought Dun, but to the point.

Swych began the Elders' reply. "Right, now you know which way is upstream. You want to begin with the path that runs along the river. It goes some way, but like most things on the map, we can't tell how it will be now. This map is quite old."

"Sorry," Padg said. "I thought Dun's father had done this one?"

"He did not begin it," Swych said. "And many have scratched its surface."

Ardg chipped in, "Yes, this map is quite a treasure of the tribe, really. Although there's a copy of it, you will take the original with you. It has been updated and altered many times in its life and while the fact that we need you to take good care of it and return it goes without saying, we would also ask you to take something else on your journey."

He pressed something thin, short metal into Dun's hand.

"This is your father's stylus. It has been sharpened for you. Please update the map as you can. Knowledge of our world is something that has always set the Bridge-folk apart from our peers. The map, so far as we know, is the most complete one in existence. We would like you to continue that task.

Dun said, "That would be our... err..."

"Honor?" Padg offered.

"Good," Swych said. "The map is of great tactical importance to us all. Now, you may well meet our nearest neighbors, the River-folk. You will certainly be within their territory once you are a span away from here, so if nothing else you will be being monitored. We are at peace with all our neighbors, but the River-folk are not really to be trusted."

"Have never really been trusted," Ebun said as the subject crossed into his field. "The trouble with the River-folk is that they don't really believe in setting out life the way we do. They have trouble with our concepts of family, tribehood, ownership. Things like that. They know to behave themselves when they come here trading, but on their own land, they set the law. What law there is."

Dark

"If you can get through their territory without a meeting, that would be an advantage, but you'll be there three or more spans so it may be difficult to avoid them," Swych said.

"I could write a scroll to carry with you saying you're on tribe business; it may help avoid trouble," Ardg said. "It's a shame we're so far from a market gathering; we could have asked one of their representatives then. No matter, needs must now."

"Next on your route," Swych continued, "if you continue to follow the river, you'll pass by the land of the Tunnel-folk and the Stone-folk on either side. Tunnel-folk on near-side, Stone-folk far-side. The actual river land at this point is disputed. Obviously, the River-folk think it's theirs, but the Tunnel-folk and Stone-folk go down to fish and use water so there's a kind of informal truce. The Tunnel-folk are fairly reclusive; you'll be unlikely to meet them. Although again, they're usually inquisitive and thorough, so they'll know you're there. Stone-folk are fairly formal to deal with but predictable. They will insist on a meeting with their Alpha if you run into them. You could use a formal scroll there too; they hold great store by such things. Then the Fire-folk." Swych paused at this point. The Skald filled the gap then.

"The legends say the Fire-folk were forged in the great vents of their home, explaining both their temper and their fierceness in battle," Ebun began.

Swych jumped in. "I, however, have not found them so. They come to the markets to trade, seem to behave themselves well enough and bring interesting trade goods."

"What do they bring?" Dun asked.

"Good question. They bring stones and minerals mostly, of great interest to the alchemists," Swych replied.

"And what do they mostly trade for?"

"Often food goods, edible fungus mainly. Sometimes our woven goods."

"What happens farther north of the Fire-folk?" Dun said, warming to his role.

A brief period of silence was followed by Ardg. "We don't really know."

"Our maps cannot be considered accurate after that point," Swych said.

"Haven't we ever traveled that far?" Padg asked, slightly mystified.

"No, not really. The trading that has taken place with the Machine-folk has been here; they have traveled to us."

"So no one has been there and returned to tell of it?" Dun could hear Padg's rising sense of adventure.

"Again only legends," Ebun said. "Magical machines with incredible powers..."

Swych cut him off again. "There are always legends. But as you rightly deduce, Padg, there is little store to be set by them, and fewer still facts to corroborate. We hope your journey may add to our knowledge."

"So, in brief," Padg said, "we are being sent on a journey far upstream, with a map that's far from accurate, through territories in disagreement, in order to find a mythical land we know nothing about through gods-only-know-what dangers?"

"A bleak, but reasonably fair summation of the facts," Ardg replied.

Padg drew breath to reply but never finished. A loud urgent clang from the center of the village and Macky burst into the Moot-hall.

"Raiders!" he yelled.

"What? Who?" Ebun said.

"Irrelevant," Swych said. Then to Macky, she said, "Militia?"

"Done."

"Where?"

"Bridge."

"How many?"

"Dozens?"

"Arm up," Swych said. "To me!"

She rushed out of the door; the sounds of weapons and shouting rushed in.

Padg, Dun, and Tali stood.

Dark

"Not you three," the Alpha said.

"But..." Padg said.

"No," Ardg said firmly. "Your path is elsewhere. Myrch?"

"Quick. This way. Packs, map. Now!" He led them out of a hatch behind the Alpha's chair and down a narrow passage, silent once the hatch had closed.

"What the hells?" Tali said.

"Not now," Myrch said.

"Who?" Padg said.

"River-folk," Myrch said, "now run!"

The passage disgorged them downstream of Dun's house. Dun recognized the feel of the ledge. They could hear echoing sounds of combat still. Occasional alto shouts that could have been Swych. It sounded brutal. Dun shivered.

"Damn," said Myrch. "You, wait here."

And with a splosh he was off.

"The natives...now there's something. 'The folk' they call themselves. Mammals, sure, but what kind I dunno. Biology was never my strong suit."

Excerpts from <Distress Beacon SN-1853001>. Found by E.S.V. Vixen Terradate: 26102225.

Dark

Chapter Seven

They scrambled down onto the path that ran alongside the river, water smacking against the sides of the pipe. At the sounds of shouting and the clash of weapons, they huddled as far back on the ledge as they could.

"We need to *do* something!" Padg said. "Let's attack from this side."

"Myrch said to stay put," Tali said.

There was a huge roar from the pipe ahead of them, anger and triumph in what sounded like accents of River-folk.

"Come on!" Padg said and sploshed off toward the sound of battle.

"Oh, gods," Dun said. "I guess we'd better go after him."

As they approached the churn of water by the bridge, the sound of cries from the village joined the storm in the pipe. Padg rushed forward but felt a swirl in the air to his left. He turned to meet it and felt himself being lifted out of the water.

"When I say stay, stay!" Myrch hissed.

"But they're..."

"Wait!" Myrch said.

A huge crashing noise came from the village. A barrier collapsing? Padg squirmed in Myrch's grip.

"Wait..."

The deafening war cry of the raiders stormed up to the bridge and into the village.

"Okay! Go now!" Myrch hissed. "Quick!"

"But..."

"Go!"

He swung Padg back onto the path and pushed him on for good measure. A metally sweet smell in the water followed them on their way.

Dark

Chapter Eight

They hurried on. The first part of the path was familiar to Dun and Padg, so they hadn't yet un-slung their traveling sticks to check the way in front of them. Usually most folk relied on air-sense in these circumstances, allowing their hairs to feel the volume of air and give them a clue of what was coming immediately ahead. It would tell of a rapidly approaching large object—a wall or a person, for example—or it would tell of the feeling of moving from an enclosed space into a large cavern. However for traveling, given the amount of stopping and sensing the air that would be required, air-sense was relegated in favor of a good stick. With this as a tool, much faster progress could be made in unfamiliar terrain without coming unstuck in the endless tunnels, random pipes, cables, and pits.

While still in their own territory, they kept up a good pace. The map told them that the path by the side of the river ran on for some time, so they took up a jaunty pace at Padg's insistence. His thinking being that any time they gained now would allow their supplies to sustain them in the event of uncertainty. It also afforded them distance from the noises in the village.

"Hold on you two," Dun called from up front where he'd made a slight lead on his friends. "I think we've just run out of pathway."

It was true. The metal walkway that had been their companion from the village had tapered away to nothing in the wall beside them.

"Dig me out a traveling stick, Padg. I want to test this water."

Padg obliged, grumbling slightly that it was his traveling stick and not Dun's own that was about to get wet. Dun ignored the low key protests and proceeded to dip the slim staff in the water. He pulled it out and felt the wetness along it until he made a resigned grunt.

"Okay. In we go."

"What?" Padg and Tali shouted in unison.

"In the river," Dun said baldly.

"It's...err...quite deep here," Padg said.

"We'll freeze," Tali cried.

"Oh well," Padg said cheerfully. "At least we won't feel it when we drown."

"Unless you two have any better ideas; this is as far as the path goes. We go on. The river seems like our only option to me."

"What about all our kit?" Padg chipped in.

"We'll carry our packs on our heads for now. If any of us get tired, another can take a stint with their pack to rest them and so on."

Padg wasn't sure he liked this new bold leadership side to his friend, but he couldn't help grudgingly agreeing that it was probably, at this point, their only course of action.

"Okay. In it is."

They tied onto their packs all the things from pouches and pockets that would suffer from getting wet, and with a slight squeak from Tali, lowered themselves into the stream. The water at this point came to just above their knees. It was cold.

***

"How much farther, Dun?" Tali tried to hide the whine in her voice but failed to hide the fatigue.

The constant sloshing gait they'd had to adopt to make progress through the pipe had been taking its toll. The three packs—at Padg's suggestion—were now all tied in a row atop two of the traveling sticks, held above the water between two of them. That way each of them could take turns resting more easily. The resting one of the trio, Tali, searched the tunnel walls to check if there were any crossing tunnels or pipes, even a small ledge for them to rest on. In half a span there had been none.

"I'm not sure. The scale on the map isn't really clear. We're right in River-folk territory, but that's about all I can tell you."

"There must be side tunnels somewhere for them to get in and out of the river. They can't live in the water all the time," Padg said.

"Could be hatches that they close from the inside," Dun replied. "No one really knows since they keep to themselves so much."

"Have you noticed the fish?" Padg said.

"The lack of them?"

"Yeah."

"I had. Not one since we've been down here."

"Oh well," Padg said. "At least you can be assured its not your lousy fishing technique."

Dun and Tali both snorted. On balance, there were few folk that Dun would rather be up to his knees in a cold river with than his best friend, but even Padg's stoic cheer wasn't going to save them from freezing if they didn't find a way out of the water soon.

"Wait!" Tali shouted from up front.

"What?" Dun hissed back.

"Shh...not sure. There's something here, a rope or—"

Then came a sharp twang and a creaking of rope and they all flew together in a melee of arms and legs. Across his back, Dun could feel a mesh of ropes and squashed against his legs, Padg. Dun's face was pressed into Tali's back. The silence of their shock was punctuated by a creaking noise, like some kind of rope animal's breathing and, in the distance, a faint metallic tinkling. They swung and twisted gently.

Dark

"What the...?" Dun said.

"A trap,' Padg said. "A net or something, triggered as we walked across it."

"I was so stupid," Dun said. "I should have felt it under us."

"Don't punish yourself," Padg said. "We were distracted, besides, I think they'd disguised it. The pipe floor felt flat to me."

"Who do you think they are?" Tali said.

"Pardon?" Padg asked.

"You said *they*, who do you think..."

"Well, well, well. What kind of strange fishes do you think we've caught here, then?" A harsh, grating voice cut through them, accompanied by a waft of an odd resiny scent.

"I think, Tali," Padg said, "we're about to find out."

Chapter Nine

Anything their rough-speaking assailant said was menacing enough already, but Dun found the point of a spear jabbing him as punctuation. The bag they were suspended in swung and twisted, slowly. Dun was sure he could sense others besides the speaker. The resinous smell, and using his air-sense while slowly rotating, was giving Dun a headache.

"What's wrong, fishy? Swallowed your tongue?"

The surrounding gang all laughed at this point, harsh and guttural. Dun estimated that there were six of them, including the leader. What use that information would be to him stuck in a net though, he wasn't so sure.

"What do you want?" Padg said coolly from the net above Dun.

"Ah, I thought these might be talking fish if I tickled them enough." More laughter.

"What do I want. What *do* I want? Perhaps, I want all of your belongings and for you to be telling me what it is exactly you're doing in my river?"

Dun drew breath in response, but the coarse bark cut him off again.

"Or maybe, I want to peg your insides out to dry in the vents for trespassing."

"Or maybe, you want to let them all down from the net and the Bridge-folk will forgive your little blunder!"

The new voice sang out cool and ringing across the walls of the tunnel. The authority it spoke with was impressive. A slight speech tic to it and he'd certainly never heard the voice used to that effect before. Myrch had followed them.

"Now, now, I don't want to hurry you but..."

Dark

The voice was closer now, about the same distance away as the leader of their captors. The "but" had an extreme gravity that even the bluff leader of the group of ruffians didn't wish to try. Dun could've sworn he heard a faintly suppressed squeak from the leader, then the new voice whispering too low for him to hear. Next, the group's leader issued a couple of barked orders in the odd River-folk dialect and with a creak of the rope, they began to be lowered back into the water.

"Come on," Myrch said, helping with the ropes. "I think we've outstayed our welcome."

"Welcome?" Padg said. "I must have missed that."

As they disentangled themselves, with the liquid floating the edges of the rope net, there was a quick swirl in the water as Myrch twirled around. There was a sharp twang and a bang as metal hit metal at the tunnel wall. The leader of the River-folk gang gave a muffled gasp.

"Do not toy with me, Darvan. The next bolt will be in your head," Myrch's voice rang out strong and clear.

The silence of the stand-off gave the three friends time to free themselves, collect their traveling sticks, and stand up again in the water.

"How...?" Dun said.

"Not now, not here," Myrch said, brusquely.

Then he leaned in toward Tali and whispered in her ear, "Right, young alchemist, we need a diversion, in about fifty clicks. Can you manage it?"

"Yep," Tali said and fumbled in her backpack.

Myrch turned back again in the direction of the River-folk and spoke deliberately, "And now we must leave. Do not think to follow us, or any of your clan, Darvan. It will be the worse for you if you do, trust me."

Then he spoke to the friends again, "Shall we? Tali, if you would?"

Tali threw a small fabric bag she had been preparing into the water between them and the River-folk. There was a splosh as it hit the water, a brief pause, and then the noise of frothing and boiling with a very strong stale smell.

"Run," Myrch said. And they did.

***

A thousand or more serious clicks of running in nearly knee-deep water and everyone's lungs started to protest. Luckily for the friends at that point, Myrch was always slightly ahead of them. Keeping up an easy lope, he shouted, "In here quick!"

There was a trapdoor in the pipe, about a hand-width above the level of the water, that opened outward and upward. They all scrambled into the cramped slimy room on the other side.

Before anyone could voice their million questions, Myrch spoke, "Tali, sorry to trouble you again, but have you the supplies to make some hunter's balm?" He referred to the smear that hunters applied to themselves, before venturing out, to mask their scent. Powerful stuff, as it effectively rendered them undetectable.

"Yes," she replied, "or at least I did. I'll check that my stuff that hasn't gotten wet."

"Good," Myrch said. "Make it up but don't apply any water. Give it to me still in powder form."

She rustled in her bag again. "We're good, I think. The pack's dry on the inside."

"Excellent," Myrch said.

There was the noise of mixing and stirring and a clean, slightly sweet, powdery smell emerged. She handed a small bag of powder to Myrch, who stuck his head back out of the hatch, clapped his hands together loudly several times, then closed the hatch silently.

"That should keep them off the scent for a while. This isn't a passage they know yet. Follow me."

He guided them to a small rusted set of steps pegged vertically into one of the walls.

"Up here," he said.

They climbed up a short way; what must have been the height of the top of the river's pipe. There a room opened out. Dun thought from Air-sense it was about the size of the main room in River-hole. Once up the metal steps, they heard a quiet metal-on-metal closing noise as Myrch lowered another trapdoor back down over the hole they'd climbed through.

"We can rest here. There's a vent over there. Dry yourselves out."

It wasn't long before Dun broke the silence, "Thank you. For helping us."

Myrch made some kind of non-committal grunt.

"Yes. Thanks and all that," Padg added. "But how did you know?"

"How did I know what?" Myrch replied evenly.

"Where should I start?" Padg said, warming to his theme, irritation rising in his tone. "How did you know the name of that bandit? Darvan was he called? How do you know so much about what's going on here? How did you know this hole was here? And most importantly, how did you know to follow us?"

Awkward silence.

"Well?" Padg pressed his point. "You were following us." It was a statement, not a question.

"My, my," Myrch said, the faintest hint of amusement in his tone. "So much indignation from one who's lucky to be alive."

"We don't mean to sound ungrateful, but he does have a point," Dun said.

"Yes, he does," Myrch said. "Yes, he does."

"So?" Tali said, less edge to her tone than her friends.

"In no order, the answers to your questions would be: I've known about this hole for quite some time, and I've prepared it for just such an occasion for quite some time. You'll find a metal box in the corner opposite where we came in. It contains food and some limited medical supplies. Darvan is slightly more than a bandit in these parts. He has been slowly removing his enemies among the factions of the River-folk for quite a while. He now holds quite a lot of power for a River-folk and shouldn't be taken lightly. I know so much, about what's going on, by taking a shrewd interest and a little care. And yes I was following you, with good reason as it turned out."

"And that doesn't answer a damned one of our questions," Padg barked.

Tali chipped in at this point, in a slightly more conciliatory tone, "I don't get it. For as long as I've known you're this nobody in the village. Hardly there, hardly noticed. Then all of a sudden, you're following us, you know all about the local goings on, have a more than passable knowledge of alchemy and you turn up armed to the teeth to rescue us in the nick of time. Who are you, and what are you up to?"

"Ah," Myrch said, his tone becoming instantly serious. "That is a different question entirely."

Dark

Chapter Ten

"Truthfully? I collect information. I watch tribes' movements and chart their power struggles. I observe, I explore."

"You're a spy then?" Padg said.

"If you like, yes."

"Who are you working for? Not the Alpha." Dun followed his friend's lead.

Padg had to fill the silence that followed. "It's not the village, is it? Or us?"

"No," Myrch said. "Right now I'm working for me."

"So explain to me why we aren't leaving you here tied up and going off on our own?" Tali said.

"I think you're all smarter than that."

"So is this some sort of kidnap? A coup? What is our relationship here exactly?" she asked.

"And why should we trust you now?" Dun finished.

Myrch exhaled slowly, then spoke carefully, "Because I'm the best chance you've got."

"Oh?" Padg was unimpressed.

"I know these tunnels intimately—all the twists and turns. I know the tribes who live in them. How they interact twists more than the tunnels. I can fight, as you know. And I know of your mission..."

"How?" Dun broke in.

"I collect information, I observe, remember?" he said without a trace of sarcasm. "I know you seek the Machine-folk, and I can help you find them... If you'll let me."

A slow metal creaking and popping was all they could hear, as if the tunnels themselves were slowly breathing in and out.

"Feel along the wall behind you, there's a door. It's a little anteroom to this one, it's pretty sound proof. Go in there and discuss it between you. I'll wait below, down the ladder."

Dark

And he left them to their thoughts. Padg was the first to break the silence.

"Obviously we shouldn't trust him. We have no idea who he's really working for, and I don't like the fact that he knows so much about us but we know absolutely nothing about him."

"It's funny," Tali said. "When he said he was working for himself, I got the impression that was the truest thing he said. If he is, maybe we can turn him to our advantage."

"Or maybe he'll turn us to his. That fighting was all rather too slick for my liking. He could kill us as soon as smell us." Padg stood firm. "Dun?"

Dun spoke then in an odd absent kind of voice. "We should take him with us."

"Don't believe that stuff he said. We can do this on our own," Tali replied.

"No," Dun said. "It's what we *should* do. We're meant to take him."

"Do you trust him?" Padg said.

Then an ear-splitting crash and the clang of a metal panel, followed by Myrch's footsteps banging up the ladder.

"Decision time!" he said urgently, another crash below punctuated his sentence. "They've found us."

"It will work out. Don't worry." Dun's tone was gentle but implied finality. Then to Myrch, he said, "You come."

"Wise choice," Myrch said.

A louder clang rang out, then air and voices rushed up to them as River-folk spilled into the space beneath them.

"Out, now!" Myrch barked.

"How?" Dun said.

"Up."

"Up where?" Padg said. "There's no ladder in here." He had been busy while they were having their discussion, Dun thought.

"The pipes," Myrch said. "There's a gap to get through at roof level. It leads into a crawl space up top, now go! Quick, I'll hold them here till you're up."

While Padg stood at the bottom of the pipes, Dun gave Tali a boost up to get a good hold on a pipe bracket halfway up the wall. She quickly scuttled up. As Dun followed her he heard the sharp clanging noise of whatever missiles Myrch was firing, colliding with metal somewhere below his position at the top of the ladder. There was a groan from below as one of the missiles struck home. Then scuffling as progress was made up onto the ladder.

Padg scaled the pipes deftly and shouted across to Myrch, "Come on!"

"Just a few clicks!" Myrch said, kicking a Riverfolk back down the hatch onto his comrades.

There was nothing to drag over the hatch lid, so nothing else to do but run for the pipes. Padg leaned out of the hole at the top as Myrch climbed.

There was another scuffle at the hatch lid. "Behind you! Padg yelled, and then followed his shout with a sword-spear. They heard the swift whirra-whirra noise of its spinning flight, and then a dull squelch as it hit home.

"Good shot, boy!" Myrch said as he squeezed through into the crawl space.

"I just saved your life. We're even now. You don't get to call me, boy."

Myrch caught his breath. "No. I suppose I don't."

"Excuse me, now you *males* have finished bristling egos," Tali said briskly, "let me get to the pipe hole, we've not finished here yet."

She squeezed past them and there was a ceramic tinkling as she crashed a pottery flask against the pipes.

"There, that should keep them out of our way for a while," she said cheerfully.

"What was that?" Dun asked.

"Slickness mix," Tali said. "We trade it with the Makers for them to lubricate things they make. I thought it might come in handy for something."

"Nice," Padg said.

Tali made a noise that might have been half a laugh but was cut off by Myrch.

"We must leave. The oil's a nice trick, but it won't hold them forever. Have you any of the Hunter's Balm powder left?" he asked her.

"I think so yes."

"Dust it round the hole. There are few tunnels or paths here, we can perhaps leave them a little confused as to how to follow us."

As Tali rustled in her pack, Dun realized what Myrch said was true. Although the space they were in didn't have much headroom, with his air-sense Dun could tell it stretched out as far as he could feel in each direction. This *crawl-space* place was massive, and none of them had known it was there. Except for Myrch.

As they set off they had to adopt a weird crouching walk and the floor beneath them was all metal mesh. How far they had to travel in it Dun didn't know, but he guessed the journey for the next while wouldn't be a comfortable one. The air in the crawl space was stale and hot, which didn't make things easier, and they were all trying to walk carefully. If they put their full weight down on the mesh in a regular rhythm, it reverberated with a metallic twanging hiss for as far as Dun's air-sense could reach. Not ideal for their stealthy retreat. He couldn't remember how long they'd been walking. He certainly felt tired and hungry, and he was about to make an estimate of what time it was when suddenly Myrch stopped ahead of them.

"Here," he said, tapping on the vertical pipe before him.

They all waited for what he might say, but instead, the answer that came was the noise of metallic unscrewing. Dun thought perhaps bolts or something similar. After four lots of unscrewing, there was a louder, larger grating noise, and Dun felt a rush of fresher air blow out of the newly created gap in the pipe.

"Down," Myrch said.
"Inside?" Dun said.
"That's the idea."

"That's quite a feat of climbing. A vertical surface, I mean," Padg said critically.

"Oh there's no climbing involved," Myrch said, "mostly falling."

"WHAT?" Tali said.

"Don't worry, the pipe's a bit less steep after a little way. And you can shout as loud as you need, the pipe is double-thickness, and I'll go last to shut us back in. Who's first then?"

Dark

Chapter Eleven

"Aaaaaaaaaaaaaaaaaahhhhhhhhhh!"

The walls of the pipe hurtled past at breakneck speed. The rush of air matched the rush in Dun's head: half primal fear, half exhilaration. Parts of the pipe were sheer drops, and the only thing he could feel was the thin cushion of air he was falling through. Parts of the pipe were only slightly sloping, but his momentum was so great he flew along these too. He could hear Padg shouting below him, and Tali's voice closer above. He banged through a bumpy section of pipe and collected yet more bruises. He'd lost count of how many clicks he'd been falling. At least the insides of the pipe were relatively smooth. Dun just started to feel the expanding air beneath him through his air-sense, when he heard a thud and a groan beneath him: Padg touching down. When he shot out of the pipe himself, several clicks later, Padg had rolled out of the way. Before he could collect himself, he heard Tali's yells barreling toward them.

Thump. Her landing was in a flurry of arms and legs, hers as well as Dun's. There was a brief awkward silence as they collected themselves.

Padg spoke first, "Come on, out of the way, Myrch won't be far behind.'"

When Myrch arrived thirty clicks later, he rolled out of the pipe, straight to standing, dusted himself down, and started walking the perimeter of the room.

"Nice trick," Dun said.

"Yeah, nice," Padg said. "Where exactly are we?"

"We are under the halls of the Stone King."

"Leader of the Stone-folk?" Tali said.

"The very same," Myrch said. "We can rest in this room for a while, the Stone-folk don't know it's here."

Dark

This part of the world felt different. Dun could already feel with his air-sense that the volume of this room was much larger than the rooms they had grown up with. The roof was higher and the floors were polished, but oddly, not cold. Dun felt his way along the walls. Every face and corner he could feel was carved and in some way ornate. Nothing written, no definite pictures, but patterns, swirls, and embellishments everywhere. Abandoned now maybe, but once this room had been grand. Dun wondered if someone important lived here, or else the room had an imposing purpose. The room even smelled of stone.

They broke out pack rations, then fell ravenously on the less-than-appetizing dried food. They'd lost track of how long it was they'd now been awake. Myrch sat off to one side of the odd dusty-floored room, so the three friends huddled close together over a warm vent on the wall for comfort. No one spoke for a long time, and Padg found Dun nodding off onto his shoulder.

"Hey, friend," he said as he nudged him. "Not quite time to sleep yet."

"Uh? Oh, sorry."

"You sleep," Myrch said from across the room. "I'll take first watch."

"Yeah, thanks," Padg said. "But we'll both take watch. Dun and Tali can relieve us in half a span."

"Okay," Myrch said brusquely.

"We can go first if you like," Tali said.

"No," Padg said firmly. "You two are exhausted. Get some rest, I'll be fine."

Padg was right and in less than a hundred clicks Tali was breathing that steady, slowing breath of the sleeper, and Dun was making quiet vocal half-noises. That left Padg and Myrch in alert silence.

"What was this place?" Padg said.

"No one knows," Myrch said distantly. "Not even the Stone-folk. They knew once, but no one comes here now."

"I'm guessing an old palace or something."

"Perhaps," Myrch said.

Padg was determined to drill some information out of Myrch, no matter how reluctant he was to talk.

"This River-folk thing is bothering you, isn't it?" Padg said.

"You're rather chatty all of a sudden for the strong silent one," Myrch replied.

"Humor me."

"This is the point where I remind you that you're in no position to make demands."

"Humor me anyway," Padg said firmly.

After a brief silence, Myrch said, "As it goes, yes, I am bothered. The River-folk don't normally behave that way and out-of-character behavior concerns me."

"Why?"

"The River-folk have been vagabonds for years. Feudal ones at that. They tend to fight among families and within families. There are alliances and blood wars going back centuries. Although they are a people with a great knowledge of the Dark, which could bring them great power, they choose instead to bicker internally. It's somehow in their nature."

"You suspect someone else is behind this?"

"Yes." Myrch's brief reply was strained.

"You know who it is, too," Padg said.

"I have some theories."

"Tell me."

"No."

"This 'non-relationship' we have is really starting to annoy me."

"Grow up, Padg. Even if I trusted you, you are not equipped to deal with the knowledge. Besides, as I said, I don't know anything for certain. Just theories."

"And you'd not impart any of that to help our chances of success?"

"No. Your best chance of survival, bar none, is to stick with me."

Dark

That closed the discussion, and they sat the rest of their watch out in silence. And silence it really was. Padg hadn't realized quite how much noise there was back home, until now. Here there was none, just a foreboding stillness. Stone silence. To one end of the room was a large stone door, mostly shut and even when he stretched his air-sense to feel what was coming through the door crack. The answer was: very little. Whatever these cavernous rooms down below the Stone-folk used to be, they were all properly abandoned now. He waited out the rest of their watch meditating. That was something he'd learned in his hunter training, and thus far on their journey, he hadn't had much chance. Resigned to getting no more out of Myrch, he sat out their turn quietly trying to meditate.

The clicker-beetle that Padg had set at the start of the watch went off in a flurry of ticking, and he woke Dun with a shove of his foot. Wake up. Your turn, Dun. The beetle needs feeding.

Dun gently pushed Tali's shoulder. "Our turn."

She groaned and stretched herself. "Anything to eat?" she inquired.

"I'm sure I can rustle something up," Dun said a little too cheerfully.

They sat and ate quietly until Dun unstopped his water flask with a "bung" noise.

"Wait," Tali said.

"Eh?" Dun replied with flask halfway to his mouth.

"Here," she said and took the flask from him. He heard a small dribble as she added something to the flask. "Try now," she said.

Dun took a mouthful and an explosion of flavors took over his tongue: sweet and bitter, sour and dryly satisfying all at once.

"Wow," was all he could manage afterward.

"There! We're not *just* about smells and melting things!" There was a smile in her voice.

"What is it?" Dun asked.

"Well, that's just it. We don't really know. We scored it last big market from an odd trader chap. He didn't speak much or say where he'd come from or anything, but we traded for loads of it. Now we're just trying to work out what's in it and what to do with it. For now, we've called it Sweet-water until one of the Elders thinks of a grander name for it."

"Wow, no idea what it is, and you're expecting me to drink it?"

"Yes," Tali said feigning hurt. "We *have* checked it's not poisonous."

"Oh, good," Dun said. "How did you do that?

"What do you think apprentices are for?" she said.

"It works great in the water."

"Yeah. I thought it might be nice to bring along if we were out here a while."

"You're a bundle of surprises, aren't you?" Dun said.

"You've barely scratched the surface." She laughed.

They cleared up their packs, putting everything away carefully in case of a hasty exit. Then Tali said, "Shall we go on an explore of the corridor?"

Dun felt a twinge of guilt immediately. "We should stay here. We're meant to be keeping guard."

"Yeah, but we could do that from a little way away, couldn't we? You can feel there's no one here."

That was certainly true. However far Dun could stretch his air-sense, there were just big volumes of still air. In the case of what was beyond the crack in the big stone door from their room, it was probably a big corridor of still air.

He was curious enough though and once the initial flush of guilt and responsibility had passed, there was something else. A foretelling feeling, of something that he couldn't quite put a name to. An odd feeling, like waiting and beginning at the same time. He shook his head to clear it.

"Come on, Dun, you know you want to!" she hissed, giggling.

"All right, but not far and be quiet!" he hissed back.

The stone door was vast. A huge slab of stone worked to a beautiful, decorated surface. Running his hand over it, Dun could feel the fine-grained texture of the tools the mason had used: heavier here, lighter there, almost like the feel of handwriting on a tablet. When they pushed it, the door moved in a graceful arc, despite its weight. They felt the brief movement of air displaced by the door until the swirls passed and once more there was stillness. Ahead of them, they could feel the shape of a long corridor with a high ceiling.

"Glad you came now?" Tali said playfully.

"It's massive."

"They were busy folk, whoever they were."

"I was assuming it was the Stone-folk," Dun said, the certainty leaving his mind as he spoke.

"I'm thinking way older than the Stone-folk. Could have been anyone. Want to explore a bit?"

At Dun's intake of breath, Tali said, "Come on. You want to be led astray, really. Relax a little."

Dun sighed and headed out after Tali's voice. "You check the river-side wall, I'll check the far side," she said cheerfully.

"Shh," Dun said. "We don't want to wake anyone."

"Okay," she hissed back.

They progressed down the huge stone passageway, feeling the walls as they went.

"What have you got?" Tali hissed, across the corridor.

"What you'd expect, I suppose," Dun whispered back. "Huge stones making the wall up, very smooth, massive columns with a spiral twist in them. In between there are flat panels carved, feels like huge images of folk, kind of. I imagine they'd be leaders or important tribes-folk."

"Odd," Tali said. "Over here I've got very simple walls; all rough regular blocks; big pillars, but simple ones. And no carvings at all."

Into the silence where Dun was mulling the implications, Tali spoke again, "You'd think both sides would match."

"Perhaps they fancied doing the other side differently."

"Yeah, but if they did don't you think it would be just as grand? Different but grand?"

"I suppose so."

"Don't suppose, I think," she said. Her voice was no longer a whisper as she got into her stride. "Think about what these people built. The level of skill in it. And whoever they were, they were bragging."

Dun had to laugh at that.

"Well," Tali said, laughing too, "they were. Feel the size of the place."

She came over to the side of the corridor Dun was on. She took his hand and traced it across the wall until they found one of the relief carvings.

"Feel the craft that's gone into it."

Dun felt odd at being led by the hand. He was feeling a queasy sensation in his stomach.

"Now come over to this side." She rushed across and screamed.

Dark

Chapter Twelve

Dun heard screaming, and then rubble falling. He ran across the corridor to get to where he heard the scream tailing off. Not checking his footing in his haste, he tripped on a floor slab with a raised edge and fell full stretch, bashing his jaw on the rubble-filled floor and biting his tongue as he did so. Dazed, he lay there for what was about thirty clicks but to Dun, it felt much longer. The screaming had stopped, the noise of crashing stone had stopped, and the corridor returned to silence.

Dun's heart leaped into his throat as he dragged himself up. He tasted blood in his mouth, but his only thought was of Tali. He stopped himself just before he leaped forward.

"Think, Dun, you're no use to her dead," he chided himself.

Instead of rushing ahead, he smelled the air and reached out with his air-sense. He could smell Tali: fear, tinged by excitement. *Typical*, Dun thought. A little blood. Masonry dust. Reaching out with his air-sense again, he got a surprise. The corridor wasn't how it had been before. A large chunk of it had fallen in. Some of Tali's mystery wall, evidently.

Dun sidled forward, following the trailing scent, careful that he didn't trip again, or worse, step on Tali if she was injured in the rubble. Dun had so prepared himself to find Tali in the rubble that when he found her standing up he nearly bumped into her. She was upright and stock still.

"Tali! You scared the wits out of me."

"Dun."

"What?"

"I think we've found something incredible. Feel."

Dun did as Tali suggested and felt with his air-sense into the room. It was long and lower-roofed than the corridor, but as he slowly stepped forward, he found the far wall sooner than he expected and he realized what she was talking about.

"Gods," Dun said. There was a mural on the long wall of the space, and by the crumbling texture of the stone, it was very old. Epochs old. Many pieces had flaked to the floor; some huge chunks, some small slivers.

"It's beautiful," Tali said, hands flat against the wall.

And it truly was. For all its age, the work and the art involved were breathtaking. It seemed to be many characters, sometimes the same ones, engaged in something. Different panels had similar characters, but different scenes. Beautiful, but disjointed and fragmented from the level of decay.

"My gods, the folk who carved this must have been so clever," Dun said.

"Which makes it ironic that it was discovered by folk who are so stupid!" Myrch barked.

"Blood and spit," Tali said, under her breath.

"I think you broke their wall," Padg said.

After a brief pause in which all of them caught their breath, Dun spoke first, "They're some sort of pictogram. They're telling some kind of story, if only we could make it out. So much has been damaged."

"There's some kind of recurring shape here too, in some of the scenes. A curve, an arch, or something," said Tali. "Feel, here?"

"There's writing too, although gods alone know what it says," Dun said.

"I don't recognize it in any writing I've learned, and we do learn ancient scripts for researching recipes," Tali added. "It's not the Stone-folk writing or at least not recently. It doesn't seem related even."

"Come on then, Myrch," Padg said, from where he'd found himself a stretch of wall to feel for himself. "You seem to be expert in everything, you must be able to tell us."

Myrch had sidled over to the wall too while everyone had been talking. He said nothing.

"You must have some kind of clue," Padg said.

"Ancient history really isn't my area of expertise," he said flatly. Then more urgently, he added, "Can we get back to the more important subject of how you two idiots nearly got yourselves killed here?"

"Must we?" Tali said.

"Yes. I don't think you're getting this. The Stone-folk are renowned for their building abilities. Their forebears were more skilled still, and they are very protective of their history."

"I thought history wasn't your strong..."

"Padg!" Myrch shouted now. "Down here is dangerous. Protections for who knows what, set here for eons waiting for someone to bumble into them and get themselves killed. Our only protection down here is caution. If you two thunder around the place then I can't protect you. Then the whole point of this journey will be forfeit."

"I thought you knew where you were going down here?" Dun said.

"I never said that."

"But your hiding place?" Tali said.

"Only ever used as just that. There's an access hatch and a series of ladders to get back up. I've never entered the Stone-folk's domain this way."

"But you have been to the Stone-folk's kingdom before?" Dun said, checking all his assumptions now.

"Yes, but only from the river level and only with the correct invitations and protocols. Down here, if we get caught..."

"If we get caught, what, exactly?" Padg said.

"Well, let's just say we're trespassing. And the Stone-folk don't react well to surprises."

"Great," Tali said. "That's just great."

"So what now?" Padg said, testily.

Not rising to Padg's tone, Myrch said, "I suggest we go back to the room and eat, and then since we can't go back up due to our pursuers, we press on *carefully*."

"You think they'd still be waiting for us if we went back up?" Dun said.

"Be careful not to underestimate our river friends' persistence."

"If we stay to eat, I want to spend some time recording what I can about the pictograms," Dun said.

"If you must," Myrch said reluctantly. "But everyone else should stay in the room, in case we need to escape that way."

"I've not even touched them yet," Padg said.

"All right! Go too if you must, but be *careful*."

So Tali and Myrch trudged back to the room with their packs, leaving Dun and Padg at the face of the mural. Dun quickly realized that Padg was waiting until he could no longer sense the others anywhere in the corridor outside. Then, in the anteroom, they were sufficiently far away not to be heard.

"I thought you hated history," Dun said to his friend once they were clear to talk.

"Of course I do, idiot, I stayed to talk to you."

"Just like old times."

"I've got a feeling nothing's ever going to be like old times ever again. But you know that."

"I know you didn't just stay to chat."

"No," Padg said. "I've been busy on your watch."

"I'm guessing not busy sleeping?"

"No. I waited till Myrch was asleep and searched his pack."

"Hells, Padg, you could have got yourself killed if he'd caught you."

"I took a chance. We needed to find some more about him."

"And?"

"He's got a lot of *weird* stuff with him."

"Like what?" Dun said, his interest piqued.

"Some stuff too weird to begin to describe…"

"You're apprenticed to the Makers chum if you can't make anything out of it, who can?" Dun said.

"Well, to start with, that weapon of his. Even that's weird. For a start, it's all metal. It's a kind of a tube, with a wooden feeling handle that's got metal bumps on it. There feels like there may be levers on it to get it to come to bits, but since I might have had to get it back together in a hurry, I didn't risk it."

"You *have* been busy."

"That isn't the half of it, Dun. There were squishy pouches with something in them. Some extremely nice writing scrolls. Not like bark or the papyrus that we trade for, but thinner, finer. And oddest of all was this weird contraption, like a helmet or a hat with a strap to hold it on, and a fabric inner, but with all this odd mechanical apparatus on top of it that seemed to be holding two round glass plates in place. *Then* it all folded up to fit in his pack and again there were a lot of levers and metal bumps to it, but I thought it best to leave everything exactly how he expected to find it."

"And breathe," Dun said.

There was a rumble, a tumbling stone sound as some piece of rubble settled in the distance.

"Hells, Padg, I don't know what to say."

"Well, whatever else he is, our friend Myrch is one hell of a trader. Any piece of his kit must be worth tens of thousands of trade tallies. Our Makers would kill to get their paws on it. Do you *still* think he's okay?"

Dun let out a deep sigh. "I trust your judgment completely, Padg, and I don't trust him. It's just I've got this sense that he's not a bad person and we should follow him."

"Is this one of those 'foretelling' feelings?" Padg shot back.

"I think so."

"And that's the best we've got to go on?"

"That's all we've got to go on, friend, sorry," Dun said sadly. "Is that enough for you?"

Dark

"It'll have to be. It's you I'm following, Dun, not him." Then after a pause, he said, "Shall we get back to these ancient scratches of yours then?"

Long after they'd finished their rough sketches of the layouts and some details of the pictograms, something that he'd felt in that place was playing in his mind. There was a recurring shape that he knew was important, but couldn't quite place. An oval of sorts. It seemed many of the scenes took place inside this shape. He noticed other things too. Often there was a horizontal line bisecting the oval. And many characters seemed to populate the many scenes, but they seemed to be of two main types: small two-legged, upright, slightly hairy types and thinner, taller, hunched-over creatures. It was almost as if he had all the words to make up a sentence, but didn't know the sequence. Later, as they walked, he was too preoccupied to notice the tiniest tickle of foretelling, like a polite cough in his brain. It was too late then to cry out, as Tali stood on the first step of a great staircase upward. They heard a click and a noise of stone grinding on stone, then a whoosh and a cloud of dust enveloped them in a split second. As they coughed and gasped for breath, the last thing they heard was a huge booming clang echoing through the great stone halls. Then they lost consciousness completely.

"It's so vast down here and so much of it made or modified by 'Folk', not from before. If I hadn't been around a bit, a feller could be quite overwhelmed."

Excerpts from <Distress Beacon SN-1853001>.
Found by E.S.V. Vixen Terradate: 26102225.

Dark

Chapter Thirteen

Dun's head swam, in a way he had never felt before. It felt as if someone had stirred his brains with a stick. His temples throbbed. He lifted his head, off what felt like a rush mat, and all the contents of his head whirled around. In a rush, he threw up, heavily and repeatedly until all he could do was retch.

"Oh great, that's just great," Padg's voice came from across the small room. Dun felt around him.

"What kind of a greeting is that for an old friend?" Dun groaned. Then he retched again.

"Do give it a rest, Padg," Tali said. "I can't even give him anything since we haven't got our stuff. You know he feels as bad as you do."

"Where are we?" Dun said, finally managing to prop himself up on his elbows. He reached about for his pack.

"Don't bother," Tali said. "Our stuff's all been taken."

"A cell of some sort. No idea how we got here," Padg said. "Last I remember was that powder shooting out of the walls, my head buzzing, and then waking up here."

"We haven't been awake much longer than you," Tali added. "Three hundred, four hundred clicks or so. You seem to feel the worst of the three of us, but whatever it was we got hit with, it was pretty potent."

"You said three of us," Dun said, more alert now. "Where's Myrch?"

"Don't know," Padg said. "When we woke he wasn't here. Do you still think we should trust him?"

"I never said we *should* trust him, just that I thought he should be with us."

"And now?"

"I'm not sure," Dun said. "My head isn't very straight at the moment."

The room felt small and stone-walled. Low-roofed as well from what Dun's air-sense told him. The rank smells of the cell drifted into his consciousness. He wasn't the only one to have been sick from whatever the ancient trap had released. He hoped their captors wouldn't take too long to check up on them. He was starting to feel ill again.

He was not disappointed. A metal key scraped into the lock of the large stone door and air rushed into the cell. Then a brief silence and a quiet gasp before a gruff voice spoke.

"Let us be getting you cleaned up before we take you to the Captain of the guard, you do not smell so good." The voice was very thickly accented but precise. An odd dialect that Dun was having trouble getting his ear attuned to.

"Who are you? Where are we?" Dun said. "Please?" he added as an afterthought, remembering his lessons about the formality of the Stone-folk if that was still where they were.

"Now then, that is enough questions for a prisoner, I think," the voice said firmly. Then after a pause, he said, "But since you ask politely, I will answer what you have asked. I am Tuf, of the palace guard, and you are in the dungeon under the Halls of Stone. Now, you two men-folk will go with me. The lady will go with Amber here."

Dun heard Tali grunt disapproval. "Lady" What an odd turn of phrase that was. Dun was sure Tali wouldn't imagine herself that way. In his disorientation, Dun had hardly noticed the second scent in the corridor, but of course, they would want to segregate males and females to bathe. It wasn't something the Bridge-folk were used to, but it fitted with what he knew of the Stone-folk. This was going to take some getting used to. And he hoped that they got used to it before committing some dreadful sin of manners that would get them all killed.

"Now if you'll permit me the inconvenience, gentle-folk. Your leg, please." He picked up Dun's foot in a firm grip and Dun heard a grinding of stone and a metallic click. There was the pressure of stone around one of his ankles.

"We have some precautions for our visitors down here. We would not want anyone to wander off and become ... lost. It is called a 'quern'. If you walk slowly with it, it is merely an inconvenience."

It was quite a heavy inconvenience; Dun reckoned it would be possible to walk in some kind of awkward way, but not run. *Clever*, he thought.

Dun and Padg were taken down the passage, Tali off in a different direction. They were led into a large room where Dun felt as soon as he entered, the presence of water. It took him a small while to hear the water; some kind of slow-running channel through the middle of the chamber. There were two other Stone-folk in the chamber. Dun assumed that they were lower status in some way, as Tuf didn't even speak to them. He merely placed Dun in the hand of one of them, Padg in the other, and they were stripped of what clothes they had and scrubbed with some kind of a light but rough washing stone. Once this was over they were led to the corner of the room, where a warm air vent blew air of a smell that was the only thing here familiar to Dun at all. Their jailer must have left the room during the ordeal, as by the time they were both dry Tuf had returned with some kind of clothing for them to wear. It seemed to go over Dun's head and right down to his feet. His arms were free to come out of the sides. Though it was the most clothing he had ever worn in his life, it was by no means uncomfortable, as the cloth that touched his skin smelled faintly sweet and spicy and was the smoothest material he had ever felt. It had a kind of sheen to it he had never felt in any kind of fabric, certainly not the rough weaves for blankets and bedding that the Bridge-folk used.

After being dusted with some kind of fragrant powder that made Dun cough, they were led back out into the corridor to wait for Tali and Amber.

Tali had found herself in a similar chamber to Dun but had no one else to help her wash except Amber.

Odd that they think I need guarding less than males, she thought.

Her quern was lighter than Dun's as well, she was sure it was. Amber was younger than her too, at a guess. Tali reckoned she could easily overpower her if it came to it, but for now, she was content to find out how things unfolded. And to do a little unfolding too, starting with Amber.

"Do you do this all the time?" Tali asked.

"I shouldn't talk to you," Amber said.

"Because we're prisoners?"

"No, I'm a servant. I'd get punished."

She spoke in such a defeated way that Tali suspected punishment would be a lot more than a stern telling-off. She had to tread carefully, but equally, she had to know more of what was going on.

"The guard, Tuf is he called? He's gone with the boys, yes?"

"Yes," Amber said in a tone of surprise, as if for males and females to bathe together was unthinkable.

"And we're the only ones here?"

"Yes."

"Then we can talk, if we're quiet. I promise you won't get into trouble."

Tali knew what a servant was, but was quite unsure how to pitch a conversation with someone who had been brought up to think themselves less than her. All the tribe of Bridge-folk considered themselves of equal status no matter what their place in the tribe. The elders were only elevated by tacit agreement and even the Alpha could be removed if they got above themselves.

Slowly, in the act of tenderness of washing another, Amber unwound. Tali asked gently about Amber's home life. She'd been an orphan but her uncle had cared for her enough to ensure she got a proper servant's place in the palace. It seemed that—tough though the life was—there were plenty of worse places to work, and worse masters to work for than Tuf. After some more careful probing, it seemed that Tuf was mostly all bluster, except when he'd been drinking something that Amber called Gava. She guessed this was the fermented product of something or other. The Bridge-folk knew about making alcohol but mostly chose not to and didn't really drink it, unlike the River-folk who did both to impressive degrees. That small insight into Tuf's character, Tali filed away with some satisfaction; and then gently pressed on.

It turned out they were not prisoners yet, but rather suspected of trespass. They were to be brought before the Captain of the Guards, a stern fellow called Skarn. Although Amber didn't know much about him directly, she did know that everyone else respected and feared him in equal measure. Then if it turned out not to be a simple matter, they would go before The Council. This she spoke in almost reverent tones, so Tali made some guesses as to what the situation was there.

Finally, she probed a little about the manner of their discovery. After they set off some kind of ancient alarm, along with the trap that was their undoing, a troop had been sent to investigate. It seemed that where they'd come in from was very deep in Stone-folk territory and not visited at all. Almost as if they'd forgotten it was there. Amber wasn't sure how they were finally found, but all three of them were unconscious when they were brought to the level below the palace. And they stayed that way for a span. Amber made no mention of there being any more than the three of them and on that point, Tali thought she'd keep quiet.

Dark

As to where their stuff was being kept, it seemed like Amber wasn't party to exact information, but there were many storerooms on the floors above, that being where cleaning and bathing equipment were kept. Tali liked Amber and thought that under other circumstances she might have the beginnings of a friendship. But Tali was done bathing, and it was time to dry out, don a robe and meet her captors.

Dun was unusually twitchy as he stood in the corridor with Padg. He had no idea how this was going to play out. And the fact that his foretelling seemed to be dormant when he most needed it, didn't make him feel any better. His jumpy mood wasn't aided by the door to his left opening suddenly and Tali being ushered out. As she bumped into him, he felt the soft cloth of the robe she was wearing and cursed himself for having any feelings like that right now. It felt like his entire mind was conspiring against him. He suppressed a laugh at his own expense, which came out as an odd grunt.

"Save it for the Captain," Tuf said and led them up the stairs.

Chapter Fourteen

They sat on a cold stone bench in the room that Tuf, the prison guard, had told them was the guard Captain's chamber. In front of them, Dun could feel a large featureless stone slab, about twice his length and waist high, that Dun supposed passed as a desk. They'd been in there for a thousand clicks, maybe more. Guard Captain Skarn was obviously used to making people wait. Dun sat in the middle of the bench and Tali astride it at one end. Padg had not sat down yet and paced the room.

Dark

Padg had not found anything interesting enough to make the extra energy expenditure worthwhile. He felt some extremely finely-woven hangings on the walls. This made the room much warmer than their cell; it also damped down the echo from the walls in a way he thought might comfort him, in a different context. There were no other interesting features to the room, apart from some kind of metal tube hanging on a stand with a short stone rod beside it that Padg supposed was some sort of a bell or gong for summoning aides. There were no documents on the desk. Padg supposed the Guard Captain must have all of that with him, and that he must store things elsewhere. The desk was a great featureless slab of stone, with its main point of interest being how smoothly it was finished. No holes to store anything, no openings to be pried or examined. The stone door they'd come in through had been closed behind them and the only feature there was a small hole; perhaps for a key or opening device. The hole was too small to insert a finger, so the massive heavy door was not to provide a means of escape either. Even the two tiny rectangular vent holes at floor level, through which air was being circulated in and out of the room, were way too small to help them. Padg was not resigned to being a captive, though, and was nearly knocked off his feet when Guard Captain Skarn breezed in through the door and to his desk.

"Sit down," he said firmly.

Padg did.

They waited. They heard Skarn unroll some kind of scroll on his desk. A report on them, maybe, Dun thought. Skarn sighed, an odd taut sound in his voice. There was the faint rustling of someone reading a scroll, accompanied by a tapping on the desk that was maybe a stylus. They waited.

"What are we going to do with you? Hmm?"

Tali drew breath to reply and was cut off.

"No, I wasn't really asking." Skarn's long-suffering voice rolled on without a break. "You were found in The Ancient Stones with no diplomatic license and no escort. Our own people never go there, for fear of setting off some long-forgotten lethal device and taking valuable time and resources from our overstretched Palace guard. So what, I am asking myself, were you doing there? Are you soldiers, spies, or stupid?"

Nobody drew breath this time.

"This would be the point you *do* talk."

Dun's mind raced. How much to say? Certainly, he couldn't mention Myrch; that would only get them into more trouble. Dun had an idea that their mysterious guide spent his life making many friends and enemies, and he wasn't sure which, if either, the Stone-folk might be. Either way, less was definitely more in terms of what he said. But just how much and how to say it.

"Now!"

Dun held his breath and hoped the others would stay quiet or follow his lead.

"Forgive me, honorable Guard Captain," Dun began.

He hadn't been told the exact form of address the Stone-folk used for a Captain, but he'd been briefed well enough to make a guess.

"We are none of those, but emissaries who have become lost."

"Emissaries, from whom and how lost? Why were you found so far below the Palace? That is surely not the proper place for envoys? Speak!"

"Honorable Captain, our party was set upon by a band of"—he paused, searching for a neutral word—"brigands and in our flight became lost. We come from the Bridge-people, on a diplomatic mission to meet your wise court and King. We knew when we fled if we continued our course we might come upon your lands, but in our flight, we did not realize how deep we had gone, or where that would place us in your domain. We humbly crave your pardon for any offense we have caused by our blunder."

Skarn sighed again. For a short while, all the friends could hear was the tap, tap, tap of the stylus on the huge stone desk. Skarn let out a breath he must have been holding in a slow exhale and then spoke, "Well, told though your story is, the truth or falsehood in it must be decided by wiser minds than mine, I think. You will be brought before the Stone-council and so your story will be examined and your fate decided."

He rang the gong in the corner. Sure enough, a scuffle at the door provided an answer.

"Tuf, take these blundering Bridge-folk back to their cells. Then send word to Lord Schist that the Stone-council should be convened at the earliest opportunity."

"As you wish, sir," Tuf said and led the friends back out into the corridor.

Amber waited for them there and took Tali away from Dun and Padg, each to their cells. The large stone door grated into place behind Dun and Padg.

"What's this Stone-council then?" Padg asked.

"It's where the Stone-folk make all their decisions. Not like the Moot-hall back home though. They have Barons and Dukes and Lords of different parts of their territory, and they seem to make the decisions for everyone," Dun said.

"How do you get to be a Lord then?"

"I think you have to be born one."

"What if you're not very good at it?"

"I don't know."

"It doesn't sound right to me," Padg decided testily.

Dun hummed in reply, non-committally. Padg paced the cell. Dun wondered if Tali being separated from them was playing on his mind.

"How many of these Barons and Lords have they got?"

"I don't know exactly, but more than you'd think you'd need to do any effective ruling."

"And they split the land between them?"

"No, I think you get that too when you become a"— he paused thinking of which honorific to insert— "whatever. I'm trying to remember from my lessons what it was called... inheritance."

"I'm so glad I skipped folk-politics," Padg said, the sigh evident in his voice. "What does 'inheritance' mean then?"

"Well, if you're male, when your father dies you get the land and possessions he had and you become Lord of it, responsible for all the people who live there."

"If you're female?

"You don't."

"Nope, sounds like an awful system to me."

Padg went back to pacing.

Then after a while, he said, "If there are so many of these Lords there must be a reasonable amount of land for them to own? Or everyone would be at war all the time."

"I don't know, I think you'd have done quite well at folk-politics, friend!" Dun laughed. "There are any number of long-running conflicts between the Great Stone Houses, but you're also right about their land. The Stone-folk's domain is enormous. Caverns upon caverns, on many levels. There are some will travel to this Stone-council meeting, farther than we have come to get here."

"That begs the question, why they aren't in control of everyone in the world."

"I suppose they're too busy arguing amongst themselves over their own land, to worry about warring with anyone else," Dun replied.

"Seems their crazy way of governing is good for something."

They both laughed at that.

"Quiet there in the cells!" Tuf's voice came booming down the corridor outside of them. "Speak tomorrow at the Stone-council!"

Dark

Chapter Fifteen

Crack...Boom. Crack...Boom. Crack...Boom!

The sound of something hard and metal, being struck on something hollow and stone, echoed around the largest chamber Dun had ever been in. He'd never heard an echo go on so long and his air-sense couldn't feel the chamber's roof to give him even an inkling of how big it was.

"The Stone-council has been called. All present will stand and be silent."

The friends stood up from another cold stone bench. Dun felt uneasy, although he thought it could have easily been down to the odd watery mushroom gruel and flaky flatbreads they had been given for breakfast. Dun could still smell the odd stale fungus on Padg's breath. He imagined the experience was mutual. The benches in here were much grander than the ones in their cell. Although they were long, each place to sit was marked by an indent, and once seated one was oddly quite comfortable. Dun suspected that might be a good thing if they were in for a long haul at this council, whatever it turned out to be like.

The voice calling them to silence was unusual too. Also massive and booming but odd in some way— a normal voice made louder somehow. Dun wondered about a huge speaking tube of some kind. Whatever it was, the voice seemed to come from everywhere at once. This chamber had been built to intimidate. Dun had a feeling it might be working.

The voice spoke again, in a strange rhythmic voice:

"As it was when the first stones were cut, so it is now.
I call forth from the Stone-lanes the deepest and the near,
All the Lords of stone.
Come Lord Schist, Lord of us all.
Chancellor Granite, come to the hall.

Dark

> Wise Obsidian sits at their hand, ready at once to
> answer our call.
> Then Lord Protectors, Marble, Basalt, and Diamond,
> protect the Carvers, Masons, and Miners.
> Next Dukes of the Realm, Shale, Pumice, and Slate.
> Follow Barons then after, Sand, Lime, and Clay.
> All voices be heard till all voice be one will.
> Let the carvers record when the stone becomes still.

As it was when the first stones were cut, so it is now."

The echoes resonated high into the roof and then the chamber was still again.

Then a different voice, older, thinner, from a definite direction directly across the chamber from them.

"Who calls us here, out of the proper time? And for what reason? Stone-speaker, be swift and tell us."

The first voice, the Stone-speaker, spoke again, "My Lord Schist, we have been called here at the behest of Guard Captain Tuf. There are strangers in our midst, and we are to determine their nature and purpose, as their arrival in the Stone-lanes was unannounced."

"Very good," Lord Schist said. "Proceed."

"Call Guard Captain Tuf," the Stone-speaker boomed.

"I am here," Tuf said.

"You know the price of speaking untruth to this gathering?" This seemed to be more a ritual question than a real inquiry.

"My words will be carved in the annals of Stone, for all my descendants to read and untruths there to read for their eternal shame," he said, giving the ritual response.

"Speak then and tell us what you know."

Tuf recounted how the friends had been found unconscious halfway up a staircase, the guards having been alerted by the noise of a huge gong. Tuf made quite a lot out of where they were found. It seemed that they had rediscovered some long-lost route into the Stone-folk's domain. There was great description of how Tuf's team of guards got there and the caution they took to avoid setting off any other alarms that may have been down there. As he listened, two things struck Dun: Firstly, there was no mention of the wall they had broken through and what they had found there. Secondly, there was no mention whatsoever of Myrch. Equally clearly, Tuf's search had stopped when they had been found. Apparently, the Stone-folk's skills didn't lie in tracking, although now Dun thought about it, Myrch didn't have much of a smell to track. The Stone-speaker's voice snapped Dun back from his thoughts.

"Who speaks for the strangers?"

There was a pause, while the three friends stumbled. Tali spoke first, "Well, we kind of all speak for ourselves."

"Is the female a noble?" the Stone-speaker said.

"The female can speak for herself, thank you," Tali replied testily.

"And, noble born?" the Stone-speaker went on.

"Well, the Bridge-folk don't really have nobles," Padg said.

"Then she may not speak here," the speaker said.

"What?" Padg and Tali spoke as one.

"I will speak for my people."

Dun's voice rose clear above the grumblings in the chamber.

"What are you doing?" Padg hissed.

"Hopefully saving us. Be quiet," Dun hissed back.

The murmurs in the chamber stilled, and the Stone-speaker began again, "Who are you and where are you from?"

"I am Dun, an Ambassador of the Bridge-folk. I am sent by my people in peace and with their wishes of goodwill, despite our unusual entrance to your realm."

"Explain your trespass into the Stone-lanes."

"We humbly beg your pardon in this matter, my Lords. We intended no trespass."

Padg whispered, quizzically, "We humbly beg your pardon, my Lords?"

Tali hissed, "Shut up, idiot. It's how they talk."

Dun was too focussed on proceedings to let that distract him. It was quite a strain talking in this weird formal way, but that was what the Elders had said he must do and he had spent some time learning the necessary formalities.

"But trespass it was. Explain how you came here."

"We became lost fleeing from a band of River-folk and stumbled into your halls on a lower level, not knowing where we were. Had we met an officer of your people we would have presented the correct greetings and a formal message from my people. I have those in my belongings if I can be allowed access."

"That is not possible. Besides, it is a little late for formal greetings, do you not think?"

Not waiting for a reply, the Stone-speaker went on, "And that is not the only thing that is impossible. The River-folk would not attack another people, much less pursue you to our borders. There are treaties in place to prevent such things. Besides, it is not in their nature. They are a nomadic folk, a trading folk, not a war-like folk."

"Treaties or not, they still chased us and held us captive."

"Why would they do such a thing?"

"I don't know," Dun said, realizing how thin that sounded. "But everything I've said is true."

"The veracity of your tale is for others to decide."

Lord Schist spoke from across the chamber, "Do you have anything else to say in your defense?"

"No."

"You know the gravity of the charges you face?"

"Yes?"

"That you trespassed here is beyond doubt. The price to be paid for that is imprisonment. What the council will now discuss, is whether they believe you to be spies. The penalty for spying is death, in the Stone Maw."

The Stone-speaker spoke again, "Now the Council will deliberate. Guards, remove the strangers and return them to the cells."

Dark

Chapter Sixteen

They were led out from the audience chamber. The silence was taut; they all desperately wanted to talk to each other, but they all saw the more pressing need not to antagonize their guards. The silence, however, gave them the mixed blessing of time to think.

The passage from the chamber led, via some stairs, to the Palace prisons. At the foot of the stairs, the corridor teed off in two directions. As they neared it they heard a small "tut". This they had come to recognize as a noise of attention and deference from one of the more lowly Stone-folk to their superiors. In this case, Tali recognized the "tut" as belonging to Amber, her "attendant". Where Dun and Padg had the rather firm attention of Tuf himself as their jailer, it seemed that the Stone-folk viewed Tali as less of a threat, so the relationship she had with her "jailer" was much less harsh. Tali had found that even talking to Amber was possible, once Tuf was out of earshot and enough of Amber's fears about being caught had been calmed. As Tali was led off down the corridor she started to think about the friendship that was forming; she knew it was a friendship that was important for all of them.

As Dun and Padg reached the door of their cell, the question that was at the front of Padg's mind finally slipped out.

"What's the Stone Maw?"

"Where we put our wrong-doers to death," Tuf said.

The enormity of how different this culture was from their own was coming home to Dun. The most serious punishment for the Bridge-folk was banishment, and even then it was mostly temporary. Most petty disputes were resolved between families, and any misdemeanors that were taken to the Alpha were sorted by facing the people who were affected, who often chose recompense over punishment.

"What kind of crimes face that?" Dun said.

"Only the most serious: murder; kidnap, great theft, despoiling our monuments or tombs. And, of course, spying."

A sudden thought in Dun's mind made him go out on a limb. "You don't believe we're spies."

"That is for the Council to decide." But Tuf's tone told Dun all he needed to know. Not that Tuf was going to prove an ally, but it was a little reassuring to know someone believed them.

"I should take you to the Maw since you ask," Tuf said. "It is at the end of the passage."

Now it had been mentioned, Padg wished it hadn't.

***

Tali wasn't expecting to get another clean, but Amber insisted on washing her hair. Amber wet Tali's hair with water that was pleasantly warm, and then rubbed some kind of foaming bar on it that smelled of pipe-mallow, a flower that Tali knew well as a perfuming agent—sweet and heady. Amber was gentle, as before, but some hesitancy in her hands told Tali that something was up.

"What is your village like?" Amber asked gently.

"Er, well, busy I suppose and a bit chaotic. Always something going on. Friendly, there's always something that's happened, that folk like to gossip about. It drives you crazy sometimes since everyone knows everyone's business. The folk who are about my age, I guess you'd call some of them my friends, are obsessed with men-folk and finding a mate, even though that doesn't happen for a few ages yet. Sorry, here's me drifting on. What about you?"

The silence that hung in the air told Tali much of what she needed to know.

"Tali?"

"Yes."

"Will you be my...friend?"

"Oh, Amber...of course I will."

"Tali?"

"Yes, Amber?"

"I know where your things are."

Tali stifled a gasp. Well, aren't you just the little bag of surprises, she thought.

***

The large stone door creaked heavily on what Dun guessed must be massive hinges, opening into an enclosed chamber that his air-sense told him would hold about forty folk standing up.

"This is the room of the Maw."

Tuf led Dun and Padg, one hand each, into the room. He stopped and placed their hands on what was a large slab at waist height. He let them feel their way around it. It seemed to be quite a similar shape to the stone beds they had been sleeping on, with a roughly folk-shaped indentation running along its top face.

"The condemned lie here. They place their head in the Maw."

Dun and Padg felt their way along the stone table to the wall where at the head end of the table there was a large cube cut out of the wall, large enough to take someone's head. There were holes under where the head would go, wider than the with of Dun's finger and deeper. Dun could smell something that might be dried blood and something astringent that had perhaps been used to clean up afterward. Dun was starting to feel the slow, sick chill of fear. He gulped to try and keep it down and hoped no one had heard him. Padg spoke.

"How..."

Tuf cut him off. "A large stone block sits at the top of the shaft. A lever is pulled, the block falls..." He trailed off for a moment before adding, "It is... quick."

"That's meant to be comforting?" Padg was more annoyed than scared sounding.

"I hope it will not come to that."

"Can you not speak up on our behalf?" Dun asked.

"It is not permitted. I have given my account. Now it is for the council to decide."

"I'm oddly not comforted by that either."

***

"Tali, I... don't want you to... go," Amber said.

"I have to go at some point."

"No. I mean, the Council, how they make... people talk."

"Death sentence? Well, I'm not keen on that either."

Tali sat on the floor of the cell with her back to Amber. Amber was combing her hair with a comb made from some carved substance that Tali didn't recognize the feel of. The sensation of it on her skin, through her hair, wasn't unpleasant. They had been talking for what seemed like a whole span.

"Will it be noticed that you've been here so long, Amber?"

"No, it is Shale cycle. That is the time that Tuf drinks at the end of his work. He will be snoring now."

Tali immediately considered the usefulness of that but decided that a botched attempt at escape would make their chances worse. This required some careful planning.

"The people who talk. What do they say? Is it not going well for us?"

"As it is Shale cycle, Duke Shale presides over the council. For each cycle of meeting it is different."

"We do something similar at home," Tali said. "Folk-moots that have a different leader each time they meet."

"It is the same then. But here each house has allegiances, reasons to cast votes one way or another; vendettas, pacts."

"And I'm starting to suspect this has some bearing on us?"

"It seems... Duke Shale is trying to sway the council, to bring a quick verdict. Have you called spies and..."

"It's all right, Amber. Any idea why?"

"No, Tali, no one knows. Many times, the Shale clan has been a peacemaker for alliances."

"Hmm... but not now, eh."

"No. Duke Shale will have you executed; I know it." Amber finally broke down.

"Now then." Tali gave the Stone-folk girl a gentle pat. "This game's not over yet. Not by a long reed. Amber, do you really care what happens to us?"

"Yes," she said between sobs.

"Okay. I need you to help us, then. It will be dangerous for you, and I'll understand if you say no. Don't say anything yet, until I've explained what kind of position I'm putting you in, then you can decide if you're foolish enough to say yes."

With Tali's new, more excited tone, Amber's sobbing stopped.

"Now explain what happens when the council decides to execute..."

As Tali went to sleep, with the plan fixed in her mind, the only missing but vital piece was how to stall the council from declaring their death warrant. What could she possibly say here, in her position as a woman, that would buy them enough time to put her plan into action? She lay back on the stone bed, calmed her mind, and waited for sleep or inspiration to claim her.

Chapter Seventeen

Later that night it was Padg, with disturbed dreams, who woke Dun. Dun wished for once it was the other way around. He had experienced no visions for days and was beginning to wonder whether that was a good sign or a bad one.

"You all right, Padg?"

"Fine," his friend said in a clipped fashion.

"We'll get out of this."

"I know." Padg didn't sound so sure.

He felt terrible; he was meant to be leading this party and he had dragged them into this. It was only his blind trust of Myrch that had got them here, and that hadn't turned out well. But was it blind trust? Or was he just doing a good job of following his instincts and what foretellings he had? He was becoming too confused in his head to tell. He felt terrible too about the fact that Tali was sitting on her own in a cold cell and not with them. He knew she could take care of herself, but still... Or was he wanting that because he missed her himself? For all her occasional accidents, she had an air of confidence; confidence that he needed right now.

"Dun?"

"Yes?"

"Do they really... kill folk like that? Crushing them... it just seems so..."

"Messy?"

"I was thinking more, barbaric, but yeah."

"It's just another set of traditions, ways of life."

"I know that in my head, knew it before we left, got ourselves into... this, but now I'm here it all seems so... other. I can't understand it, and it scares me."

"I know, Padg."

Dark

Dun didn't know why the "otherness" that Padg spoke of bothered him so much less. It wasn't just all the time spent studying the cultures of other folk when they were pups. Padg had had that too, if he'd been listening to any of it. It was as if Dun knew, understood, straight away, that even the oddest cultures had a reason for what they did. Knowing that was enough, for him, not to be bothered; and it gave him time to adjust. Then it came to him; a way, at least, to increase their chances—pool their resources...

"We should ask for a last request," he said.

"Very cheering," Padg said. "I feel so much better now."

Dun chuckled, the first real lifting of mood he'd felt for spans.

"No, you daft pup. I've had an idea. If we can't think of anything ourselves, at least we can get our heads together."

"But they won't let us get to Tali. She's being kept somewhere else," Padg said.

"That's where our last request comes in."

"We don't even know if they allow such things."

"I suspect they will. They might seem barbaric, but they are great observers of form, and every culture believes itself to be capable of merciful acts."

It didn't take long for Dun to establish from Tuf that last requests were indeed granted to the condemned. It took a little extra time to persuade the gruff guard that, although they weren't actually condemned yet, a last request should be granted now. It seemed that since the process was taking so long, if they were indeed condemned they'd get little enough chance for last requests when the time came. When the door to their cell was opened and the warm scent of Tali drifted in, Dun caught himself feeling slightly smug. His guess had paid off.

"Good work," Padg said.

"Greetings men-folk," Tali said as the door closed. Then they fell upon each other hugging until Tali broke it up. "Hold on, lads, I've had an idea."

She spent some time explaining her plan in detail: how her relationship with Amber had developed, and how it appeared Tali's newfound friend might become a co-conspirator. She filled them in on all the little nuances and political relationships that Amber had shared. The allegiances and rivalries, vendettas and pacts that seemingly made the Stonefolk who they were. A strange people of many rules, but seemingly there was always a way around if the reward was high enough. A people of hard work and long memories.

"What about Amber?" Dun asked, in concerned tones.

"Yeah, can we trust her?" Padg said.

"No, that's not what I meant," Dun shot back. "I was more thinking what happens to her if she does help us? We're not exactly popular folks here, are we?"

"I... I had thought about that, have been thinking about that. I... don't know, I..."

"I'm sorry, Tali, I didn't mean to imply..."

"Yeah, I know," she said in almost a whisper. "I like her..."

"But she's the best chance we've got?" Padg always had a way of cutting to the point.

"Listen, we don't have to ask her," Dun said. He felt torn both ways. Did he have the right to be noble about Amber on behalf of the three of them?

"I think she's going to decide that for herself. She may seem quiet, but that's just the way they made her here," Tali said.

Dark

When he heard the sound of Tuf shuffling and coughing outside their cell two thoughts struck Dun. How quickly the time had flown, and how long had Tuf been there? Their plan, such as it was, was a fragile raft and any one of its reeds could snap with the slightest nudge in the wrong place, leaving them floundering. And this particular river, Dun suspected, was heading nowhere good. They were still missing one vital straw to weave in too. How to stall a decision from the council long enough to even get their raft in the water. And aside from that, as if there wasn't enough for Dun to worry about, the conversation with Tali had brought up something new. The attitude of some of the Stone-folk factions, to them, bothered him; more than just fear of spying and intrusion, more than fear of someone unknown and new. Something else was fueling this, Dun was sure, but he couldn't pin down what it was. And why did it seem to be the two farthest upstream Dukedoms? He could feel all the pieces but couldn't grasp the whole. It reminded him of a game the pups played—each with the pieces of a reed doll, sticks, and strands. The first to assemble the toy won. A simple game, stupid-seeming now and so far away. But as simple as it was, Dun felt the pieces mocking him; challenging him to make them into something. As they drifted off to sleep again, Dun arranged and rearranged the sticks and straws obsessively in his head. Padg twitched next to Dun, his voice just too faint to be a whimper.

Tali, though, dreamed of something else. She dreamed of the Stone-carvers, slowly chipping their names into a massive monolith.

Chapter Eighteen

Something was going on. Tali noticed Amber was almost silent, monosyllabic at most. After a hurried breakfast, they were ushered back into the hallway to stand by the stone counter that served as Tuf's guard station. It quickly transpired that they had been summoned. The Council had reconvened. A decision had been reached. Once they were sitting on the benches in the hall, the same formalities were observed. However, this time everyone seemed at a more heightened state of urgency. And when the Stone-speaker's voice echoed off to silence, this time, the distinctive crack-boom echoed out twice, quickly. Then everyone in the chamber began to hum. An eerie low drone built up a resonance in the chamber's massive space.

The Stone-speaker began again, "The Council has spoken. After deliberation, a decision was reached. As it has been since the annals of Stone began, it falls to me to speak the sentence. We meet in all solemnity to do the gravest task that can be done..."

Before Dun's stomach could fall too far, a loud female shout rang across the humming in the chamber. "Carvers!" Tali's voice almost tore as she projected, to cut through the massive sound of the drone. She had done enough though, as the humming stopped short.

"What is the meaning of this?" the Stone-speaker screeched, apoplectic with rage at having been interrupted. "A female may not speak here!"

Tali didn't feel the need to stop there, though. "The carvers!" she said, finding her feet now.

"Who speaks our name and why?" came the distinctive high clear voice of Lord Marble, the Carvers' Protector.

"We have found something important. A piece, lost from your records. If you execute us now, you will never know of it. Only we can show you!" Tali sounded triumphant.

Dun shared the elation, the first he'd felt in many spans and from beside him he heard a quiet "Yes!" from Padg. Now the chamber had a different kind of silence; not ominous, but warmed with a faint hope of their escape.

It was the kind of silence, Tali decided, that she enjoyed. It was not, however, long-lived.

"I declare this council session adjourned! Take them away!" the Stone-speaker commanded.

Dun, Padg, and Tali were bundled back toward their cells. Padg couldn't resist a comment. "Well, Tali, if your plan was to make the Council unspeakably angry, I'd say part one was working. What happens in part two?"

The comment earned him a growl from Tali and a poke in the ribs from his guard. Padg considered it worth it; he hadn't felt so cheerful in spans.

They were in their cells only briefly before Tuf arrived. "I must take you to Skarn. Come now."

In Skarn's chamber, when they arrived, Dun could hear the shuffle of feet. Skarn was pacing. It seemed that the impact of Tali's performance had rippled throughout the Stone-folk in quick time. When he spoke his voice was taut. "Tell me what you know."

"No." Tali was quiet and defiant.

A crack that echoed around the chamber was followed by a half whimper from Tali. Dun felt sick; Padg felt incensed; both stood.

"Sit down!" Skarn barked. No one moved.

"Sit," Tali said gently. Then she turned to Skarn. "Really, as a civilized folk, is that the best you can do?"

"I could have your two friends tortured until you do tell me."

"We both know that's desperation talking. Currently, you're planning on executing the lot of us. What exactly have we got to lose?" she said. "Here's how it's going to work. You are going to tell your masters that we will be taken back to where we were found, and we will lead you from there. Any more violence or threats of violence—we don't go. Any sense of us being tricked—we don't go. We are civilized folk, you are civilized folk. Let's behave that way."

"Tuf!" Skarn shouted. "Take them back to their cells."

It didn't take long before they got a response to Tali's bold move. A deputation arrived in the corridor. It consisted of Lords and Dukes and various hangers-on, judging by the fuss and bustle. Tuf explained as he opened Dun and Padg's cell.

"You are to take Lord Schist and a deputation from each tribe to show them whatever it is you claim to have found. If this turns out to be a trick, then you will be thrown back in the cells immediately and you will return to the next council session for sentencing."

"Seems fair enough," Padg said.

"There is a palace guard cohort to lead us to where you were found. Everyone follow their instructions carefully; we are going somewhere uncharted and dangerous. We wish to keep everyone safe. Does anyone have any questions?" Tuf said.

Silence was his answer.

"Then let us go."

Dun realized he was suppressing excitement. This was the first opportunity they had to experience some of the Stone-folk's homeland. Prior to that point, the extent of their range had been cells and council chamber, which wasn't far on balance, and the small part of forgotten territory they were returning to. They climbed a helical staircase, and Dun couldn't help but marvel at the eons of craft that had gone into making it. Every piece carved from solid rock, so the legends of the Stone-folk seemed to say. It was an awesome achievement.

Dark

They passed through lanes of homes, where Dun could hear the flurry and blather of everyday life: the shouting of cubs, the shouting of mothers after their cubs, the aroma of some kind of sweet-smelling powder accompanied by an odd, stone-scraping noise. They climbed over a bridge that arched sharply upward as they walked it. Beneath the bridge, he could hear the ding of metal on rock face. Was it mining? Carving? They crossed a space that Dun's air-sense told him was pretty large, seemingly packed with noises and smells that resolved themselves into a market. Dun listened hard to try to make out what was being sold. He tried to make out the smells of the food, all of which smelled much more palatable than the fare they'd been offered since being there. They passed schools of cubs echoing a list from a teacher, a family arguing, soldiers being drilled, and an eerie stone-clomping sound; some kind of work bashing stones together? Dun couldn't even guess.

Slowly, the signs of civilization dwindled to just the faint moan of air movement through distant passages. The smells faded from life to staleness, abandonment. The passages slowly leveled, then eased downward as they went on, and Dun's sense of direction was told him these passages were more curving too, as if they were moving in some huge arc. He imagined them as a stylus inscribing the tail of some serpentine, mythical beast. If it was a creature of stories, then its tail was forked. There were many choices of passage as they continued deeper into the dark reaches of the Stone-lanes. Sometimes the guards stopped and conferred. *This really wasn't somewhere they came often*, Dun thought. After much deciding and backtracking they reached another set of stone stairs, wide and straight this time. Dun felt dust shushing under his feet and listened to the hushed chatter of the party and the sound of fingers being run across stone, as they realized the walls on either side of them were intricately carved.

"Please don't touch the carvings," Tuf said. "They may hide traps or triggers for things we have not yet investigated. Stay close and try to remember how dangerous this place is." He sounded tense.

The staircase was long and massive and it took a good deal of careful time to get the party even halfway down.

Then Tuf began again, "Now we will need to lead everyone one at a time across this last landing. It is very important you follow your guide closely; there is a trap here and it is dangerous. Follow my instructions and everyone will be safe."

So the nobles and the hangers-on were led across the landing one by one and eventually Tali, Padg, and Dun. Dun instinctively felt his throat tighten, and he could remember the sinister smell in his nose from last time they were here.

Once they had reached the bottom of the stairs, Tuf spoke to them, "We have arrived. Lead us to this place you have found."

So with a guard holding each of them, to prevent escape, they returned to the breach in the wall and the huge wall carving beyond it was just how they'd left it. Tali and Dun just had time to remind themselves of the strange shapes and the story they might tell before the quiet cold voice of Lord Schist's advisor, Obsidian, spoke out, "Lead me, Bridge-folk, to where you strayed. What did you find, I wonder?"

They led him to the stone face with the series of carvings. They heard the hiss of his old fingers, running the grooves and edges of the stone. He muttered under his breath, but his quiet, steely voice meant it was hard to make anything out at all. Dun thought he heard him say, "Can't be..." or another word that might have been "fakery," but he was too distracted to tell. Now he was here at the carvings again, he knew there was something the shapes should be telling him. Something very important he had all the facts to piece together, but couldn't. It was something about that recurring motif, the odd curved shape, and the two figures on it. He needed to talk to the others about it, share their ideas, but his thoughts were disturbed by Obsidian's call across the chamber. Even Obsidian shouting was oddly quiet.

"Where is that historian? What's he called? Gneiss? Come here. And a carver. Lord Marble, who is Master Carver now after Tuck-pointer's death?"

"That would be Bolster, wise Obsidian."

"Is he here?"

"Yes..."

"Then send him forth. Quickly now."

They came to the wall too. This time, some of the thoughts and conference were loud enough to hear.

"No, it is genuine. Feel the quality of the grain, the chisel strokes, firm, even, smooth."

"Countless eons old, before the Stone annals of our time."

"Do you know what it depicts?" It was Obsidian's voice this time.

"We would need more time to study."

"You have a suspicion?" the historian asked.

"There is a possible..." Obsidian said, almost to himself. Then aloud to the chamber, he said, "Lords all, we must leave now. Guards, take the prisoners and have their sentence carried out."

"But Counselor Obsidian, surely Lord Schist must be present for a sentence to be passed?"

"Take them and execute them!"

"It will take a little time to prepare the Stone Maw."

"Do it as fast as you can. Go! Now!"

Dark

Chapter Nineteen

So this was really it, Dun thought, as the guards hurried them, pushing and prodding them back to their cells. But why all of a sudden? What did that mural say that was worth killing them over?

Should he even be worrying about that at all? Were they about to be put to death? He chastised himself for being distracted. But that didn't stop him thinking about it.

"I always thought these Stone-folk were no appreciators of art," Padg said after a particularly vindictive poke from his guard. Although they had become used to the heavy quern-stones on their feet, hurrying in them was neither comfortable nor easy.

"Quiet you," the poking guard said.

"Oh come on," Dun chimed in, bottled annoyance rising in him. "It's hardly like you can threaten us. Let's agree that we'll hurry not to get you into trouble, and you'll let us talk on our way. It is kind of our last chance."

"Well," the guard said, pushing Dun, *who seemed more senior*, Dun thought, "I don't suppose it'll bother Tuf none."

"There," Dun said in what he hoped were pacifying tones. "Speaking of Tuf, where is he? I thought he'd have come this way with us if it was fastest."

"It isn't."

"Oh?"

"There's a quicker more dangerous way. He'll have taken that to get there first."

"I'm not being picky here," Padg chimed in. "But would it have made any difference taking us that way, if you're all so keen to get rid of us?"

"It has ladders," Padg's guard said.

"Ah," Padg conceded. He was particularly feeling the weight and chafing of his quern-stone, in the rush to their doom.

Dun had noticed that Tali was unusually quiet.

"You okay?" he asked.

"Yes. Fine."

"It'll be okay."

"You *know* that?"

"No, I've not had a foretelling but..."

"Well, then," she said sharply. Then, realizing quite how she'd lashed at Dun, she continued, "I'm sorry, it's just... I'm... I..."

"Scared?" Dun offered.

"Yes."

"If, you know, if- we'll all be together..." Dun said.

"If it does come to that," Tali said. "I want to go first. I don't think I could stand it... you know."

"Yeah, I know," Dun said.

They drifted back into a silence surprisingly easy for what they'd just discussed. The air clearer now, they'd broached what they needed most to say. *At least they were returning by a less populated route*, Dun thought. Somehow he felt less bad because of that. Or maybe it was a rest span. He'd lost track since he'd been a prisoner and wasn't sure what times they were being kept to. All he knew was that he was tired, and he didn't want to die when he was tired. *Did everyone get stupid thoughts like that when facing death*, he wondered? Of all the times that a foretelling would be useful, now would be good. It was just that the part of his brain that was tired and scared seemed to be the part he was supposed to be calling on to produce a result.

The journey seemed to be slowing down and not just due to carrying the weight of the quernstones. The guards gave them a break and issued flasks of faintly brackish water for them to drink. Dun panted and Padg's leg was bleeding where his stone had rubbed him. He adjusted the stone and tore some fabric off his other trouser leg to stuff down where it was rubbing. It would have to do. The break wasn't as long as either Dun or Padg had hoped, but the new pace the guards set was mercifully slower. Dun wondered whether this was just because they were closer to their destination. He caught that thought and reminded himself he must keep his head straight, despite everything. Tali and Padg, despite their bluster, depended on him. He was responsible for leading them, wherever they had to go, and if he allowed himself the luxury of wallowing in fears of his own doom, then what kind of person did that make him?

Slowly, Dun detected smells of civilization on the gentle breeze moving through the corridors. They were nearing the end of the journey. They threaded their way back through the market and back through houses to the stair that led down to the prison level. All three of them were made to stand in front of Tuf's desk. He had reached there before them, as they'd all expected. They could smell something pungent on his breath.

"The two males will follow me," Tuf said. Dun thought, he knows our names. He wondered Tuf had to disassociate himself from people he's supposed to execute?

"The female must wait here with a guard for her escort—wherever she is, curse her. Well, we cannot wait, we must proceed."

Dark

Dun and Padg were led to the chamber that they'd bathed in when they arrived. Two guards were there to meet them. It seemed to Dun there were a lot more guards around. Their clothes were taken, and Dun and Padg were roughly scrubbed with stones then doused in warm water. The guards guided them to a warm air vent, and they waited while they dried off. Next, the guards pulled them into fresh-smelling, loose-fitting clothes. Finally, they left the chamber and walked back out into the corridor. It felt refreshingly cool after the humidity of the bath chamber. Then they were walked back to their cells. Tuf was there to meet them. He reached for Dun's face, held his chin, and smeared something in the middle of his forehead. It felt greasy and cold.

"Gods, decide your fate," Tuf said.

He repeated the ritual with Padg. Now Dun felt really scared.

***

Tali stood at the guard station with her guard, for whom she hadn't managed to overhear a name. It was definitely a male though, she could smell that, and a nervous one to boot. She heard his feet shuffling on the floor as the time clicked by. At least she could enjoy the fact that she wasn't the only one who was nervous. She wondered where Amber was. Somehow, whatever happened, she wanted Amber to be there. It seemed right. Although equally, Tali could understand if Amber didn't want to be.

Her guard finally cracked.

"Right, we will wait here for Amber no longer. I will return you to your cell and search for her."

I can sit down, thought Tali, as she was ushered back. She was trying to stay cheerful, but the remainder of her morale was ebbing away. She was hurriedly pushed into her cell, caught her foot, and fell to the floor. As she rubbed the parts of her that stung, she wondered what she'd tripped on; she knew her cell pretty well by now. She felt across the floor.

It was her backpack.

Tali's heart leaped. Now she had an ally and they had a chance. There was only one question left to answer: Would she still have time?

Dark

"Who knew, a whole... a whole everything, could spring up out of what we left behind, the first time."

Excerpts from <Distress Beacon SN-1853001>.
Found by E.S.V. Vixen Terradate: 26102225.

Dark

Chapter Twenty

Dun and Padg, now dressed and anointed with odd, heady-smelling ointment, followed their guards down a short passage to a room they'd not been in before. In it, they were led to a stone table with stone benches either side.

"Sit."

They did as they were told and waited at the benches. It seemed like time had slowed almost to a stop. Dun found himself experiencing everything with a complete intensity he'd not felt before. Everything seemed more real, every tiny detail stood out. At the same time, he knew they were racing toward their fate. Another guard came in along with a smell—food of some description, smelling relatively palatable. With a clatter, bowls were placed before Dun and Padg.

"Eat."

The smell that wafted up was something that they had never experienced since being here. Food that you might want to eat immediately, rather than an offering that in some way was not quite right—an off smell here, an odd stale taste, a particularly slimy texture, or just plain cold. They'd had all of that in their short stay here, and that had made everything slightly longer. Was the food so much better for some people here then? Were they experiencing "underclass" food? Would Amber eat like this? Her family? Or was this grade of catering usually reserved for prisoners, the condemned? Dun shuddered. Surely a folk as sophisticated as the Stone-folk had worked out for themselves that how you treated misbehavior in a group said more about you than almost anything else. How could you ever hope to reform, or address, by treating misdemeanor with contempt? Dun didn't suppose the Stone-folk much cared what anyone else thought. How could they? He caught himself. All this supposition was fruitless in their position anyway. And what made it all worse was that the particular contempt they were being treated with was political; Dun was sure. There was some metaphorical market stall they had upset here, and they were reaping the consequences. Some of it was to do with that godsdamned mural, but that had only been the tipping point in their visit here. Something else had altered the normal course of diplomacy amongst the peoples here. Normally, straying visitors would be returned with a reprimand and appeasement gifts would be necessary, but there had been none of that. Nothing in Dun's careful preparation had warned him that the Stone-folk were so quick at wanting to execute people. Maybe not being returned was what it was about. Could it be that some of the tribes here were behaving *so* peculiarly, they didn't want any outsiders to know? At any cost. He really needed some time alone with the others to start discussing that, but it seemed as if that was just not going to happen. Dun supposed that true to form for the Stone-folk, Tali would be being kept somewhere else and being fed, alone. He sighed and started to eat. At least it tasted as good as it smelled, and it was warm.

Dun drifted off into a reverie. He couldn't remember the last time he'd eaten food that'd been anything but a test of endurance. He started to feel drowsy. He felt warm and pleasant inside and was just hoping for a gentle sliding off to sleep when a horrifying thought occurred to him. Had the food been poisoned? Or if not poisoned, had they been sedated in some way, perhaps to make it easier to get them to go to their fate? Or worse still, to make it seem—to those chosen to attend such things—as if they were calmly accepting their lot. He felt sick and cold and panicky. He felt his heart start to thud louder in his chest. Long and slow, but louder. It was all he could hear in his ears.

Then there was an awful smell, a rotting, reeking, death and decaying stench. Through his slightly drifty state, he could hear the guards vomiting heartily. Then he felt his arm being forcibly grabbed and dragged off the stone bench, the rest of his drowsy body following behind.

"Come *on*!" a voice in his ear hissed.

His mind searched around for a personality to attach to the voice. Tali! This was their chance and she'd created it. He wanted to wrap his arms around her and congratulate her on how brilliant she was but he felt so drowsy. All he could do was let himself be dragged. Now his panic was easing off, he could hear Padg groaning not far from him. Tali reached around Dun to grab Padg too and pulled both of them, staggering toward the doorway. Dun found himself feeling light-headed and distant, but he was enjoying the odd feeling of not being entirely in control.

"Gods, I knew I'd used too much," Tali said, grunting as she dragged them. "You two helping at this point would be really useful!"

"Sfargh," Padg said.

Once in the corridor, Tali began pulling at right angles and dragged them toward where they now knew Tuf's guard station to be. This bothered Dun. Oddly, less than he thought it should. They brushed past the stone table. There was a ceramic rolling noise, and then a small wet pottery smash onto the stone floor. Dun felt a small splash onto his foot.

A waft of another familiar, faintly sweet, powdery smell drifted toward him. Gods, his brain was slow. Who was it? Smell was normally his strongest sense.

"Quickly, down here!" a quiet, insistent voice called out. Amber, of course. Dun felt slow in every way, but gradually his brain was crawling out of whatever mud it had become mired in. Amber felt for Dun's hand then dragged him off at a sharp angle, down a very narrow passage that he had not noticed before. Padg was behind him, being pushed by Tali, which seemed to be some kind of struggle. Amber squeezed past them to the entrance of the passage, then, after a brief scraping of stone, Dun's air-sense told him the passage had been closed.

"Where is this, Amber?" Tali asked.

"An old, forgotten passage. My father was a mason. I learned a thing or two."

"Didn't you just!"

"I used to follow him everywhere. I wanted to be a mason. I couldn't because..." She paused, then said, "I learned all the tools and strokes, and used to love to rescribe all the old maps."

Dun's brain was rolling something around. Something Tali had said. Something about "*Using too much*".

"Myooou", Dun said.
"Pardon?" Tali said.
"Mmmm... youw."
"Me?"
"You," Dun said, gaining confidence.
"Yes?"
"You... poisoned... us," Dun said.
"Only a little," Tali said.
"Eh?"

"Only a little, and I didn't mean to. The poisoning thing was only a by-product anyway. I was trying to mask the effects of the stench for you."

"Y've hud meuh... muh... m-y fa... ther's coo... cooking then?" Padg said.

"Oh, you've come round too now have you?" Tali said.

"You used a scent?" Dun asked.

"A vapor, more like. Some natural, some not."

"How come it's affected so wide an area?" Dun said.

"Ah, you apply the right vapor to the right vents and airflow does the rest. Amber helped with that."

"Thank you, Amber," Dun said. "We couldn't have asked you to help us, and we can only guess what you've risked. Thank you."

Amber made a humming noise.

"What now?" Padg said.

"Well," Tali said, "we wait a little for the chaos to build then we use some more of the hunter's balm to hide and we make a run for it."

"Which way?" Dun said. "I'm not sure we could even get out the way we came in."

"No," Amber said. "It's too far and too dangerous. We thought the easiest way is through the main upper stairway and out through the Grand Entrance."

"Won't that be busy?" Dun said.

"Ah, but busy helps us. We can sneak away undetected through a crowd. The hunter's balm works very well that way," said Tali.

"You're enjoying this aren't you?" Padg said to her.

Tali grunted. Their conversation was broken by the noise of loud shouting and rushing feet coming from the main corridor.

"I think that might be our cue," Dun said.

Dark

Chapter Twenty-One

Dun opened the door to the passage they'd been hiding in. It swung inward noiselessly. Dun couldn't help but wonder how the carvers had achieved that. Chaos still reigned outside, but seemingly much farther down the corridor from them.

Once the door was open, Amber squeezed past.

"Quick! This way," she said and led them firmly in the direction of the noise.

"Shouldn't we be heading *away* from everyone else?" Padg said.

"Not if you want your things back," Amber said over her shoulder. "They are in a storeroom, down here."

She led them, single file, down the passage to a room that smelled of old cloth. She shifted inside and called for them all to follow.

"Check it's all here quickly, then let's go," Tali said.

"I'll listen out," Amber said, moving back toward the door and pulling it over.

Tali led them to a series of shelves carved into the rock, along the wall farthest from the door. Sure enough, Dun smelled his familiar travel pack before he even touched it, and some fumbling around on the shelves discovered Padg's pack and the remaining sword-spears. Padg started back toward the door.

"Hey you, not so fast," Tali said. "There's the small matter of those quern-stones to deal with. I've waited til here because I don't want to be leaving odd smells in that secret corridor. We might not have finished using it yet. Right. Stand still. I need to be quick."

Tali was right about the smell. Dun heard the hissing noise at the same time the astringent, ferrous stink reached his nose. Then there was a dull metal plink, and the two halves of the quern-stone fell away. He limped around in a circle trying to restore his circulation and quickly discovered that was only going to pose slightly less of a problem than his balance. He heard the fizz, then plink, of Padg being freed. Dun was still rubbing his calves.

"The quickest way back is toward the Council Chamber," Amber said.

"That takes us past some quite busy places," Padg said.

"I've still got a few tricks in my pouch," Tali said.

"You're *definitely* enjoying this," Padg cut back.

"Wait." Dun's slightly urgent voice stopped them. "The map. It's not in my pack."

"Bones and ashes!" Padg cursed. "Skarn will have that for sure."

"His chamber is back the other way," Amber said. "Going back for it would double our chances of being caught."

Dun sighed. "Going on without it would do that for us too, at least when we get out of here. We've got to find it and take it back. Or destroy it. We can't let it fall into the wrong hands." Then when he thought about what he'd said, and how Amber might interpret it, he added, "You know what I mean."

"I know," she said quietly. Then said, "So, we must go back for it."

As they hurried along the passage, Dun fell in alongside Tali. "How much hunter's balm have we got left?"

"To make it effective? Maybe two doses each for us," she replied.

"I think we need to use one now," Dun said. "It's the quickest way of getting in and out."

"It's still a big risk," Padg said.

"The map *is* one of the reasons we're here," Dun said.

"Okay," Tali spoke quickly to Amber and they pulled into the mouth of another adjoining passage.

She applied the ointment. Dun had always been impressed at how quickly it worked. He could instantly feel the cold tingle of the salve on his skin where she'd briskly rubbed it on. He had always wondered how it worked quite so well. Although she didn't apply it to any of the things he was carrying or his loose clothes, the vapor permeated everything so quickly that within sixty clicks he couldn't even smell himself. He shivered. It was an experience he found extremely disquieting.

"Quickly," Amber said, breaking his thoughts. "He is two doors farther along from here. We will wait. Go now. You must go alone; any more than one of us and we'll be caught for sure."

Dun rounded the corner into the passage, running his hand along the wall, ears spiked high listening. He could hear no one, but a still cloud of scent in the air told him that Skarn had been there recently. Dun slowed his breathing and crept toward the door. The scent was stronger, although he could hear nothing in the room. His other ear was picking up fainter sounds from the corridor, of urgent shouting and running. The search was on for them, just not here. He inched himself around the doorway. The scent was dense in here. But still, nothing to hear. Dun crept along the wall nearest the door, away from where he knew Skarn's desk to be, checking gently for shelves.

"GUARDS!"

Skarn's voice was so loud and so close, it was everything Dun could do not to jump. He knew that if he did, disturbing the air would give him away to Skarn's air-sense. If that was as good as the Guard Captain's ability for stillness, then Dun was caught for sure. Frozen, he waited, listening hard. Now he could hear the slightly raised breath sounds after Skarn's shout and, outside the room, running feet coming closer. He hoped they didn't find the others on their way.

With his air-sense, he felt Skarn moving, possibly toward the door, certainly away from his desk. Dun slid himself slowly, back against the wall. He could feel stone edges against his back now. At last, a shelf. He edged his fingers behind him and started feeling along the stone-work for anything that might prove interesting. Some flattened scrolls: an odd spiky stone and another stone, abrasive and light. Then he smelled something. The familiar scent of the fabric straps of the map case they'd been carrying the scroll in. Dun went to reach farther into the shelf, and then heard a brief scrape behind him. His pulse leaped to clicker-beetle speed, as he realized Skarn was aiming for the same shelf. Dun knew that if he moved his feet Skarn would hear him. All he could do was lean in place, slowly away from the hands as they reached toward him. Too quick and the eddies in the air would give him away. Too slow, and... He didn't dare think about too slow. Heart hammering, Dun felt like every muscle in his body was clenched. The air brushed past and a scraping noise across the stone and parchment on the shelf told Dun that Skarn had found one of the things he was seeking. All Dun could do was hope he wouldn't find one of the others. As the scraping stopped and the object was lifted into the air, a waft of its scent followed; it was the map case. Dun had no time to process that. Skarn had paused. If he lifted his hand back to the shelf, Dun was easily within reach. Skarn gave a characteristic searching sniff.

"Are you here, little Bridge-pup?" Skarn's voice was low and menacing, but becoming clearer as his head turned. Dun could hear the voice getting closer still, the air from the words starting to brush his face. "Would you dare be here? Is this why we can't find you, hmm?"

Dun's mouth was dry. The urge to swallow rose in his throat. He somehow felt his body was conspiring against him. He focussed what attention he could to try to suppress the reflex. If he let it run its course, it would be the death of him.

"Come on out, little Bridge-pup..."

The air on Dun's face was warm and stale and if Skarn's air-sense was sharp, surely he would be able to feel the resistance in the air that Dun's own face was providing.

"Come on out..."

Dun felt a shape, possibly a hand, closing toward him. He leaned as far as he could, he was as far as he could stretch. Any farther and he'd overbalance. The hand still got closer.

"Captain Skarn!" a loud voice shouted from the doorway.

As Skarn whirled to answer it, Dun took his chance. He followed in Skarn's wake, latching onto the scent of the map case. From the wake, the case was probably on Skarn's left-hand side.

"Reporting as ordered, Captain."

"Why are you not bringing me the hides of the prisoners?" Skarn barked.

"We are still searching, sir."

"Not good enough. Bring a guard cohort back here now and search the detention level."

"We have searched it, sir."

"Then... search... it... again. Now!"

As Skarn finished berating the guard, he swung his body away from the door, and Dun felt a bump against him. He grabbed. It was the map case. This was his one chance. Knowing where Skarn was standing, Dun kicked out hard and connected with a knee. Skarn yelped—as much out of shock as anything else—and as he flinched, Dun yanked the map case, ducked low, and ran for the door. Skarn was quick though, and Dun was already flying through the air before he had a chance to process the information that Skarn had stuck his uninjured leg out in the doorway for Dun to trip over. Dun hit the ground and grazed the edge of the doorway at the same time. He used the momentum to roll to the wall of the passage and stand.

"Now I have you!" Skarn shouted triumphantly.

"Afraid not!" Padg's voice came loud from the passage beside them, as did the butt of a sword-spear, which crunched as it connected with Skarn's jaw.

"Time to go, lovely though it's been," Padg said as he grabbed Dun's arm. "Any time you like, Tali!"

In response to this, Dun heard two swift fizzes overhead, and then a bizarre whistling, whooping noise followed by a curious acrid, charcoal smell. The noise and smell seemed to be reaching some kind of a crescendo, even as they were running away, in the opposite direction.

"That should keep them occupied for a little while," Tali said.

"Nice trick," Padg said.

"Howl-bombs," she replied. "Glad you like them."

"Where now, Amber?" Dun said, breathless.

"You have the map?" she asked.

"Yes."

"Then up."

Chapter Twenty-Two

Tali smashed another flask on the stairs at the top. As Dun listened to the tinkling shards dancing down the steps, he reminded himself why he liked her: She was smart.

"That should be slippy enough to keep them amused for a while," she said.

"Where now?" Dun said.

"Through the market," Amber said.

"Won't our scent give us away if we're being searched for?" Dun asked.

"There should be enough distractions going on there that we will slip by if we are swift."

"Won't the market be guarded?" Padg said.

"Yes," Amber said simply.

"Great. I was enjoying your plan until then."

"It is the only plan there is Padg," Amber said to him quietly.

Noises drifted up the staircase to them, a melee of shouting and swearing punctuated by the definite sound of a skull connecting with stone.

"Time to go," Dun said.

The passage to the market became wider as they neared their destination. Amber reassured Dun that if the market were to be guarded, then the main route in, the one they were taking, was so wide at the market end that guarding it was impractical. There were many other narrower passages in and out that made a two guard scent-search of all passers-by much more effective. She reassured him getting *out* of the market again would be their real problem. Reassurance wasn't what Dun was feeling.

His unease started to lift when the sounds and smells coming down the passage fully permeated his consciousness and were too big to ignore. There was something intoxicating to Dun about the bustle, noise, and smell of a strange market. At once safe and predictable: everyone everywhere needed, food, tools, something to smell nice; but at the same time wild and different. Dun could hear the sounds of stone being hand ground, next to a hawker crying "yip, yipyip yiii!". He smelled talcum, sweat, sand, and old dust. The irresistible magic of the mundane and the exotic. Dun felt happy, then his next foretelling arrived. The swirling feeling came so quickly it caused him to lose his balance and he slid sideways into Padg.

"Easy there, feller!" his friend said. "Hey, are you okay?"

But Dun soared on the foretelling, which was his most vivid to date. And it was very simple: He was at the market buying something. This market. Buying something hand-sized, no, something that would fit in his hand. Something carved. A totem. The things that all folk carved. Small statues of animals, portraits, abstract shapes. Made from different materials depending on a tribes traditions, but the common thread to all of them was texture. The carvers often picked raw pieces for their feel before they started, and then a slow process of etching, scraping, writing, smoothing. They were sometimes finished with blobs or glazes of scented resin, sometimes left plain. The totems were widely sought and traded and on market stalls, kept on woven thongs or strings to prevent thieves.

"Thieves!" the shout from the totem stallholder was shrill and very, very loud.

Dun felt jolted back to the present, and then felt the totem in his hand. He felt his hand being jerked nearly out of it's joint as Padg dragged him. The four of them ran in a line, hand in hand, Amber at the lead as she knew the market the best. A fact displayed by her deftly kicking the leg from a stall on their way past, spilling the stalls contents to the ground and its owners curses into the air. As the chaos spread like a stain behind them, Amber led them along the wall of the massive market chamber and pulled them smartly down a small passage, away from the main chamber. She reached down to check her position, and then grunting her satisfaction that she was in the right place, kicked a grill at floor level. She bundled the others through the tube it revealed and reinstated the grill once they were all in the tube.

"Forward!" she hissed at Dun's backside. "There is a small chamber ahead."

The tunnel was claustrophobic and had a small amount of water running in a groove beneath them as they crawled. It had the effect of making an unpleasant trip into an unpleasant damp and fusty trip. Ahead was longer than any of them really expected. Finally, Tali, out front, found the passage widen.

"Here," she whispered.

"They won't hear us down here. We're safe for a while," Amber said.

"Good!" Padg said. "What in the hells were you thinking?" He rounded on Dun.

"I don't know. One minute I was in a foretelling trance, then I was being dragged here."

"What seems like a harmless, odd quirk in an old friend is less amusing when it's about to get us all killed!"

"I know, I'm sorry."

"What did you steal?" Padg asked. "I hope it was worth nearly getting us all killed."

"A totem," he said quietly.

"Is that *it*?"

"Yeah." Dun's voice sounded small even to him. "It's not as if I intended that to happen. I didn't even know it was."

"I know," Padg said, half in apology. "What is it anyway?"

"The totem? I'm not sure. I haven't really had a chance to examine it."

He took it out of his pocket and felt its surface, turning it, and exploring the egg-shaped item in his hand. The ovoid was stone and seemed to have two "faces". Half of its surface was polished smooth, its opposite side pitted irregularly, possibly the natural surface of the stone. There was something about this object that Dun felt he already knew. A familiarity not with the object itself, but somehow with what it was. That was the thing with totems, many were not simple. There were levels of meaning to them, sometimes spiritual or political. There were portraits, caricatures, maps, toys, puzzles, animals, abstract shapes. Some even had embedded scents, small crystals of incense, or perfumed wood, sometimes blended to create an artful olfactory layer on top of the tactile one.

But what did this one mean? And why did Dun feel like he knew it so well?

Chapter Twenty-Three

Dun felt a firm poke in his ribs from something blunt and woke with a start.

"We cannot stay here forever." It was Amber.

Dun didn't even realize he'd been asleep, or how long he'd been out for. He just knew he felt better, very much better.

"Here," Amber said, poking something warm into his hands. "You are not the only one who steals."

Dun felt a comment rise in his throat but thought better of it. It was the first warm food he had eaten since they were about to be executed, and it tasted fantastic. Some kind of spiced nuts ground up into nearly a paste and wrapped in a leaf. It was a satisfying combination of sweet and slightly bitter, and the spices warmed him as it went down. He could hear similar noises of satisfaction from the others in the bolt-hole and smiled to himself. As he finished, he put his hand back into his pocket to feel for a rag to wipe the sweet grease from his hands. Instead, he found the totem nestling warm against his leg. It was odd to find the thing comforted him, as much as it unnerved him. And that was before he answered all those nagging questions about it. The shape of it, the odd one-half textured, one-half smooth, feel of the thing. He knew it, somehow.

"Come," Amber said from the end of the room nearest the exit. "The noises of searching have died down now. We must leave."

There was surprisingly little noise of bustle coming from the cavern outside. Dun figured it must be sleep-cycle.

Amber marshaled everyone in the corridor. "Ready?"

One noise each from the Bridge-folk was enough, and Amber slid the grating free and edged out.

Dark

She paused briefly then, said, "Okay. Clear. Come."

They followed out as quickly and quietly as squeezing would allow. Amber grabbed Dun's hand, and they quickly formed a chain with Tali bringing up the rear. The route through the sleeping market that Amber picked took the folk through a trail of fading aromas. The smells stranded together in Dun's mind. He thought of the weavers in the village, taking different textured fibers in their great peg looms to make beautiful rugs, to go underfoot in special places. This place was certainly special but too dangerous to enjoy now. An impatient pull on Dun's wrist from Amber snapped him back to the present.

"Come."

"Wait," Tali's voice came hushed but urgent from the back of the snake of hands. She pulled Padg and so jerked all the others to a stop.

"Listen, above us."

When they stood, stopping even breathing, the hissed voices over their heads carried enough to be audible.

"...still not apprehended! They are only Bridge-folk: a simple people. Why can we not find them?"

"We have all our guards searching now. We have called on volunteers from the common-folk too; traders and the like."

"It is not good enough. They must be found. You all know what is at stake."

"We cannot be sure how much they know."

"Why else would they be here?"

"Accident?"

"I am no great believer in accident."

" Truly spies then?"

"Yes," the voice said impatiently. "But from whom? I always believed the Bridge-folk to be too naive."

"You think them not to be Bridge-folk?"

"I think merely we should inform our allies that we may all be being observed."

"Impossible, how could anyone know? The Ri—"

"Silence!"

"I merely..."

"Quiet! I can hear something. Below us..."

"Run!" Amber hissed.

They did. Still holding onto her hand, they ran zigzag through the stalls. And all the time, through their panted breathing they could hear the gathering calls and voices of militia and soldiers closing. When the calls became shouts they knew they were surrounded.

"We were so close to the gates." Amber tried to keep the tone of desperation from her voice.

"Now we shall find who these spies are and what they are really doing here!" Skarn shouted.

"Well, that would really spoil my fun," Myrch said. His voice so close; he was as close as the guards.

Then came a low concussion wave and everyone was knocked flat, ears ringing. Dun felt his arm being roughly dragged and followed where it went, too dazed to do otherwise. He was pushed down to some wide steps and fighting to keep his balance, was encouraged down. He was starting to get enough wits to use his air-sense around him. Tali and Padg were above him on the steps, below them all, some kind of water. There was another loud explosion from the top of the stairs and they continued down hastily. At the bottom of the staircase was the river, quite deep, wide and fast there and moored at the bottom of the stairs bobbed some kind of crude raft, made from found things. It smelled of rusted steel and thermoplastic. Dun felt someone hurry down the stairs behind them.

"Get on!" Myrch shouted. They climbed awkwardly on, Dun getting feet wet in the process. The raft lurched as some kind of tie was hastily cut and the flow carried them away.

"Well," said Myrch, "did you miss me?"

"Where the hell have you been?" Tali shouted.

"I'll take that as a no then."

Dark

Dark

"You can adapt amazingly quickly to extraordinary conditions, if you have to. Maybe they're not that extraordinary. Maybe they're just ordinary, transposed, shifted sideways somehow."

Excerpts from <Distress Beacon SN-1853001>. Found by E.S.V. Vixen Terradate: 26102225.

Dark

Chapter Twenty-Four

"Amber!" Dun had started to come around from his daze. "We've left Amber!"

"If Amber is anyone you care about you'll lower your voice. We may be being followed."

"Hells," Padg said, "we can't go back."

"We can't leave her!" Dun cried.

"I believe we just have," Myrch said and returned to pushing the raft along with something long that made an odd short scrape on the bottom with each push.

Dun drew breath to speak, then stopped himself. What was there to say? He slumped, head propped against one of the edges of the raft. The raft smelled oily. Dun found himself twiddling with the bindings that held the raft together. Although the poles themselves were natural, some large river reed Dun guessed, the binding material was not. One of those "found" cords that was plaited and sold by some folk. A mix of different materials whose individual manufacture was long lost. It was strong enough, it had that for it, although depending on what mix of fibers made it up, it had the occasional surprise: becoming unexpectedly loose, getting tighter as it rubbed, even becoming permanently knotted once tied. Dun preferred ropes make from plant fiber. You knew where you were with that.

Something flat and long landed on his chest with a thud.

"Make yourself useful. Steer," Myrch said.

"Steer it yourself."

He felt the thing lifted off him. "Give it here," Padg said, quietly. "I'll do it."

"Get over it quickly," Myrch said. "We don't have the luxury of time to mope."

"Leave him alone," Tali said, distant.

They sank back into a gentle rhythm. The bump-scrape of the punting pole, the occasional splish of Padg performing a small course correction to Myrch's grunted orders.

"If we need to be so stealthy," Padg said after a while, breaking the bump-scrape rhythm. "Why is our punt-pole so damned noisy?"

"Do you know, that's the most sense any of you has spoken. Do you know how to scull, with oars?"

"Of course I know. I'm Bridge-folk. Bridges tend to go over rivers."

"Good," Myrch said. "You scull, I'll attend to the pole."

The bump-scrape stopped, to be replaced with the gentle swish-splish of Padg sculling from the back of the raft. After some rustling and Myrch making some kind of subvocal yell, there was a kind of brief hissing, ripping noise from whatever Myrch had found, another subvocal noise of what could perhaps be satisfaction, and then quiet again. The bumping noise, dampened, resumed again, the scrape had ceased entirely.

"So after all this fuss, are we actually being followed?" Tali said.

"Not anymore, no," Myrch said. "Thankfully, since stealth is not our strong point."

"Damn, and I'd have guessed politeness," Padg said.

"Sarcasm on the other hand," Tali said.

"Ah, yes," Padg said cheerily. "We're rather good at that."

They settled into a quiet rhythm of a bump of pole then a swish of oars. Bump, swish. Bump, swish. Dun thought of a heartbeat followed by a rush of blood. Maybe they were like some kind of bug in the bloodstream of the Dark; bump swish toward what kind of dark heart? Dun desperately wanted to cling to being awake, keeping some kind of angry vigil, as if allowing himself to drift off would let his memory of Amber ebb. In the end, his fatigue overtook him.

He woke some time later having the oddest feeling that something had changed. He yawned and stretched. As his consciousness returned, he began to get the oddest feeling; he could only just feel where the roof was above him. It was there, but far away, and the floor, all of the floor, was moving. He sat up slowly but found he still had to balance himself. The odd moving floor was making bizarre echoes, his air-sense and hearing were not telling him the same as his balance.

"It's called the Sea of Sevens," Myrch said. "To my knowledge, the largest body of water in the Dark."

"I heard Gatryn sing a song about it once," Tali said. "He knows all the old songs."

"The Alchemist knows much more than that," Myrch said in an odd tone that invited no questions and ended the exchange.

Dun was lost in the slap and slosh of the water on the raft. "It's amazing."

"It's amazing how you've ducked your turn for so long," Padg said. "Grab hold." He poked Dun with the end of one of the oars which the other dutifully took.

The rowing resumed. Dun realized there was no bump noise anymore. "No pole?"

"Too deep," Myrch said.

"The songs said it goes down forever," Tali said.

Myrch made a low snort.

"Any fish in it?" Dun said.

"Fish, sure," Myrch said, like a response to a challenge. There was further rustling from his end of the raft. "Hey, hold this."

Dark

Dun felt Tali shift to the end of the raft and a slight tweak in their course. Then the distinct plop of a baited line being dropped. Dun nearly smiled. He remembered fishing with his father when he was small. They sat close on the bridge. He remembered his feet swinging, and he could feel the warmth of his fathers arm against him. Oddly, he even remembered some of what they talked about. How fish were smart, was it? Dun wasn't so sure. They wound up with enough of them to eat, but his father was quietly certain. It might seem like the odds are always stacked against the fish, but they can outsmart even the best fisher-folk. Maybe swim the wrong way, maybe not fall for the bait, maybe even wriggle off the hook at the last minute. The smartest fish could even have the bait and not bite the hook.

"There you go!" Myrch said, a mix of genuine pleased and smug. "Tooth-fish."

"Really?" Tali said.

"Yup."

"Didn't realize fish was so much your thing," Padg said.

"If you weren't such a peasant, you'd know what one was," Tali said.

"Er, I do. Scaly, finny things. Wet heads."

"Tooth-fish, you idiot pup. I've never found one, much less tasted it," Tali said.

"It's massive!" Dun said as he felt the weight of the fish rock the raft.

"A delicacy throughout the Dark," Myrch said. "But oddly, for some reason only ever found in this lake. Rarely swim out of it. Highly sought after, so anyone with anything to trade or fight with will mostly get them before they get all the way down to the Bridge. This cycle we eat like kings."

The fish had some weight to it and just needed skinning. Tali offered to do that straight away. She muttered something about making finings with some unspecified part of the innards that Dun didn't want to think too deeply about. And once he'd tasted the fish, he was distracted from any thoughts like that. It was delicate, and they ate it raw. It had a sweet and meaty texture. He now knew what the fuss was about. The one fish Myrch had caught was enough to feed all four of them, with some left that Tali salted and rolled into a cloth from her kit. Dun wondered how many trade tallies what they'd just consumed would muster. Pleasantly full, he drifted back to sleep.

Dark

Chapter Twenty-Five

Bump.

The whole raft lurched. Myrch gave a waking-up shout and swore loudly. "That was not our smartest move." Then, he hissed, "Wake up!" He needn't have worried, the lurch had shaken everyone awake already.

"Where are we?" Tali asked.

"Damn good question," Myrch said. "If we hadn't all been asleep at the oars we'd know that by now." He paused, then said, "Godsdamn. Lakeside."

"For such a charming name," Padg said. "That doesn't bode well."

Myrch snorted.

"Nice village?" Padg pressed.

"No," Myrch clipped back. "Gods forgotten scum-hole."

"Good," Tali said. "Sounds lovely. We're here why?"

"Wait, I got that one," Padg said, "because our glorious leader, or kidnapper, or whatever he is, fell asleep too."

"And still, we're here because...?" Tali's sarcastic edge was hardly hidden.

"Because it's two full spans to the place we should have left the lake," Myrch said.

"So what now?" Dun said.

"Find somewhere to moor, away from the village, and I check things out," Myrch said.

"We can't come too?" Tali said.

"Sure," Myrch said, "if you'd like to take your chances with death in less than ten strides on the shore."

"Such a performer," Padg said under his breath.

Myrch grabbed an oar and began rowing the raft, seemingly along the hard face of where they'd landed, one bump at a time.

Dark

"Here," he said handing the paddle to Dun. There was a chink and a rustle of fibers. *Tying up the raft*, Dun thought. Once the rustling had stopped, Dun felt the air shift toward them, and he heard the sound of a crowd. A raucous crowd at that. Raucous in a way that Dun hadn't really heard before. The most riotous assembly Dun had ever heard was festival time in the village. A night of free-flowing mead in the Moot-hall could get quite out of hand at times. But the noise that Dun could hear from farther around the lake sounded more, dangerous, somehow.

The raft lurched again, but slowly. Then the slow gloop noise of someone entering the water. There was a brief gasp as Myrch started to feel the cold and the wet.

"What do we do?" Dun said.

"Stay," Myrch said. "I'll swim around. Don't move. Lay low til I get back."

"Okay! Great!" Padg said.

"Yeah. Lay lower than that," Myrch hissed and then swam off toward the noise of the settlement.

When the noise of Myrch swimming had been drowned by the sounds drifting on the water from Lakeside, Padg spoke, "Did I say, 'great?'"

"Yep, you said that," Tali said.

"Loudly," Dun said.

"And we are..."

"Going to stay here, yes," Tali finished.

More rustling and ripping noises from Tali's side of the raft.

"Good, good," Padg said. "And you are?"

"Preparing," Tali said.

"Better prepare quicker," Dun said. "I can hear voices."

"You always hear voices," Padg said.

"Outside my head, Padg. Outside."

"And who have we here?" a strange, harsh, nasal voice said. "Mmmh, eh my friendly sea rats, they smell like visitors to our fine town. And what have they brought us, mmmh? A nice present and all. Lovely rafty, eh? Nice made too. Found ropes and all, mmmh? You get off now. Swim from here."

"Who says?" Tali said, annoyed.

A gulp from Padg. "Err, they've got a knife. Ow, steady."

"Ah, smart pup, eh? Off the raft!"

Dun lowered himself off the side of the raft. Then he felt for Tali who was already climbing down.

"Now put the smart pup down, Royg. Good. Now scram!"

There was a splash. Dun and Tali heard a gasp, and then a pant for breath as Padg surfaced.

"You..." Padg was cut off by a kick in the knee from under the water.

"Hey, smart pup!" the nasal shout from off the raft said. "You be alive or dead, I'm easy either way. Don't be a dumb, pup. Go."

"Shh, let's go," Tali said in Padg's ear.

"But..."

"It can wait," she said.

He felt one arm each being dragged until they were farther away. Then they all swam in long, slow strokes toward the crowd noise. Lakeside seemed quieter now than before, but occasional bursts of noise broke through. Odd sounds, things breaking, shouts, screams. They swam on.

Then when they were out of earshot of the raft.

"I saved our stuff."

"Wow, Tali, you don't hang about," Dun said.

"Pays not to."

"Isn't it drenched?" Padg said.

"No," Tali said. "I bagged it."

"Where is it all?"

"Following us. I tied it around my waist before we jumped."

"Okay. Amazing," Padg said.

"Mmm-hmm."

Dun was nearest to the shore of Lakeside. The steep metal wall felt of rust and rivets and smelled of oil. They swam along it for a while looking for a way up, glad that the sound of the thieves on the lake got increasingly quieter.

Dun stopped. "Hey, I've found something. Feels like a ladder."

"And a ladder it is!" A friendly sounding voice boomed down to them. A deep voice with a laugh in it somewhere, but with something else too. "That will be ten tallies if you please."

"Ten tallies for what?" Padg said, tired and outraged.

"Call it embarkation tax."

"And you've got the right to extract that, how?"

"On two counts: Firstly on the count of how you're down there cold in the water, and I'm up here in the warm. Second, I'm Old Fryk, the watchman, and I just asked you real nicely." He paused. "I could ask you, not nicely."

"I'll pay," Tali said resigned.

"Where did you..?" Dun started.

"Prepared." Tali cut him off. She reached up the ladder with the stick, and the watchman took it with one hand, and then in a smooth sweep swapped hands and with the other pulled Tali up onto the side. *Not so old*, thought Tali. The others waited.

"So!" Fryk said, "Are you going to bob around in there all span, or are you coming up here to get dry? I'm easy either way."

"A lot of folk seem to be that easy around here," Padg said, starting to climb.

They both reached over the top rung of the ladder to a flat surface of old worn chequer-plate, slightly sticky.

"Hey," Tali said to the watchman. "Can you give me a hand with our stuff here?"

The place smelled of stale sweat and gone off chemicals of all kinds, mead certainly. A loud crash and a thump sounded in the distance, and then a peal of hysterical laughter.

"Welcome to Lakeside!" The watchman laughed.

Chapter Twenty-Six

Old Fryk led them all to a hot vent not far from the edge of what he called the quay. Dun and Padg took a brief time to dry themselves, while he talked.

"So any old fool could fathom that you are not from here. And Old Fryk is not just any old fool, eh?"

Dun was starting to guess that the conversation being peppered with "ehs" was some kind of local affectation. He also had the thought that as much as he liked Fryk on first impression, that they should keep themselves to themselves.

"No. We're from downstream."

"You're not river-folk though, eh?"

"No," Dun said.

"You come here alone?"

"Yes," Dun said.

"Mmm, well, suit yourself, eh? We all gots secrets to keep. Matter of fact, that's what brings most of us here. Keeping 'em. Running from 'em. I reckon you'll fit right in."

"Hey, where's Tali?" Dun whispered across to Padg.

"I'm here," she said, closer to the waterside than the two of them.

"Are you coming over or do you like being soaked?" Padg said.

"Patience," Tali said, testily.

"Hey, come away from the edge now, young folk," Old Fryk said, addressing Tali. "If you fall in, it's only going to cost you another ten tallies for me to fish you out, eh?" He chuckled to himself. "Now. You young folk got a place to stay here? No? I thought not. Well, here is some advice I'll give you for free. Along the quay from here, about two hundred strides, where the chequer-plate stops, there's a set of nice chimes. That's the sign of Madam Bana's hostel. It's the quietest, easiest place you'll find for a new traveler here."

"Sounds boring," Padg said.

"I'd have thought you'd had enough excitement for one day," Tali said.

"Aye," Fryk said, "and boring is rare and highly sought after in these parts. Like free advice. Now dry up and git! I've got a quay to mind."

They followed Fryk's instructions til they came to the chimes. They turned toward the sound but instead of a doorway filled with drape or reed door, it was filled with folk. Or a folk. And the largest example that any of them had ever come across. Dun reckoned that this folk-door-person must be as wide as he was tall and a good two heads taller than Ardg from the village.

"It spoke, eh?" A deep voice, calm sounding said. A voice that brooked no argument.

"Eh?" This time more insistent.

"Er, hi," Dun said. "We were trying to find somewhere to stay?"

Silence.

"Old Fryk sent us."

"Hmm? Oh." Then over his mountainous shoulder, he said, "Bana? Madam Bana!"

They heard shuffling from behind him. "Yes?"

From what Dun could guess from voice and scent, Madam Bana and the door were related. Mother and son? Grandmother and grandson? That was hard to tell.

Dun said, "Hello? Madam Bana? Have you lodgings for the night, please? Old Fryk sent us?"

Madam Bana pealed laughter. When she had calmed down, she said, "I'm sorry, dear, we just don't get many manners here in Lakeside, and here's me forgetting mine. Its six tallies a night each. Its only straw on the floor, mind, no pallets, but its clean and its safe. A meal at first cycle is three tallies extra. That's it, take it or leave it."

"We'll take it," Tali said over Dun's shoulder and handed across a tally stick.

"Good!" Bana said. "Gryk!" The door had a name.

"Weapons!" Gryk said. Then after a brief confused silence. "No one comes in with weapons. Take yours off now."

"How did he know..." Padg started under his breath.

"Everyone has weapons." Gryk carried on in his calm monotone. "It's Lakeside."

"But how will we know to get them back?" Dun said as politely as he could muster, removing a knife he had strapped to his calf.

"Now there's the oddest thing, dear, he's always been able to do that. Give him a sack full of weapons and a week to forget and he never will. He's never forgotten one, nor yet given one to the wrong owner. Gods know how he does it. This way, dears..." And Madam Bana led the way past Gryk, storing the sack and past the clinking chimes to a warm and cozy interior, smelling faintly of yeast.

They slept soundly for the first time in cycles, and everyone except Dun had fervid dreams. He woke to the smell of something fantastic. Light and sweet and subtle. He found himself dragged from sleep, leaving Padg snoring softly, to the low table in what he assumed was a dining area.

"Good sleep, my pup?" a cheery Madame Bana said.

"Yes, thank you," Dun said.

"And what do we have planned today? I presume you're travelers?"

"Oh, I hadn't really thought," Dun said, sidestepping to not reveal too much.

"Oh, do tuck in, by the way. The hubbou is fresh made this morning."

Hubbou turned out to be a beautiful, fresh, fluffy substance with a slightly crunchy outside. He fell on it like a starveling.

When Tali and Padg woke and joined him, all that could be heard from Dun was the scraping of stylus on parchment.

"Hey."

Tali and Padg joined the food, greeted Dun, and then briefly joined the Hubbou induced silence.

"Where would you go to find someone, Madame Bana?" Tail asked when their host's smell filled the doorway.

"Why, dear, is someone lost?"

"No, not really, but it would be good to know where he is."

"He, hmm?"

"Oh, not that kind of he."

"Oh?"

"No."

"Well, then. The best place to find someone who's lost, or not lost, around here, would be the Bocado."

"Where's that?" Padg said.

"Oh, it's in the center of Lakeside, where the Great Throng is,"

"The Great Throng?" Dun said.

"One thing at a time, dear. It's where the Great Throng is and listen out for the squeak of the doors. The Bocado doors swing all the time, wake and sleep. So many folk, in and out. If you hear them squeak quick and loud though, do be careful to duck."

"Sorry to interrupt, Madam Bana," Dun said.

"Such lovely manners. You must be Bridge-folk, eh? Few enough of your kind wash up here. Too busy about your own business and no one else's, I'm sure. Mmm, and here I am getting all off down a side passage. What was it you were asking me?"

"The Great Throng."

"Ah, yes. Well, I guess you folk from way down by the Bridge might call it a market, and so might any folk else. And you might be imagining stalls and wares all set out and so. Well, the Great Throng ain't so much arranged around folk who are laying out their wares and haggling for a fair price for a fair piece of craft. No stalls, or much laid out. More arranged around folk who might want to run away."

"Oh," Dun said.

"Mmm," Madame Bana said, "more racta, dear? I'm making more for myself."

"No, thank you," Tali said. "We should be getting on, I think."

"I don't need to tell you to be careful, do I, dears?"

Dark

Chapter Twenty-Seven

"We smell like simple folk," Tali said.

"Eh?" Padg said.

"You heard."

"But we are simple folk," Dun said.

"Which will simply get us robbed," Tali said.

"Or worse," Padg said.

"Okay, point taken."

So they found themselves in the rather rough-hewn wear of the Lakeside folk, including some rather interesting lace-up leg greaves that seemed to be in fashion. Tali found the attentions of the aging proprietor of the shop they'd found rather creepy, but she bit her tongue for the sake of the party, making minimal fuss. Once in the street again, they headed toward the main noise of the town, down a wide main street lined with ramshackle dwellings.

"I may need to scrub myself," Tali said.

Dun said, "They don't smell that bad, a bit of oil-skin maybe, but..."

"Not the clothes you idiot!" she snapped.

"Oh, sorry... him."

"Yes, him, paws all over me. 'Oh, let me just check this fits properly there, and let me adjust that here.' Gah! When this is all over, I'll remember to come back and adjust him."

"You did nearly have his finger off tying up that last lace," Padg noted.

"I think the best revenge we can take is never to come back here again," Dun said.

"Or you could melt his legs together with some of that Alchemy stuff," Padg said.

"Yes, that would work too," Dun said, cheerily.

"When I want an opinion from either of you two idiot-folk, I'll be sure and ask for it."

"And I wasn't."

Dun swallowed a giggle at Padg's revenge plans, for fear of retribution and they padded on toward the Throng. They noticed as they walked, that the dwellings either side of them had noises from way up high, as well as at street level. None of the other folk that Dun had any knowledge of built dwellings other than on the ground. Seemed like an odd thing to do in the Dark. There was always another tunnel you could annex, or in some cases a trapdoor to go down, but these smelled like reed and mud dwellings like the ones in the village back home. Sure the Stone-folk had raised walkways, but even all of their cave dens were at floor level. Dun found the enshrouding noise oppressive. Or maybe it was the fact that everyone here seemed to be having some kind of grudge with the other. At varying levels of threat and volume. Dun could imagine how Lakeside had earned its infamy.

The Throng became a wall of noise, long before they got to it, but oddly a wall where each brick was a different texture to the next. As a whole, the soundscape of the market was a cacophony, but each component had its own madly unique edge: brazen rough-edged singing, a barely audible high-pitched trilling, scores of resonant clicker beetles, the schiwng-swish noise of metal being sharpened, and distant mournful ululation. As they approached, the air became thicker with the breath of hundreds of hawkers, the pushy, the wheedling, the desperate, all plying their trade. "Come buy..." this, "Never known before..." that, and "How could you possibly survive without..." those.

"This is fantastic," Padg whispered into Dun's ear, so as not to be overheard. A precaution, probably not necessary under the circumstances.

"It's making my head ache already, and we've not been here two hundred clicks yet," Dun said.

"Well, I'd rather be here than in that clothes shop," Tali said. "It might be an eel-pool, but at least we all know what we're getting ourselves into. Everyone is clearly out for what they can get, they're going to try and con you, but at least we're all aware of that. Seems more, honest, somehow."

"Now there's a word I wasn't expecting to hear today," Dun said.

"Or at least not in that context," Padg said. "Maybe, 'Nah, mate, I wasn't trying to rob you, honest.'"

"You two could be less amusing and more helpful by listening out for the Bocado," Tali said.

They walked and listened and listened and walked. Even Dun starting to enjoy what was quite an experience and for once, one that didn't seem to be utterly life-threatening. They braved some snacks from a vendor, a spice-dried version of the fish they'd enjoyed in the lake. And, Tali seemed to think, they didn't get stung too badly in the bartering of it. Padg and Tali both came away from a weapons hawker with matching small, found metal knives, very sharp. They spent a brief moment in a small space between two stalls, admiring their purchases, when there was a loud squeaky crash, a dusty thump, and loud squeaky cursing.

"If you ever come near my bar again, you miserable, scum-eating, misbegotten, folk-toad, I swear on all the gods that I will rip off a hind leg as you flee and use it to beat your sorry carcass into jelly!"

The voice was loud, harsh, and carried a long way, without the need to shout. The level of threat in the words, however, was apparent. The squeaky cursing came from a position lower down near the floor and was interspersed with spitting.

"I think we've found the Bocado," Padg said.

Dark

Chapter Twenty-Eight

The interior of the Bocado was filled with a choking haze from gods knew what. Tali suspected it might be stimulant in nature, but whatever it was, in this bar, it was popular. The other main addition to the decor of the place was the music. A loud and insistent female voice, that seemed due to the acoustics of the place, to carry everywhere, was being accompanied by two stringed instruments that used a set of musical notes Dun hadn't experienced before. Not an unpleasant sound, just an alien one. It needed to be pretty alien in Dun's opinion, to stand out from the amazing range of noises outside in the Throng. The song was unfamiliar in itself, but it didn't take much of a listen to peg it as someone's lament over a lost love.

As they explored, carefully, they found that around the edge of the bar were cozy booths, a table that seated four or six at a squeeze and a bench on either side. With low spoken voices, a reasonable degree of privacy was to be had. Tali, still having the majority of their tally sticks, went to what passed for a bar. To Tali it felt like some kind of found piece of wall or roof structure co-opted for the purpose of serving and laid sideways. She ordered a racta for Dun, the mead that Padg had insisted on, and a herbal tea for herself. It seemed the local drink round here was a thing called "Good-drip", by the temperament of the clientele in there she wondered just how good it really was. Her brief reverie was broken by a tray being slid across the bar gently coming to rest against her upper leg. She felt to check the drinks and discovered a bonus: There was a small bowl of some kind of chips. She tried one, which seemed to be some kind of salted dried local plant. Since she didn't have to pay for it, Tali assumed that the salt in there was to cause them to drink more. Well, she felt like something to nibble at while she thought. And there was a lot to think about. She carried everything back to the booth.

"Here y—"

"Shh!" Dun hissed.

She put the tray down on the table in the booth and as she did Dun grabbed her hand. She suppressed a cry. Gently but firmly, he guided her hand to a piece of parchment he'd laid out flat. She ran her hand across it. In his small precise writing he'd written:

Quiet! I've been listening to a booth about three tables away behind us.
I think its Myrch.

She tapped his hand on the wrist. She paused but nothing happened. She took her forefinger and drew in squiggles on his hand. He finally understood and pushed the stylus into her grip. She scribbled hastily back and both Dun and Padg reached over to read it.

Has he said anything yet?

Then in Padg's long spidery hand, he wrote,

We think he's been negotiating a way to gain passage through someone's territory. Faeries? Never heard of them.

Tali scribbled back.

Listen. Can talk later.

They strained and could make out two voices, that of Myrch and another with a River-folk accent.

"...too much," Myrch said.

"Well, my friend. I don't believe you have much choice. Besides, your employers will pay."

"...just plain extortion."

"I'm in business, just like you. We, freelancers, have such expenses. Covering your trail and ensuring my friend's involvement is secret, well..."

"... have died because of that knowledge."

"... mrgh..."

"... much do you want the package..."

"... bandit-folk!"

"... have a deal... good!"

Drink up. Back to the hostel.

So hastily, but as quiet as they could manage, the three of them navigated the edge of the bar farthest from the discussion and fell into the Throng. Then holding hands Padg, threaded them back through the crowds at as fast a pace as he could in the chaos. Tali was glad she had taken the pre-emptive step of paying for two stays at the hostel for all of them. It kept their room and it saved time. Since it was work-cycle, when they got back to the digs, it was empty except for them and Gryk on the door. He greeted them cheerily, though he did briefly stop them to remove their newly bought knives.

"How does he know?" Dun said when they got back to their room.

"Habit?" Padg said.

"I tell you what. I'm glad of him now. He'll keep strangers away from the door and listening in at windows. Not the kind of thing I'd have thought he'd tolerate," Tali said. "So what the hells was that wheedling mercenary up to? And what did I miss while I was at the bar?"

"Well," began Padg, "there was all that stuff about the Faerie, whoever the hells they are."

"Fire-folk," Tali said. "It's an old name for them. I've come across it before in ancient alchemy scrolls. They used to be the go-to folk for potions and stuff as they used to be the only folk with enough hot vents to do any real alchemy. Of course, since then we've all learned to adapt and find new vents all the time but it's still said that the vents of the Fire-folk are the hottest. "super-heated" or "high-pressure" so they say."

"Sorry, you've lost me into alchemy speak," Padg said, feigning a snore.

Tali kicked him. "Well listen up, dozy, it might be important."

"So, if it's the Fire-folk we're talking about. What do we know? They are supposed to be really secretive," Dun said. "And they have a whole lot of rituals unique to them, that no one else has experienced. Supposedly no one who learns their secrets gets to escape alive."

"Sounds like a traders tale to me," Tali said. "Much truth in it do we think?"

"Not much to go on," Dun said. "Almost all the stuff passed down about them is rumor. There is an area on my father's map where he thought their tunnels began. It says, 'Fire-folk. Beware!' on it."

"Not massively encouraging then," Padg said.

"Well, hard to tell what Father meant by it. He wasn't one for overstatement, so the warning is genuine, but then again, by the rough way he's sketched out the boundaries of their realm, he never went there himself."

"Let's move on, I presume that's where Myrch was trying to negotiate passage. Let's just hope he did an efficient job."

"Yeah, he's efficient all right," Padg said bitterly. "Efficiently double-crossing all of us with the damned River-folk."

"That doesn't really bother me that much," Dun said.

"What?" Padg said.

"No, really. What does bother me is: Why? What are the River-folk up to and why is Myrch needing to stay on their right side?"

"Two very good questions," Tali said. "Any thoughts?"

"Not really. I just get a feeling that the plans of the River-folk and Myrch aren't in the slightest bit related. They've just crossed each other's paths and proved mutually useful."

"Is that a feeling or a *feeling*?" Padg said.

"A guess a hunch more than anything."

"What do we think is in the package that they were talking about?" Tali said.

"Knowing that pack of tricks that Myrch carries around with him, it could be anything. Those found weapons he has are deadly and to anyone in the Dark he could name his price." Dun said.

"Too simple," Tali countered. "If it was the weapons, he wouldn't be so free with using them. I think he's got something else."

"One last thought. Do we face him with it?" Dun said.

"Are you mad?" Padg said. "Half of what they said could be 'knowledge enough to get us all killed', and gods know who else in the process."

"We should go back and tell the village," Tali said.

"We can't go back."

"No, not without having found the Machine-folk."

"No, we just can't go back," Dun said.

Dark

Chapter Twenty-Nine

"We just can't go back? What kind of cryptic shaman nonsense is that you're talking now, Dun?" Padg said.

"I don't know," Dun said. "I just found myself saying it. I don't know where it came from."

"Well, can you kindly refrain from *just saying* things that haven't been through the conscious part of your brain because it's beginning to creep me out!"

"Okay. Sorry."

"What now?" Tali said.

"Do we think he knew we were there?" Dun said.

"Nah," Padg said, "we were careful, didn't say much at all. Didn't even smell like us."

"I've noticed his smell-sense isn't that great anyhow," Tali said.

"He's a wily one though that Myrch. I wouldn't put it past him to somehow *know*," said Dun.

"No *somehow knowing* is your job," Padg said. "Woooooohhh!"

"Oh give it up you two, this is serious. What do we still need to do before we go and find Myrch, if indeed we still want to go and find him? I for one want to check that market out properly for some any reagents I might be able to use. There's stuff from my kit I could do with refreshing and, who knows, way out here, I might find something unusual. You two might manage some useful reconnaissance of what's ahead of us, maybe find out a little more about the fire-people?"

"Do we want to go and find him?" Padg said. "Not sure I'm that keen."

"I think we have to," Dun said. "If what he said has wider implications for other folk, ours for example, then we don't want to let him know that we've overheard. We need him to think we're unaware for as long as possible."

"We don't need to meet him just yet though, do we?" Padg said.

"No, I don't think so," Dun said. "Right now he just thinks we're lost, or still stuck on the raft. Or he's forgotten about us for now. When it enters his mind again, *he'll* come after *us*. Until then, let's make the most of it."

The Throng was less dense when they returned to it. That was somehow more unsettling than the experience of a full-on crush of not completely trustworthy folk. When they were in the thick of it Dun noticed the odd ululating noise again. It was quite faint the first time they visited the market, just one note in a song, but now it was a whole tune to itself. A new much nearer voice joined in loudly not far behind them. The trader that they were stood with where Tali was haggling over some form of rock or other, noticed Dun's silence and abstraction.

"Tinkralas," the trader said.

"Eh?" Dun said, the word not familiar at all. Even the sounds used were odd.

"New god around here. Followers call themselves Tinkralas. All do that odd singing thing at the same time mid-cycle, they sing at other times too, but everyone sings mid-cycle."

"Recent thing?" Padg said, curious.

"Yeah," the trader replied, "spread real quick too. Don't hold with it myself, I'm an old-gods kind of folk. But each to their own, eh?"

Tali finished her business with the trader and the three moved on. The singing tailed off. A thoughtful silence hung over the three Bridge-folk. They moved on through the rest of the throng.

Tali said, "Have you got any room left in that map case of yours, Dun?"

"I think so, why?"

"Can we stop near the Bocado? I thought I heard a seller touting some stuff that might be worth reading."

"Why? Is our charismatic company not enough entertainment for you?" Padg asked.

"Too much entertainment, sometimes," she said. "No, it's just there might be something interesting, you never know."

"We never do," Dun said. "Let's go."

After some time studying the wares of the scroll-seller, Tali haggled for a sheet that contained some kind of ancient recipe and a couple of history texts at which point Dun intervened, citing the capacity of his map case. They bought some kind of insect-related local delicacy and a bottle of mead each, then retreated to the hostel to assess their purchases.

Sitting around in the hostel room later, with the faint snoring of Padg in one corner and the faint scratching of Dun making more amendments to the map, Tali lay on the straw against one wall of the room. She made a humming noise of interested surprise.

"Hey check this out." She tossed the scroll in the direction of the scratching.

"Careful!" Dun said half-catching, half-deflecting the roll and its bamboo inner.

"It's mostly about general folklore, but there's a mention of totems in there."

"Oh, right..."

"Last but one paragraph."

"I've got it. Oh yes, it says, 'Sometimes totems aren't always of imagined forms of the gods, there was an ancient fashion of the Stone-folks of the Gabbro dynasty to carve representations of stories, lays and folktales onto the surface of rounded stones.'"

"Sound familiar?"

"Should it?"

"Gods, for someone who's a trainee shaman you can be immensely dense sometimes. It's that thing you picked up at the Stone-folks market. That's what it is. It's a totem of some kind of tale, or..."

"Song," Dun said.

"Yeah, or a song."

"Definitely a song. It's the Ballad of Yarra and Jarris. It's the egg from the Ballad, '...And half was warm and half was black...' The texture is different on one side than the other. Good gods. I wish I could remember the rest of the song."

"Ask Padg when he wakes up; he's the singer here," Tali said.

"Hey! Shake your tail," Dun shouted. "Might as well wake him now, it might be important."

"Whaa..?" Padg said sleepily.

"What's the rest of the Ballad of Yarra and Jarris?"

"Rest? Huh..? What are you on about?"

"Okay, listen carefully," Tali said. "We've found something interesting in those books from the market, but we need you to fill us in on a detail."

"You woke me up for music class?" Padg said, disbelieving.

"More like history class, really," Dun said with a smirk in his voice.

"Great," Padg said. "I hated history."

"That's enough reminiscing about our schooling," Tali said. "How does the Ballad of Yarra and Jarris go?"

"Give me a second," he said and cleared his throat.

"You don't need to sing it," Tali said, "just recite it for us."

"Okay. Here it goes."

"In the place of long ago, outside the egg upon its back
Yarra looked upon the deep—and her shimmered hair was black
Resplendent in the void and deep—and her shimmered hair was black.

Jaris came and warmed her heart—he came to her along the track
Came from the deep and warmed her heart—he came to her along the track.

*They loved as one an eons breadth—and half was
warm and half was black
They loved as none before or since—and half was
warm and half was black.*

*And then a one came in between—she felt her heart
begin to crack
The darkest face came in between—she felt her heart
begin to crack.*

*Then he was gone and never seen—and none was
warm and all was black
He faded went and never seen—and none was warm
and all was black.*

*Then we climbed back inside the egg—how long to wait
till he came back
Returned ourselves inside the egg—how long to wait
till he came back?"*

"Chuck the totem over here?" Tali said.

"Knowing what you're like at catching things, not likely," Dun said. "I'll bring it and hand it. How's that?"

"It's definitely our song all right." She felt the cool polished surface of one side and the textured surface of the other. "And half was warm and half was black. Clever."

"Hey, pass it here," Padg said. "I wonder." There were fumbling noises from him exploring the surface. Then a sharp crack.

"What the..?" Dun said.

"I'll be a river rat," Padg said. "Get a load of this. Careful when you take it. It's not how you found it."

And that was true. Somehow when Dun got the egg back, it was in two halves along the mysterious divide of texture.

"How did you..?" Dun said.

"I thought about the line where it says, 'We all climbed back inside the egg...' and I wondered how literal the Stone-folk had been when they made this. Pretty literal is the answer. It twisted and pulled and twisted again and there you go. Feel the inside too."

Dun did. "Wow! There's some kind of pattern here, a motif. Here, Tali, you feel the other half. The pattern is on both sides. It's lots of intersecting lines. It feels like..."

"A map," Tali said. "It's a map."

> *"I know I'm no expert at this, but I always felt like eco-systems were more finely balanced, more knife edge. Precarious, even. But here in the Dark, it seems like the creatures don't just cling to their niche, they chisel it out. Fiercely, vibrantly. I've never felt the fight to be, to exist, so strongly as here, so close to the edge."*

Excerpts from <Distress Beacon SN-1853001>. Found by E.S.V. Vixen Terradate: 26102225.

Dark

Chapter Thirty

"Now what do we do with it?" Padg said.

"Try to study it now, I guess," Dun said. "Compare it to what we know on our charts and check if there's any comparison."

"Then close it up and keep quiet," Tali said. "The less Myrch knows, the better, I suspect."

And so they studied and pored over Dun's recent marks and the ones his father had made before them. All to no avail. There did not seem to be any similarity at all.

"Maybe it's not a map?" Padg said.

"Definitely a map," Tali said finally.

"No wait, Padg might be right, or partly right. Maybe its a picture of a map."

"Now you are talking nonsense. A picture is a map," Tali said.

"Yeah, friend, I hate to disagree with you when you're standing on my bank here, but what are you on about?"

"A map is meant to be an exact representation of what's there, right?"

"Yeah..." Tali said.

"Well, maybe this one isn't meant to be."

"What would be the point of that then?" Padg said.

"Art maybe? Just to show how clever they were. I don't know, but I don't *think* it's a map you're meant to follow."

"Okay. We're none the wiser then."

"No, I didn't say that. I think it's got a meaning. It's just not a step for step map."

"Close it up we've got company," Tali said.

They could all hear approaching footsteps.

"Ah, good," Myrch said. "I wondered where you'd gotten to. Now, what exactly did you do with my raft?"

"Well," Padg said, "I'm going to guess if you didn't already know you wouldn't be asking us."

Myrch laughed, a deep genuine laugh. "How perceptive you are, young pup. Shall we go?"

"Which way now, if we haven't got a raft?" Dun said.

"I'd have hoped you'd have thought of that before you let those dreary River-folk thugs take it off you. Luckily, I have thought about it. I have hired the services of a guide. We will travel through the realm of the Fire-folk."

Myrch paused, as if expecting questions. There were none.

"In order to get there, we need to travel through a place called the Disputed Zone. It has no jurisdiction to speak of, although the Lake-folk and the River-folk have fought over it for years. It is said that the Disputed Zone has its own people too. A lost feral folk, long since turned to barbarism and savagery. Folktales and travelers fancies, I'd guess, but you can never be too sure. And the Disputed Zone has no one to maintain it so it's very fabric is dangerous."

"Isn't it full of collectors then?" Tali said.

"Although there may be a wealth of found things waiting in the Disputed Zone, collectors have enough to contend with the things they find, without risking an area they *know* stands a good chance of killing them. Collectors do come here, but mostly the desperate and the foolhardy. And all with a guide, like my friend here. Meet Jarn."

The friends murmured assent and Jarn grunted in return.

"We go?" he said.

"Shall we?" Myrch said.

"Sounds great, I can't wait," Padg said.

***

They crossed the last border post, a ramshackle affair of piled boxes and spars of wood and metal. Two folk stood guard, in that alert way guards who occasionally meet action do. Dun could tell by their clipped speech and manners that these folk were professional soldiery as opposed to lackaday militia. Their guide, Jarn, handed something over to the guards. Some kind of permit, Dun guessed, that seemed to be acceptable and the guards grunted their assent for the party to pass.

"We go, eh?" Jarn said. He was as strange to the nose, as he was to the ear.

They moved beyond the barrier. Dun felt a large space. Under his feet, the floor was metallic and smooth, but old. It had none of the usual clutter of places at home or lakeside. Even the relatively organized Stone-folk had the odd box of this or the odd unswept pile of that around. This place was empty. Truly empty.

"This has been cleared," Padg said.

"For a good spearthrow, I'll bet," Tali said.

"Silence!" Jarn hissed.

When quiet fell across the area, it took a moment for Dun's ears to readjust. After days in the hubbub of Riverside, the silence was unnerving. They walked slowly and carefully, following Jarn with Myrch bringing up the rear. They reached another barrier ahead, more makeshift than the one they had left.

"Stay," Jarn said. He shuffled off ahead. There was some clunking and scraping, then he said, "Come!"

They did. Forcing their way through a tight doorway between a smooth, flat, vertical plate and something spongy and stale smelling. They followed into a crazy, chaotic, twisted pile of all the possible things any folk in the vicinity had ever left behind in their lives.

"What *is* this place?" Tali said.

"Borderland," Jarn said.

"Why all the stuff?" Dun said, panting and feeling for a new foothold above his head.

"Blocks the Disputed Zone off from... unwanted visitors," Myrch said.

"Does it work?" Padg said.

"It makes everyone feel better," Myrch replied.

Their route changed from being steep upward over rough and sharp metal pieces, to the interior of a massive rusty pipe that seemed to be sloping slowly down. As they fell into silence again, Dun noticed something new. The whole place around him was making noise. Distant clanging, nearby but quiet creaking; sighing of air slowly let out. The whole place seemed alive. Padg gave voice to Dun's fears.

"This place gives me the creeps."

"Creepy noises are the least of our worries," Myrch said.

"Worry about things you don't hear," Jarn said.

That was enough to settle the party back into quiet brooding again. Fatigue started to set in as, with every step, there was something new to process or circumvent. Dun never really liked the word chaos, it was too easily bandied about, but this place? That was the only word to describe it. They walked on, carefully, listening to the clipped, almost hissed instructions and warnings given by Jarn. Sidestepping gaping holes and razor-sharp edges in just enough time was enough for them to diligently follow and begin to trust their taciturn guide.

"Wait," he said. Everyone stopped. "Give me hand," he said to Padg, still out in front. "Walk here. There, is nasty.

Padg walked as directed, needing the help of Jarn's calloused hand, as the floor sloped alarmingly underfoot and apparently whatever was nasty was downslope. Once he had made the few steps required on the slope, he reached back and relayed to Tali the same instructions, and then she to Dun. Myrch crossed last.

"Now we camp," Jarn said. "Wait."

They heard Jarn strain slightly ahead and above them, to shift something metallic that squeaked when it moved. Then a faint hiss.

"Up here. There are two steps."

They all followed. The two steps turned out to be a short ladder that took them up to a small, clean room with a level metal floor. Jarn ushered them all in. There were slightly more sounds of straining as the door closed and then the hissing noise, this time accompanied by the worrying feeling of the pressure rising, just slightly, in the room.

"We are safe here," Jarn said. "Rest. The door secures from inside. No one hears from outside."

They broke out rations, with the special treat of spiced lake fish from the market. Tali had had the sense to visit before they left. Tali, Dun, and Padg ate with a companionable murmur between them, Myrch and Jarn in silence. When they had finished they brought out bedrolls, a market purchase of Padg's.

"So do you really believe that there are some kind of lost people out here?" Padg said.

"I don't know," Jarn said. "Is easy to let ears play tricks on you, eh? No good for a guide. Deal with what you know."

"Why does anyone think there are folk here at all then?" Tali asked.

"Old travelers tales. Traders looking for an audience in the cantinas of Lakeside." Myrch's tone held an edge of scorn.

"Not all traveler tales untrue," Jarn said.

Myrch made a non-committal grunt.

"There are many tales, Lakeside folk superstitious, but some tales woven from the same thread maybe, eh?" There was silence from the rest of the group, Jarn had his audience.

"The tales all tell of a folk, not lost, but here before us, before Lakeside. Ancient folk. But things here change. Something becomes different, some say a Gods punishment. The folk here become warped, altered, decaying but still live. Some tales tell of travelers go missing, that's true enough. Dangerous here, eh? Some tales have folk who hear strange noises in these caverns. That's true too, you can hear. But many tales tell of a noise that travelers hear before they go missing. A chattering. Like teeth. Quiet at first, then louder and more. Stories say if you hear that noise, you never reappear."

There was no noise now, inside the room until Padg spoke, "Charming though that tale is," he said. "If no one ever returns, how does anyone know about the noise?"

For the first time in their journey, they heard Myrch laugh. Not his usual sarcastic bark, but genuine laughter. They all joined in.

"Hey!" Jarn said, with a faintly hurt tone. "You ask. I tell. Those are the tales."

In a better mood than Dun had felt for days, he slept.

Chapter Thirty-One

Although Dun dreamed, they felt more distant, and when he woke he had no headache and felt fresh. After a brief breakfast, they broke camp and headed back out of the strange door and began their trek again.

They went in, then came out of another tunnel and along an uneven surface that felt very high up.

"Watch step, eh?" Jarn said.

They were walking on what felt like curving metal pipes. Dun couldn't help the uneasy feeling of walking on the ribcage of a giant metal beast. A sudden whoosh of gas jetting somewhere ahead and below them didn't belie that impression.

Behind him, Tali squeaked. "Gods!"

"What?" Dun said. "You okay?"

"Yeah. That... whatever it is we're walking on, shifted," she said.

"Watch step," Padg said behind them both.

Dun sniggered.

"Shh! It felt like it moved." Tali spoke more firmly.

"You said," Padg said.

"I think this place is starting to give everyone the gibbers." Dun tried to sound reassuring.

"No, it wasn't that. It jerked like *someone* moved it."

"No one is supposed to live here," Padg said.

"I know what I felt," Tali said.

The three friends began walking forward again, increasing their stride slightly to catch up with Myrch and Jarn. When they drew near, Myrch and Jarn were already in hushed conversation.

"Your ears play tricks," Jarn said.

"No," Myrch said.

"What?" Dun said as they stopped.

"Nothing," Myrch said. "Shall we get on?"

Dark

"Wait!" Jarn said. "Now we must climb, eh? There is rope here, at feet. You climb down, one at a time. You wait till you hear me reach bottom, okay?"

And with that, grunting, he disappeared over the edge of what Dun still thought of as a metal ribcage and they heard regular rustling as he lowered himself, hand over hand, down the rope. The sound became fainter. They waited. The rope went still. Dun shuffled uneasily.

"Quiet!" Myrch hissed. "I'm listening."

There seemed to be nothing to listen to. The tension stretched out.

"Curse him." Myrch sounded venomous. There was a rustle as Myrch unshouldered his pack and further noise as he undid straps and fished inside. There was a faint click and a smooth sliding noise, and then a clack. Dun thought it sounded like teeth biting on something metal.

"Dun," Myrch said through whatever he was evidently holding in his teeth. "Feel the rope as I go down, as soon as my weight goes off it. Follow. Then Tali do the same, then Padg. Quickly now."

Myrch's descent was more of a whizz of rope on fabric and Dun heard him all the way down to a soft thud, and then the rope was slack. He eased himself over the edge holding the plant fiber rope and braced himself against the last of the metal *ribs*. There were two more ribs spilling over the edge, and then nothing. Dun was hanging in midair with only the rope to guide him. His air-sense gave him a feeling of nausea as his brain tried to reconcile the moving world to his unusual motion. Slowly, he waited to stop swinging and began to climb down.

At the bottom, he steadied his wits and his stomach, and then Padg slid down next to him. Last to plop down beside them was Tali.

"Where's Jarn?" she said unable to feel him close by.

"Gone," Myrch said.
"What?" Dun said.
"You heard."
"But where?"

"I don't know. Just gone," Myrch said.

Dun noticed patches of damp under him as he slowly shifted foot to foot. "What now?"

"I don't know," Myrch said. "I'm thinking."

"Well, think faster," Padg said. "I can hear someone coming."

"Or something," Tali said.

They waited, ears straining into the cavernous junk filled expanse.

It was the chattering sound of teeth.

"That is not good."

"Thank you, Dun Obvious," Padg said.

The sound came to them faintly but distinctly, like a single instrument, performed from far away. An instrument made of bones. Then, slightly louder, the rest of the distant sinister orchestra joined in. The chattering grew louder.

"Where is it coming from?" Myrch said.

"I can't tell," Dun said. "There are too many echoes in here."

"Listen more carefully! Ahead? Behind?"

"Above," Tali said. "It's coming from above!"

The noise seemed to get louder all at once.

"Quick!" Myrch said. "Back to the safe room!"

They didn't need telling twice.

***

As the door slammed and the seals hissed into place the terrifying noise was accompanied by a terrible, keening cry.

"What the hells was that noise?" Dun said.

"It's like they're predators like they've got the scent," Padg said, edgy.

"No," Tali said, "there's more to it than that, I just can't think."

"Think about this instead. We are now trapped in here, there seem to be a lot more of them than there are of us," Myrch said gruffly. "We need a plan to get out. Break out a bit more food and let me have a think."

They broke out more rations and ate slowly. Padg rustled through his pack for what seemed like an age. Tali disturbed the reverie. "That noise. The cry. I think I understand now."

"Oh?" Myrch said.

"I think it's distress, anguish."

"Go on."

"I think I might have a plan. I think we need a hostage."

"Now *that* is a plan I can get behind," Myrch said.

Chapter Thirty-Two

"So, talk us through your crazy plan, Tali," Myrch said.

"Well," she said, "first we need to set a trap."

"Okay..."

"And the stunning?' Padg said.

"Ah," Tali said, warming, "leave that to me."

They huddled down and shared rations in the room that had become their fort while Tali rattled about in her backpack doing something alchemical sounding and certainly alchemical smelling. Occasionally there would be sotto voce cursing interspersed with gurgling and hissing. All of the smells seemed to be different degrees and variations on the theme of "acrid". Finally, with one last grunt of triumph, the noises abated to be replaced with more polite gurgling noises.

With Tali quieter inside the room, the din outside grew by comparison.
CHAKKA CHAKKA CHAKKA OOOOUUUURRRRRAAAAIII OOOUUURRRAAAIII!

"I hope that stunning potion is coming along, Tali, it sounds like our friends outside are getting restless," Myrch said.

"I think so," Tali said.

"Good. Now I think I've found some likely metal cartons slotted into the wall at the back here. If I can pull them out... I can drag them behind the door, and you can stand on them behind it. Reckon you can get it on target?"

"It will affect all of us anyway, but we should come round first as we'll be farthest away from the bottle when it breaks."

"Did I mention how much I was loving this plan?" Padg said.

"Yes!" everyone said else in concert.

Dark

Once Myrch dragged the makeshift metal step into place behind the door, Tali took her place behind it. It had been decided that Dun and Padg should fake a quarrel with the door open and then hope for the best.

The door opened with its characteristic hiss.

"Take your sorry furry hide and drown it!" Padg yelled.

"At least my furry hide's worth drowning!" Dun screamed back at him. "Get the hells out of here and take your chances with the natives."

"Not before I give you a piece of my mind, you pipe-rat!"

"I'll give you pipe-rat!"

And they set to, in what sounded and felt, to Tali like a very realistic fight. She was just thinking, *I hope the idiots don't really hurt each other* when there was a smack, then a dull metallic bunk sound and the other side of the door rattled slightly. Then a slight hiss and a thump and the "fight" was over.

"Serves you right, ass-hat," Dun shouted. There was no reply from Padg. Then a brief moment of stillness, inside the metal chamber and out.

chakka chakka chakka chakka chakka chakka chakka chakka

CHAKKA CHAKKA CHAKKA CHAKKA CHAKKA CHAKKA CHAKKA!

CHAKKA CHAKKA AIEEEEOOOUUUUUGGGGHHH!

OUGGHH!!!!!!

Then Dun and Tali's air-sense bulged as the "Chakka-folk" burst through the door. Their noses bulged to the scent of sweat, blood, and an odd smell of rotten meat.

"Now!" Myrch yelled.

There was a crash of glass and a whizzing noise as a moisture that smelled sickly sweet burst into the room.

"Get the door shut!"

CHAKKA CHAKKA CHAKKA

"I can't; it won't move!"

CHAKKA CHAKKA

"There's something blocking it..."
CHAKKA CHAKKA CHAKKA
"It's one of them, I can smell it."
"We've already got one in here, kick it out."
"... feeling dizzy..."
"That's the gas... move quick..."
"... can't... I..."
CHAKKA
chakka

Dark

Chapter Thirty-Three

Dun woke slowly, his ears coming online first.

"Hey, sleeping pup." That was Padg. "Wakey, wakey!"

"Ow!" That was Tali. "My ribs, you dung beetle!"

"It seemed to be the only way to wake you."

"Hmmph. Where's the *Chakka-folk*?"

"We tied him up. He's still out for the count."

"Let me check," Tali said.

Dun sat up. "He smells funny."

"Yeah, I thought that," Tali said. "Like a burned smell."

"It's giving me the creeps," Padg said.

"His face, he feels distorted somehow. Wounds, burns," Tali said. "His lips are almost completely gone. I can feel all of his teeth, and his mouth is shut, such as it is. Tissue, fluid leaking out. And so hot, inflamed. No," she said, feeling more carefully, "there's something else. Ulceration, like the tissue fluid and the burning have been there for ages. He's folk though, I think. Or used to be."

"Can you do anything for him?" Myrch said.

"Yes, I think so," Tali said. "It'll take a few days."

"Hmm..." Myrch said. "What have we got left for rations, boys?"

"Well," Padg said, rustling. "I reckon we've got a few days left without having to resort to any real hunting and foraging. Problem is, in this place, I don't think there's going to be all that much to catch."

"Wait a few clicks," Dun said. 'We've still got Jarn's pack. There should be the same amount of rations in there. That'll give us another day each."

"Blimey!" Padg said. "I hope you won't be quite as quick splitting my pack up..."

"No," Myrch said. "Dun's right. If Tali's plan doesn't pan out we're no nearer finding Jarn anyhow. Til then he's fending for himself anyway."

chakka...

"Hello, I think our friend is waking up," Myrch said cheerfully.

chakka...chakka...

"Hello," Tali said.

chakkachakkachakkachakkachakka...

"It's okay. We want to help you," she said.

chakka...chakka...

"I don't think he can understand you," Dun said.

"Can't you do some of your crazy mind stuff on him and find out what he's thinking?" Padg said.

"Doesn't work like that, idiot."

"Just trying to be helpful."

Tali jumped in, "Be helpful, Padg, by dragging my pack over here, and we'll check what I've got already that'll help. I might have some leaf-balm in there, at least that'll manage the pain for now while I work on something more specific."

So she went to work, the males taking turns checking the hostage/patient, and Tali working grinding things in her pestle. They settled into a routine, taking turns to sleep, Tali even accepting help from Dun and Padg in doing simple things like stirring and fetching. They were all pleased that the taking of a hostage had brought some peace to the noises outside. In fact, it seemed like the friends of their captive had left them completely. No one could say they weren't relieved.

After Dun, with Padg's help, persuaded Tali to sleep for at least one rest, she finally left off her frantic mixing. It was Myrch's turn to keep vigil over their captive, who had become strangely quiet. Dun, drifting off, wondered what kind of trouble they'd have stored up for themselves if he died while in their care. He decided that worry could wait until morning and sleep claimed him.

In the morning, there were fresh new things to worry about. Dun woke to Tali scrabbling in her backpack again.

"I'm sure I had some. Positive. I've been through every container."

"What?" Padg asked, feigning interest.

"Vent-moss."

"And you've not brought any?"

"Thought I had for sure, I've got the container it should go in but its got hearts ease reed in there instead."

"Oh," Padg said. "And that means?"

"It means," Tali said testily, "that you two lazy cave bats will need to go and get some for me."

"Go... and get some?" Padg said.

"Yes, go and get some. It only grows by warm vents. The vent in here is tiny and this room is too clean. I remember there being a vent by where the chakka-folk ambushed us. Reckon you can find it?"

"I think we can," Dun said.

"Be careful they don't find you," Myrch said. "And hurry yourselves, I'm not sure our friend here is all he should be. If he dies after all the rations we've fed him, I shall be cross."

So Dun and Padg strapped their remaining sword spears across their backs and eased the great metal door open a crack to listen and smell. The oddly clanking-hissing noises that gave the impression that the whole of the place was breathing, continued gently, but unabating. The smells of the chakka-people were only an imprint trace of what they had been before. Slowly they opened the door and eased themselves out.

Although the place they'd been attacked wasn't far away, it took a while at a careful pace to get back there. They stood stock still ears cocked, straining for the slightest indication of attackers. There was none.

"Now what?" Dun whispered.

"Search for this vent, I suppose," Padg said. "If it's here at all."

"And you've known Tali to be wrong how many times?" Dun said.

Dark

"All right, smart-whiskers, don't rub it in."
"Wait, listen! There!"
"What?" Padg said.
"A vent. Quite faint, but it just started up. Must be one of those intermittent ones. Come on, over here."

Sure enough, at the level of their knees was a long, thin vent blowing warm slightly fetid air.

"I hope there's some here," Dun said.

They scanned the walls, feeling carefully every hand-span, but it was only until Dun had gone down on his knees to feel between the vent and the floor that their search paid off.

"Down here," Dun said. "Get that bag open."
"I hope there's enough."
"Pass me your knife, I'll scrape the rest."

So they returned with their bounty and tapped on the metal door in the pattern they'd agreed.

"Come on, open up!" Padg hissed.

The door opened.

"Is he still okay?" Dun said.
"Yeah," Tali said, "Quiet, but okay."
"Here," Padg said, handing over the bag, "will this be enough?"
"I hope so," Tali said, less than reassuringly. "I've not really made this salve before."

Padg drew breath

Tali cut him off. "Don't say it."

Chapter Thirty-Four

The salve began to work. Tali taught them all how to apply it and where. It seemed that the sores of the chakka-folk were extensive, but worse on exposed skin. And the quiet of their patient seemed to be resignation rather than any sign of deterioration. That was a relief at least. It seemed that the loud noises that they had become used to in the chakka-folk were reserved for confrontations only. Once he'd resigned himself to capture and decided he was to be treated fairly, his noises seemed to center around gentle hissing variations with the odd one or two teeth clicks here and there.

"I'm sure its language," Dun said.

"Yeah, I think so too," Tali said.

"Does it much matter?" Padg said.

"Yes, it matters. If we want to negotiate, it'll make life a hell of a lot easier," Myrch said.

"Suppose," Padg said.

"But will we get a chance to learn it in time?" Dun said.

"Chakk, CHAKK."

"Did you say that to us?" Tali said.

"CHAK."

"I think we can take that as a yes," Padg said.

"Chakk, CHAKK."

"He's either a really quick study or he already understands a common folk language," Myrch said.

"Chakk, CHAKK."

"Which?" Dun said.

"That makes a fantastic yes or no question, idiot," Padg said. "Are you a quick study?"

"Ssssstthhh."

"That could be no," Tali said.

"CHAKK."

"So you understand us clearly," Dun said.

"CHAKK."

Dark

"But you can't speak like we do?" Tali said, warming to her line of questioning.

"Sssssth."

"Is it because of how your mouths are?"

"CHAKK."

"You can't make the same noises we do?"

"Sssth."

That sounded sad to Dun. They weren't dealing with a terrifying group of fabled monsters here.

"The wounds you've got," Tali said, "are they to do with where you live?"

"CHAKK."

"Are they burns?"

"CHAKK."

"From a chemical, is it a liquid that burns you?"

"Sssth."

"A heat then? Like from a vent?"

"...chakk?"

"Is that a *kind of*?" Dun said.

"CHAKK."

"So something burns you," Tali said.

"CHAKK."

"Where you live..."

"CHAKK."

"It's like the heat from a vent, but not that? Correct?"

"CHAKK, CHAKK!"

"Good work, Tali," Myrch said. "At least now we've got an idea what we're getting ourselves into."

"More importantly," Tali said, "do you feel better? Is the pain less?"

"CHAKK, CHAKK, CHAKK, CHAKK!"

"Good, I'm glad," she said. "The medicine seems to be working. We can teach you how to make it."

"Do you have a leader?" Myrch said. "Someone we can talk to. Someone who speaks for all of you?"

"CHAKK."

"Right then," Myrch said, "let's go on a house call."

***

It was particularly strange, following someone whose language you don't really speak. Especially since, Chak as they'd decided to call him, insisted on hurrying on ahead then "chakking" impatiently. Strange and deeply worrying since they weren't sure, even after Chak's seeming successful course of treatment, how they'd be received. And in this weirdest of abandoned cavernous places, there was always danger. The route varied greatly in altitude and texture underfoot, seeming like the farther they got into Chakka-folk territory, the more they felt like there was no ground anymore. The disorientation wasn't helped by one set of chakking coming from above and ahead of them.

It seemed the way to reach the home of these strange people was to climb and steeply too. Dun tallied this with the idea of the original ambush on them, coming from above. Why they couldn't be hoisted up in the opposite way he wasn't sure. He *was* pretty sure that a conversation like that was too complicated to get a sensible answer out of Chak playing the yes, no game. His thoughts were disrupted by the increasing trickiness of the climb. It seemed that the chakka people had treated the holds and ledges that made up the route, with something tacky and faintly resinous. That made gripping easier but didn't lessen how hard work the vertical climb was. Padg, always the fitter of the two called up from below.

"You two doing okay?"

"Yeah," Tali said.

"Uh-huh," Dun panted.

"Not much farther now," Myrch called down from above them.

Dark

Chak seemed to have reached as far up as he needed to go and was making impatient chakking back down to the climbers below. Dun heard a grunt as Myrch pulled himself up what must be the last stretch. Three more handholds and he was there himself, a right-angled ledge that would give them a new level to walk on. He heard Tali behind him pulling up the last reach, he felt stable enough underfoot to offer her a hand up.

"Thanks."

"Chakk, chakk, CHAKK."

"Okay, we're coming!" Padg said. "So impatient these Chakka types."

Dun walked along the ledge. It was wide enough to walk or stand on but not wide enough for two to pass. The high flat stretch of the wall was rougher on one side of them, the expansive dropped to the ground on the other side pressing on his awareness. He put it all to the back of his mind and tried to close down his air-sense before the vertigo made him sick.

"Chakk chakk" came the voice of their guide distantly from the front of the column.

It seemed Chak's voice resonated from wherever he was ahead. As Dun neared he realized why. Once off the ledge, he let his air-sense expand again, whiskers twitching, and took in what was in front of him. A space in which everything was confusing. There was a roof just high enough for each of them to stand, but the space was massive in length and width. Metal walls and roof from the sound and bounce back from Dun's air-sense, but some other substance for the floor, mineral based, but not quite rock. Smooth, but not quite flat either.

Dun slowly adjusted to the feel of the place as they very slowly banked and climbed on the odd smooth mock stone surface.

"Chakk, chakk." STAMP.

"What's up with him now?" Padg said.

"I think he's trying to tell us something," Dun said.

"Well done," Padg said. "Perhaps he's cross."

Tali sighed. "Have you been paying any attention at all? That's not cross. I don't know what it is, but it's new."

"Meh," Padg said, "linguistics was never my, aaaaaahhhhh."

Dun heard a whoosh, a slap of flesh on flesh, and Padg disappeared from his air-sense.

"I think," Myrch said, grunting, "that he was saying 'Be careful of the holes in the floor.'" Dun rushed to the noise, Myrch had somehow caught Padg mid-fall by his hand and held him as he walked blithely into the hole and fell his full height. *Gods, that must have hurt*, thought Dun. He reached round Padg's other side and grabbed him by his shoulder and pulled. They grunted and groaned Padg back up.

"Thanks," Padg said, breathlessly.

"Take slightly more care, there's a chap," Myrch said.

"Is your arm okay?" Dun said.

"A bit bashed, but not broken. Thank you for asking."

"Hold on," Tali said. "I've got some bruise-wort in my pack,"

"No, thank you."

"It's no trouble for me to put on, easy in fact. Won't take a..."

"No! Thank you."

"O...kay... just asking."

"Shall we move on?" Padg said, feigning cheer.

"Not until we're all a little more careful," Myrch said.

When Dun concentrated and reached out carefully with his air-sense he felt something other than the odd surface of the floor. The whole floor expanse itself was pocked with holes leading down. He felt down by his feet at the hole they'd just extracted Padg from. It was rough-hewn, but the sides were worn with use. Slightly sloping inward, clearly a good way for someone not paying attention to fall foul of. Literally.

"Chakk, chakk, aaaahh." Chak sounded, what? Cheerful? Proud? Pleased? He was quite close to Dun by the hole.

"Chakk, chakk, aaaahh." This time the entreaty was accompanied by a heavy metallic chink-squeak sound overhead. The squeak echoed on for a while.

"Aahh?" again the chink-squeak.

What was the thing that Chak was telling Dun about? It was metal, attached to something else metal and swung freely. Chak touched Dun's hand.

"What is it, Chak? What are you trying to tell me?"

Chakk held Dun's hand gently and lifted it up overhead to the roof. There over the hole, Chakk led Dun by feel, to a metal ring, bolted into the ceiling, exactly over the hole.

"Aahh? Chakk, chakk, aahh?"

"The ring is something to do with the hole?" Dun said.

"Chakk."

"Okay, and it's important."

"Chakk."

"Why? Why is it important?"

"It's how they get down," Tali said, suddenly understanding. "You use ropes through the rings, Chak?"

"Chakk!"

"And you abseil down," Myrch said.

"Chakk?"

"Slide down the rope? Yes, clever. And getting up?"

"Chakk, chakk, nnnnnhhhh! Chakk, chakk, nnnnnhhh!"

"Ah, more folk pull them up from up here?" Padg said.

"Chakk!" he said brightly.

"Clever," Myrch said again. "Very clever," he muttered walking on.

"Chakk, chakk!" Chak had held out his palm and Dun walked into it.

"What, Chak?"

"Chakk, chakk!" He held his palm firm against Dun's chest.

"I think he wants us to wait here," Dun said.

"Okay," Tali said.

"And we trust him? Just like that?" Myrch said.

"Yes," Tali said, "I think we do."

"After all the stories of folk disappearing and never returning?" he pressed.

"Yes!" Tali said firmly. "I think he's honorable and if he's a reflection of his people, then we can expect them to be honest too."

"And if not?"

"We'll just have to wait. I trust him."

"So we wait," Myrch said, statement more than a question.

"We wait."

Dark

Chapter Thirty-Five

Dun and the others had not been waiting long before they sensed a creeping presence on all sides of them and the disturbing scent of more Chakka-folk drifted into them. Dun counted about twenty and filed the count under "outnumbered" and waited. The fainter scent of Tali's balm ointment was there too, so Dun wasn't too worried.

"Chakk, chakk!" At least Chak was still representing his people. The rest gathered round them and seemed to be prodding them with blunt sticks of some sort.

"I think we're being encouraged to move on," Dun said.

"I can't help thinking of herd beasts," Padg said. History had it that thousands upon thousands of cycles ago, the River-folk used to herd giant rat-like creatures and milk them, sometimes kill them to eat. Current River-folk always denied it. The example, Dun thought, was unnerving, but outnumbered as they were, he could find little choice but to follow.

Their shepherds prodded them from time to time to speed them or warn them around the gaping holes in the floor. They came to a steep-facing wall. Dun thought it was made from rusted metal, pitted surface. He could smell two more chakkas awaiting them in front of it. Guards maybe.

"Chakk!" Chak held out a hand to Dun's chest again.

"I think he means wait here," Dun said.

They heard a low hissing and chakking murmur between the guards and Chak as he presumably negotiated. It seemed like it had gone positively as the guards didn't move and there seemed no flurry of activity that could be associated with apprehending intruders. They heard a huge noise of metal grating from the direction of the wall and felt the air move. It seemed like some kind of huge door was opening.

"Chakk!"

Wait again, thought Dun.

"I think he'll be a while in there," Dun said and hunkered down on his haunches ready for a wait. Tali sat next to him on the floor and stretched her legs out.

"Well, if we're all sitting," Padg said and sat himself.

Myrch paced.

They waited.

"If you could sit down now," Padg said, "you're making us all nervous."

Myrch continued pacing.

He was disturbed by the sound of footsteps approaching from the door Chak had disappeared into. It wasn't him coming back. All the folk approaching were doing so in step. Dun counted ten he thought, maybe more.

"Welcoming committee," Myrch said. "Nice."

The guard company coming out of the massive doorway seemed to split into two cohorts, the sound of one column flanking them on one side, the others down the opposite. Then they broke up into four small groups: behind, in front, left and right. Nowhere to run, then.

"CHAK!CHAK!" came the loud echo from all around them at once.

"CHAAAAAAAK!"

"Chak...chak...chak...chak."

"Chak...chak...chak...chak."

Foot stamps matched the beat of the clacking noise, it seemed they were to be marched inside, but whether as visitors or guests, it was hard to tell. They marched anyway.

It seemed their feet reverberated in huge booming sound then suddenly into a sharp, close staccato bark as they crossed the threshold into the Chakka-folks chambers. The guards fell into two lines left and right as it was only possible to move three abreast in this corridor. Dun knew they were the first people to visit this place, at least he hoped they'd be the first folk to visit and report back. Progressing down the corridor, it became hotter.

The corridor stretched on ahead of them and widened out into a largeish chamber. Once inside, there seemed to be a huge edifice in the middle of the room and the hissing noise of Chakka-folk all around them as if they were stacked on top of each other lining the walls, were there galleries around the room? The heat inside this sanctum was stifling. Dun wondered about it, as well as stifling, the heat was unlike any other he had ever felt. Unlike the vent's heat that jetted on a cushion of air however hot, this heat was still, flat somehow, seemingly coming straight at them from the surfaces of the monolithic cube at the center of the chamber.

A voice came from the top of the cube. "I am sspeaker for the Chossen-folk." The voice was odd, affected, but resonant nonetheless. "Who vissitss the womb of the ssacred energiess? And why?"

"Err, I am Tali! Speaker for the Bridge-folk. We have traveled many ways and pipes to meet you and we come with..."

"An offering?" Dun hissed.

"...an offering to your people, for, er..."

"Safe passage," Myrch added.

"...in return for safe passage through your lands and territory."

"We will think on thiss," the voice said. "Who among the chosen would speak for you?"

There was silence while they all internally panicked.

"Wait! There is one among you who I hope would speak for us." There was no point in calling him Chak in here. What then? "He was one, who... who..."

"Brought us here," Dun said.

"Yes, the one who brought us here."

"It iss well then. Come forth." Then a word that seemed too much chakking and hissing to quick to make sense of. Was that Chak's real name? There was a brief exchange of clacking and hissing and then silence.

"Come to us, speaker for the Bridge-folk. We would know of this strange comfort you bring to us."

Dark

So Tali edged forward, prodded gently by the guards. Each step took her closer to the cube and so hotter in turn. How could they stand to be so close to whatever the hells it was? She guessed you got used to anything with enough time. She nearly reached the face of the cube, but her face bumped a wooden structure with flat, spaced horizontal edges. The guards poked her again. She had no idea what they wanted of her.

"Ascend," the voice of the speaker said from above. Slowly, feeling for the wooden bars in front of her, she climbed.

The heat on Tali's face was almost unbearable, she focused on putting one foot in front of the other and tried not to think about anything else. When she got to the top, two hands reached down to her and pulled her up. Dusting herself down, she oriented herself. There was a great flat expanse on top of the cube and some kind of a raised area in the middle where the *speaker* sat.

"Come to uss."

Tali walked forward.

"What iss it you offer?" the Speaker said.

"I have a treatment that can help you, has helped one of you, I hope."

"Do we need help?"

"Your skin, it has burns. I think I can help heal them and make the painless."

"But we live with the pain, it iss part of who we are."

"It doesn't need to be. Speak to Cha... our friend and find if he feels its helped him."

"And how would you make all of this medicine of yourss?"

"I could teach you how to make it, or your shamans or wise-men."

"And in return?"

"You grant us safe passage through your territory."

"I will conssider."

"One more thing, we believe you have our guide Jarn. He must be returned."

"We will provide you with a guide."

"No, that's not what I mean. He is our friend we would like him returned."

"That is not possible."

"Err... why?"

"CHAKK, CHAKK, CHAKK, CHAKK."

"Chakk, chakk, chakk, chakk..."

"SILENCE! I will answer her, we are not barbarians. She has a need to know what has happened to her friend."

Tali waited, the hissing of the Chakka-folk subsiding.

"He is to become the new speaker for the Chosen-folk."

"Okay. Does he want to?" Tali said.

"That is immaterial. There must be a new speaker, he is the one."

"But aren't you the speaker?"

"I was chosen, as he is chosen, but my time is brief. Each speaker must speak while he can until the spirit of the chosen overwhelms him and he can speak no more."

"I don't understand. Why is your time brief? You sound only young."

"So I am." The speaker sounded amused. "But the fires of the spirit of the chosen burn bright, so I will teach the new speaker as I was taught, then I will join the ranks of the chosen."

"You'll die?"

"No." Again the amused tone. "But I will speak no more."

"Hmm." Tali felt the heat rising up through the soles of her feet.

"You understand?" the Speaker said, kinder now.

"I think I might be starting to," she said. "The fires-of-the-spirit-of-the-chosen; they are what we can feel all around us here? The heat?"

"Yes," the speaker said. "What else would they be?"

"And the fires, consume the speaker, in the end," she said. Knowing more now than asking.

Dark

"Yes."

"Literally? It affects your face, so you can't speak?"

"Yes."

"You were captured, sorry, chosen, yourself?"

"Yes."

"How long does it take? Until you can't speak anymore?"

"I am privileged to be the speaker for a little while yet." Again the amusement.

"But how long?"

"Five hundred spanss maybe. A little more. It takes one hundred spans to teach a new speaker. Less if they have a sharp ear."

"Gods," Tali said.

"It is the gods who chose uss. It is a privilege. Now as a speaker for your people, it is your time to choose. Do you leave with a blessing and a guide, or do you stay?"

"What about Jarn?" Tali asked.

"That is not a choice."

"I must consult with my friends."

"But you are the speaker for your people?"

"That is not how we do things."

"Here it is how *we* do things. You must decide, they must abide by the decision."

Tali had not been expecting that. It seemed like she must sanction abandoning Jarn to the Chosen-folk, at least to get them out of there and on their way. It was not something that she was happy about at all. In fact, there was very little about the whole situation that she was happy about like the mysterious source of heat that they stood on, that seemed to have permanently damaging effects on the Chosen, or the fact that their hosts seemed to kidnap folk entering their territory to become the next leader in who knew what kind of ritual. She was pleased that she'd created a salve that dealt with the pain, and without too much time to test it thoroughly, she thought a reasonable chance of improving healing and preventing infection to boot. And that was all she could settle for to comfort her. They had to go and leave Jarn to his chances.

Tali sighed. "We'll go. I'll show some of your people how to make the salve and where to find the ingredients. They're pretty common."

"Good luck, Tali of the Bridge-folk. May the gods follow your progress."

Dark

"Prolonged exposure to darkness is a funny thing. First it made me frightened, then annoyed. For the longest time, I didn't feel anything. Now I feel everything."

Excerpts from <Distress Beacon SN-1853001>. Found by E.S.V. Vixen Terradate: 26102225.

Dark

Chapter Thirty-Six

Tali spent the next three cycles while they helped the Chakka-folk, in near silence, at least when she wasn't explaining to the carers of the tribe. It seemed they had little concept of healers perse, as hardly anyone got better from anything that ailed them. When the onset of the damage from the Sacred Source or whatever it was, was complete, healing from anything became extremely unlikely. Wounds became infected and quickly too. The colony had resting rooms that seemed to do as makeshift hospitals, but no one seemed to get better in them. The smell inside them was nearly unbearable.

Tali asked for a new room. Ther was no point in making her task any more difficult than it had to be, and she set about training some of the folk, including Chak, how to make the salve. Then she made rounds of the resting rooms with her new trainees to apply it to the sick. In some simple cases, she could help with other things like setting bones and cleaning wounds. It seemed that the Chakka-folk hadn't developed much medicine at all. In the end, Dun and Padg were roped in too, to teach as many and as much as possible, while moving on as quickly as they could. At no time did they even catch a scent of Jarn. Neither did they find the Speaker again after Tali's initial audience.

Tali was woken on the morning of their third cycle there, by being shaken firmly by Padg.

"Get off me!" It came out harsher than she'd intended.

"Sorry," Padg said. "Myrch says we've got to leave, now."

"But there's so much to do."

"Yeah, still. He's been wafting around some kind of hissy gadget, and he says there's too many rads or something. Anyway, it's not safe to stay any longer, and we've got to leave."

"Okay." It didn't sound like she had a choice. Life seemed to be turning out that way a lot.

"You okay?" Padg said.

"Not so much...I—" but then Myrch was there with Dun.

"Come on, you two," Myrch said.

"Okay!" Tali said.

"What's up with you? We need to go." Myrch was short.

"But without Jarn?" she said, really angry now.

"Why do you care?" Myrch said, not a trace of anger in his voice.

"Why don't you?" she snapped back.

"He was a professional guide, he knew the risks. It's not like they're going to eat him."

"I just worry whether you'd sacrifice one of us so quickly," Tali said.

"Do you know the risks?"

Tali didn't even begin to understand the question, let alone how to answer it.

She sent a messenger to the Speaker to say they wished to leave and in return. Chak was sent back to them as a guide. They bade what passed for farewells with the folk they'd become most familiar with in their new nursing teams, collected their things, and left.

With a Chosen to guide them, the terrain became much simpler. It seemed they were being led the simplest, not the shortest way out, and they were glad of that. When they camped at the end of their first cycle Tali realized that they had all brought something with them. Every face and every hand, hers most of all, carried a glow from the *source* they had all brought with them. She quickly made to apply the ointment to all of them. Chak didn't need any, his wounds healing nicely from the first time Tali had applied the cream. Myrch refused point blank. Tali was half expecting him to before she even offered.

They made good progress, with their Chakking friend leading the way being an efficient guide. Dun couldn't help noticing more places where that had heat but with no vents. It seemed the *source* wasn't the only source. Dun pondered how the heat had gotten there, and what it even was. At the very least, it made an interesting caveat on his ever-expanding map. *"Here be source."* He still spent time worrying whether he'd ever get it back to the Bridge-folk to show them.

The last part of their journey through Chosen territory was a perilous descent down a tube that seemed to be part of a giant tunnel network. The Chakkas seemed to have a smoothed pipe gadget that allowed them to clip on to a rope and slide down it, braking their descent by lifting the trailing end of the rope. It seemed that with enough practice more than one of them could rappel down a rope at a time. This must be how the rapid ambushes took place.

As they descended, Dun could hear trickling water from the pipes below, then as he got closer he detected a faint smell drifting up the rope to meet him. Adrenaline banged into his bloodstream. He felt the rush of blood to his face, to his ears. He felt dizzy. Slowly, he realized where he'd smelled that scent before: He'd smelled it in a dream.

"What's wrong, Dun?" Tali asked.

"That dream, the one of the thing hunting and attacking us?"

"Uh-huh,"

"It took place here."

"But how could it?" Tali said. "You've never been here."

"It's foretelling, isn't it," Padg said. "That's what happens."

"So what happens in the dream?" Myrch said, last to land in the pipe behind them.

"There isn't really an end to it if that's what you're asking. It's just me sensing what the creature senses and being aware of what it's thinking."

"What is it thinking? Out of interest," Padg said.

"Mostly that it wants to hunt and bite and taste blood."

"Sorry I asked now."

"Is it in front of us or behind us?" Myrch said.

"I can't really tell," Dun said. "Sorry. You still believe me, don't you?"

"It certainly can't hurt to be prepared," Myrch said. "Is it bigger than us, smaller?"

"No, smaller. ?hhhygIts the size of a large rat, but there's something odd about it. Its mind isn't like ours."

"Well, no," Padg said, "its a rat."

"That's not what I meant slick-whiskers, part of its mind is rat-like, I guess. Savage, ravenous, but rat-like. But there's another part of its mind, somehow inside it, or maybe alongside it, that's cold, calculating, like its giving instructions, processing. Either way, small or not, it's fierce and sharp, and its killed things before, lots of things."

"Then we'd better make sure we're not on its menu," Myrch said. "I'll take the front, Padg, spear out, you're in back. Tali, anything in that bag of tricks of yours we can use?"

"I've still got a couple of compression flasks left."

"Good. Fish one out, we can do with all the help we can get. Okay." There was that small metal sliding sound and a click that accompanied Myrch when he was preparing. "Let's go. Move off slowly."

"Err, we should say good-bye to Chak first," Tali said.

"Okay, but hurry," Myrch said.

Hurried farewells were said, and they moved off into the pipe. The party tried to make less noise than the trickling stream that soaked their feet in the bottom of the pipe, Padg having the least luck on account of him walking backward guarding their rear.

Chapter Thirty-Seven

There was a twitch of whiskers then the smell of fear. Padg didn't even have the time to cry out. The beast was on him.

Sword-spear already drawn, he thought he'd caught it with the blade as it crashed into him but he couldn't tell. Gods, the thing was fast. He was bowled off his feet with the momentum and sat in the watery pipe with a splash.

"Where the hells is it?" Padg shouted.

"It went over my head and up the pipe," Tali said.

"Everyone okay?" Myrch said.

"I'm bruised but okay," Padg said.

"Tali? Dun?" Myrch asked.

"Missed me," Tali said. "Dun? Dun..."

"I... think. I think it got me, I'm... cut. It cut me. Something metal, I think."

Tali was there in a click, "Hells, Dun, sit down."

"But the pipe... it's... wet."

"Sit!" she said.

He was bleeding badly from his stomach. Tali's hands were sticky already and the sweetly metallic smell didn't normally turn her stomach, but somehow it being Dun's blood made the nausea worse.

"You two, guard us here while I patch Dun up," Tali said.

"We'll give you as long as we can," Myrch said.

"Got that flask, Tali?" Padg said.

"Backpack, side pocket. Fish me a needle and twine out of the same side while you're in there."

"On it."

"Thanks," Tali said as Padg handed over the needle and headed to the front of the party. He found a tense Myrch when he got there.

"Any signs?" Padg said.

"None," Myrch said. "Damn, but that thing was quiet."

"Hmm, and fast too."

"Can you two pipe down back there? I'm going to see if Padg can listen," Myrch said to the groaning noises and shushing from behind them. "Well?"

"Nothi..."

"What?"

"Wait... there's something. It's right at the top end of my hearing. It's higher than bat-noise. A tiny, tiny, squee kind of noise. It's nothing like any creature I've ever heard before."

"I don't think it is like any creature you've ever heard before. Not any natural one anyway."

"What do you think it is?"

"I'm guessing, but I think its some kind of machine," Myrch said.

"But I heard it, smelled it; it's like a rat."

"But it's not one, is it?"

"What else did you smell?"

Padg thought. "Something chemical, inorganic. Like that oil stuff that Tinker-folk use on found things to make them work again."

"Oil. Exactly."

"I don't understand," Padg said.

"I think, it's part machine, part beast. A rat missile, if you like. Smart enough to have its own intelligence and behaviors, but with a machine half to give commands and maybe weapons."

"Gods, that's terrible," Padg said. "Who would do such a thing?"

"Honestly," Myrch said, "I don't know, but whoever it is, I think that thing wants us dead."

"But wh—" Dun said.

"It's coming!" Padg said.

"Above!" Myrch shouted.

A low rapid series of fut noises battered out while Myrch cursed. Padg flailed his sword-spear. A whish of air and the creature crashed into the weapon and threw Padg back off his feet.

"Dang!"

"Watch..."

"Tali!"

"No!"

Then it was gone again.

"Oh no!" Tali spoke first out of the chaos.

"You okay?" Myrch said.

"Yeah," she said, "which is more than I can say for my backpack. That blasted thing shredded it on the way past. I had it over my head to fend it off."

"I think it's trying to get me," Dun said. "Why would it want to do that?"

"Time for that later," Myrch said, clipped. "Ready for another attack."

"Padg," Dun said, "toss me that flask. You've got your hands full. I want to feel a bit less useless."

Dun clicked his tongue and Padg threw to the sound. Then the rush of air again and the thing was on them. There was a crash of glass and liquid splished. A screech that was neither animal or mechanical.

"Ahhhhh!" Dun shouted.

"You little... nnng!" Padg shouted. "Got you!"

Gone again.

"Winged it properly this time, did you?" Myrch said.

"I think I got the spear tip into it. I felt it snap. Yeah," Padg said, feeling the weapon, "the ends gone."

"I think Dun got it too," Tali said. "He got us anyway."

"Yeah, urgh, what is that stuff. It's awful," Dun said.

"It's sticky," she said.

"Yeah I know," Dun said.

"It'll slow it down, hopefully," she said.

"Better had!" Myrch shouted, "Here it comes!"

The *futs* rattled out again. Myrch splished forward in the pipe, the *futting* continued. Thrashing, splashing, screeching noises. More futting, screeching, and then more futting. Keening, thinner, silence. Then just the trickle of the water in the pipe.

There was a faint wet crunch as Myrch toed the creature with his foot.

"Careful," Padg said.

"Don't you worry about me," Myrch said, amused. "You go and get patched up."

"Who's going to patch me up?" Tali said.

"Moaner," Padg said. "You always land on your feet regardless!"

A little beyond the remains of the rat-missile was another short intersecting pipe. Padg explored it and found it to be a dead end. They dragged themselves and the remains of their kit into the pipe and holed up.

"Gods, this backpack's trashed," Tali said.

"Have you lost much stuff?" Dun said.

"A good load, yes."

"Sorry," Dun said.

"Idiot," Tali said, poking him.

"Ow!"

"I think I've still got some wound cream in here, and I'll give you something to drink for the pain. It may make you drowsy."

It did. He slept soundly, woken only by the aching in his stomach wall. That was a hell of a fight. He tried to sit up but whatever it was that Tali had done to help his wounds start to knit hurt like hell. He supposed here was as good a place to rest as any and drifted back to sleep.

Chapter Thirty-Eight

Dun's nightmares woke him again, but not with a foretelling. At least not one that he could recognize as one. What he remembered was a fragmentary clash of noises and smells and gods knew what else. The only cogent reminder of his cycles rest was the banging headache he woke with and the ache in his guts.

The others were bustling around readying to break camp. Upon stirring, Dun found a small leaf wrap thrust into his hand.

"Nice, thanks," Dun said.

"Make the most of it. We need to eat them before they spoil," Tali said. "My pack got drenched and loads of stuff got wet. Bottled stuff is okay, but we're going to be really stretched for food."

"Back to weeds and rats then, yum," Padg said.

"Hopefully, it won't come to that," Myrch said.

"Why do you know something we don't?" Dun said.

"Maybe. I think I've got an idea."

"Oh, gods." Padg sighed. "It always starts like that."

"Going to tell us what this adventure might entail?" Tali said. "No, thought not."

"Why spoil a good surprise?" Myrch said.

They shouldered their packs and slid down the pipe, splishing back into the shallow stream in the bottom. They settled into a steady pace, making good time. They walked in silence, lulled by the noise of the trickle. Dun noticed the pipe widened gradually as they walked. When they stopped for their next break, the stream in the bottom of the pipe seemed shallower, slower somehow.

"Nothing to hunt or forage here," Padg said after a cursory search.

"No," Dun said, "not a scent of anything except that water and the pipe."

"The pipe smells a bit plasticky here though," Tali said.

"Doesn't help us catch fish," Dun said.

"Plastic fish?" Padg said.

Dun sniggered.

Tali said, "Yeah, I'm laughing, but I'm still hungry. I can't fix Padg's sense of humor, but I have a couple of things left. Give me a few clicks."

While they leaned against one wall of the pipe to stay out of the water for a while, Tali mixed from her remaining bottles. There was a strong smell of crushed grass and maybe milk. Dun couldn't swear that he found it enticing.

"Here." Tali handed him a bottle. "It's not fantastic, but it's got energy in it and bulk so it'll stave off the hunger for a bit at least."

They passed the bottle around, making some kind of noise from each in turn as they drank. Myrch refused and drank from some kind of faintly bitter smelling flask of his own.

"So we're going where again?" Padg said.

"I didn't say," Myrch mumbled around another gulp of whatever he was drinking.

"No, so you didn't," Padg said, hoping Myrch would fill the space. He didn't.

"Machine-folk," Dun said simply.

Myrch paused mid-swig and then continued drinking.

"It's obvious," Dun said. "Partly by how far we've traveled, but also by how hedgy you are about any questions."

He paused. "Not so much that you're bothered that we know we're going there, we always were, but something else."

"Oh?" Myrch said.

"You're worried about something when we get there? You don't like seeming like you don't know what's going on. And you don't."

"Yeah?"

"No. You kind of know where we're going, but you don't know what we're going to find when we get there."

"Have you finished?" Myrch said.

"Not quite." It was Dun's turn for the bottle, and he sipped slowly before passing it on. "Have now. Shall we go?"

"Let's."

***

Dun couldn't tell when the pipe had turned into a corridor. He guessed a while back. They'd walked nearly another whole cycle, stopping little. With no dry rations left, there was little left to stop for. Between his buzzing head and growling stomach, he really hadn't been admiring the architecture. But it had definitely changed. Now he'd thought it, he pinged out with his air-sense. Definitely changed from round section to square section and smoother. Not just a utilitarian pipe anymore, but first a smooth tube, and then a smooth corridor. And made from what? Smooth to the touch but not without texture. A nap even, smoother one way than the other. Brushed metal then? Not cool either. Or warm. Ambient. Not a trace of rust or wear in the pipe where the water still trickled underfoot.

"You've sensed it too then?" Padg said at the sound of Dun's running fingertips along the wall.

"Yeah…"

"What do you make of it?"

"Civilization to be sure. Someone *lives here*. Or did. Nothing here feels accidental, natural."

Then, as if from nowhere, a breeze began behind them. From still air, very slowly building to a strong, steady force.

"I don't think that's natural either," Tali said.

"No," Padg said, "not gusting."

"And listen. That whine again."

The very faint high-pitched squeak that seemed to be the life-blood of the rat-machine was back. A different, resonating noise this one, but way up there in the so-hard-to-hear-you-nearly-can't-register.

"I wonder if..." Dun said and edged closer, trying to cock an ear to hear better, make more out of it.

"STOP!" Myrch barked. "Take one step backward."

That was harder to do than Dun imagined. It was almost like the wind was forcing him forward, toward the noise. He dug his heels in and backed away. He bumped Padg on the way backward, who grabbed his arm.

"What *is* it?" Padg said, responding in kind to the tone of Myrch's command.

"Very dangerous," he said. "Got a glass stopper from one of your bottles, Tali? Preferably one you won't need to use again."

"Sure," she said, proffering a bottle, stopper first to Myrch. He took the stopper, leaving her holding the rest of the bottle.

Myrch hurled the stopper toward the noise.

The stopper ricocheted off the wall of the tunnel with a clang.

"What the hells is that thing?" Padg said.

"A fan. An enormous great fan. From what I can tell it fills the corridor. If we'd have bumbled into it... Well, you're bright, folks," Myrch said.

"How do we get past it?" Dun said.

"I don't know," Myrch said. "I don't know."

Chapter Thirty-Nine

They stood in front of the massive fan, a respectful distance away, pondering.

"Without stating the obvious," Padg said, "if it's just a fan, can't we stick something in it to stop it going around?"

"How many sword-spears have we got left? I've got one," Dun said.

"Two here," Padg said. "Worth a try then."

"Sounds extremely dangerous to me," Myrch said.

"Got a better plan?" Padg said.

"At the moment, no."

"Well, then," Padg said.

"At least put a rope around him," Myrch said. "Maybe we can reduce disaster, if not prevent it."

So they tied some of their remaining rope around Padg's waist and paid it out as he advanced slowly toward the corridor and the high-pitched noise, proffering his sword-spear, point end first, holding firm to the butt end. He edged farther.

With a loud 'whang' noise the sword-spear was ripped out of his hands, his shoulders nearly ripped out of their sockets, and Tali, Dun, and Myrch grabbed the rope for all they were worth and pulled. Padg wound up ingloriously on his behind in the thin trickle of water. It was enough to wet him through. Oddly he found it pleasantly distracting from the pain in his shoulder. He hoped it was only a pull and not a fracture. He could still move it, so that was a start.

"Maybe we could get around it?" Tali said.

"You first," Padg said.

"No seriously, hear me out. The passage is square here, right?"

"Seems to be," Dun said.

"Well," she went on, "a fan goes around."

"...a fan goes around?..." Padg said.

Dark

"Shush!" she said. "A fan goes around, and therefore it is round."

"O..kayy..."

"So there's..."

Dun finished for her, "A gap in the corners! Clever."

"Here," she said, unshouldering what was left of her pack. "Let me have a go. Pass me your spear, Dun."

"Careful!" Padg said.

"I've got no intention of doing what you've just done. Trust me."

"I do."

"Good."

She shed other extraneous things that might stick out, her belt and the scabbard with her knife then advanced slowly. Slowly, she lay down, feet toward the fan and wriggled toward it caterpillar style. She couldn't hear the boys over the thin whine the fan made and the whish of the air that she could now feel when this close. Why she wondered, could they not feel it before? This thing was powerful. Why did it make so little noise and have so little air-sense signature? She started to feel the air on her toes; she must be under the fan edges. It didn't really feel like a breeze, more like a constant push on one side of her. Luckily, away from the whirling blades. She stopped heart pounding.

"You okay?" Dun shouted.

"Yeah, I think there'll be enough room for me."

"Good," Myrch said. Tali continued shuffling.

"It does raise the question," Padg said, "of how we get the rest of us through. Since Tali's the skinniest of us all."

"Let's cross one bridge at a time," Myrch said.

Tali groaned.

"What's up?" Padg said.

"Cramp," Tali said.

"Oh good," Padg said. "Well, not good, but, you know..."

"Padg?" Tali said.

"Yeah?"

"Shut up."

He did. The shuffling recommenced. Tali got her legs through and slowly edged her way farther. The air was pushing her flat into the corner of the corridor. *It would be quite comforting*, she thought, *like being cuddled, if it wasn't being cuddled by huge sharp whirling fan blades of death*. She felt that she'd progressed far enough under the fan to risk raising her knees, the better to give her purchase. She did and then her face was under. It was the most horrible feeling: air pushing flat onto her face, forcing its way into her mouth. She needed to breathe and couldn't. She also needed to stop, the cramp was back, knifing her legs and her diaphragm. She knew that she couldn't stay under there for much longer, the not breathing not helping with that. She clamped down those unhelpful thoughts and clenched everything for another pull. There was a massive blast of air across her head, pulling her hair by the roots, and then she was out.

"Through!" she gasped. "I don't think we're going to get any more of you through there though."

"No, we were thinking that," Dun shouted back. "Stay put and we'll think."

"Not going anywhere for a few clicks." She panted. "While I get my breath back."

"Now what?" Dun said.

"First, grab the end of that rope and tie a knot in it. Then use a spear butt to push it through to her," Myrch said.

"Okay, I get it," Dun said. Then he said to Tali, "Hey, Tali! We're going to poke you this end of the rope through, and then we can tie your stuff on and you can pull it through."

"That's good, but how do I get you lot through," she said.

"Let's get your gear to you first," Myrch said, "Then I'll talk you through it."

Gear duly transferred; Tali felt marginally more secure alone on the far side of the fan.

"Right," Myrch said. "There'll be some kind of a panel to make this thing work somewhere. Check along the walls on both sides; it'll probably be at about your head height."

"What am I trying to find?" she said.

"Some kind of box, or a place where the wall where there's a panel screwed in?"

"Err... hold on. Let me check..." She scuttled off for seemingly an age. It became too much effort for Dun to strain to hear her running her hands over the walls on the other side of the fan noise, so he stopped trying.

"How far should I go?"

"Not more than ten strides or so, it won't be farther away than that," Myrch said.

"There's another passage off here about nine to ten strides from you."

"Don't go farther than that then," he said.

"Hmm... no... no... and no... oh... mmm... wait, I think there's something here. Ever so slightly warmer than the rest of the wall. So smooth though, I nearly missed it."

"Will it..?"

"Push? Yes," Tali said. There was a satisfying 'click' from Tali's side of the fan, and instantly the tension around them died with the high-pitched whine.

"Thank the gods for that," Dun said.

"That noise was starting to drive me crazy," Padg said.

The fan began to make all kinds of interesting noises as it very slowly lost momentum. It took a lot longer than all of them expected to finally come to a stop.

"Wow. Feel the edge on these blades, Dun," Padg said, awed.

Dun ran his fingers along the edges of the fan blades, carefully at first for fear of them being sharp. They weren't. Instead, they felt for all the world like fabric. Hard as steel, thin as paper, soft as fabric.

"Amazing," he said in the same hushed tones as Padg.

"Now we've all finished admiring the handiwork, where's that panel?" Myrch said.

"Sorry, I'm over here," Tali said, "also admiring the handiwork."

"Are we all on this side, all kit, and chattels?" Myrch asked.

"Yeah, I brought the last of the bags through," Dun said.

"Okay good. Stand clear down by that side passage, I'm not sure how strong this will be on this side," Myrch said.

"It's not too bad," Tali said. "Strong, but not enough to push anyone over."

"Good," Myrch said.

The sharp click again, then, immediately the whine and a slow whirring sound built speed gradually.

"Shall we?" Myrch had to shout. "The side passage, I think."

Dark

"If I was a betting man I'd say they developed from some kind of species the first colonists brought as pets, or protein."

Excerpts from <Distress Beacon SN-1853001>.
Found by E.S.V. Vixen Terradate: 26102225.

Dark

Chapter Forty

They hadn't progressed far down the side passage when they all stopped short. The fan noise, always louder on this side of the fan, ceased, abruptly.

"Can you...?" Dun said.

"No, it's gone," Padg said.

"Wait," Tali said, retracing her steps. "I can still hear it back here. And then, one stride and... Wow, try it."

It seemed that a definite line existed in the corridor, beyond which the noise did not seem to pass. They spent some time playing backward and forward, working out if they could hear each other—they couldn't—and experimenting.

"Boo!" Tali said, gently into Padg's ear.

"Meh! Could smell you coming," Padg said.

"Can we get on now?" Myrch said.

"Killjoy," Padg murmured.

They fell back into line walking. Then there was the music. Wonderful, complicated, rippling music. Strange unfolky voices in perfect harmony, instruments delicately tinkling high up and others in all-encompassing rumbling basso below. As they walked, the melody and instrumentation changed subtlely to measure their progress. Dun was dumbstruck.

"So beautiful," Tali said.

"Hello?" Padg called out. "Who's there?"

"I don't think there is anyone there," Myrch said.

"I don't understand," Padg said.

"I think it's recorded," Myrch said.

"What does that mean?" Padg said.

"Stored away; to be played later," Myrch said.

"Stored away how?"

"Well, on a machine. I think we're where we wanted to be. Welcome to the halls of the Machine-folk."

Dark

***

They walked on, Dun suspended somewhere between amazement and terror. The twisting musical braid wound and unwound down the corridor. Slowly, it became quieter step-by-step until it petered out completely. Then silence. Like before, even the echo of the sound from farther away did not reach them. Dun suspected another "silencing curtain" like after the fan.

"Wait," Myrch said. "There's a pad here on the floor. Step back you three. Dun, pass me that spear."

Myrch took the spear from Dun and tapped on the floor. Then, loudly, seeming to come from everywhere they heard, "Bee ba. Ebovra cheacava deanus bactri. Cha banna etho banna madga. De doo."

"Who in the hells was that?" Padg said. An edge of fear now in his voice.

"Recording again," Myrch said. "Listen."

He tapped again.

"Bee ba. Ebovra cheacava deanus bactri. Cha banna etho banna madga. De doo."

"Oh," Padg said.

"What do you think it's saying?" Dun said.

"A greeting maybe?" Padg said.

"Or a warning?" Tali said.

"I think its more mundane than that," Myrch said. "Some kind of information update. I recognize a few words."

"How?" Tali said.

"They're a little like old Stone-folk tongue."

"Oh," she said not quite hiding her suspicion.

"I studied it," Myrch said.

"Right."

"Shall we go?" Myrch said.

"Sure."

They all walked into the land of the Machine People, to strains of:

"Bee ba. Ebovra cheacava deanus bactri. Cha banna etho banna madga. De doo."

Underfoot was flawless, as were the walls, even the temperature, and the humidity. Completely, uncomfortably comfortable. The Machine-folk were nothing if not fastidious. The floor became softer, just in the center for a certain width. They found themselves walking two abreast. Cushiony. Dun took the liberty of reaching down since he was now next to Tali at the back to reach down and feel. So soft. Not natural, not fur, not plant hairs. Soft, warm. Like it should be alive. But not. On the edge of his hearing, Dun picked up something. Clicking. Their own clicker beetles were long since dead. A noise so familiar that it seemed odd for it to be there again. But a definite series of regular clicks, way in front of them, but there all the same. As they got closer, the clicks became more evident.

"Who knew," Padg said, "a civic clicker."

And he was right. As they got nearer, there was one larger click: to mark a hundred, maybe. Then back to the regular rhythm. Interesting, useful certainly, but what must it be like to live and work under such a clock. All the time. In the village people kept their own clickers if they were timing something, like the alchemists measuring potions or the healers measuring pulses, but the major times of the day were marked largely by folk's own circadian rhythms. Odd how other folk lived.

The corridor opened out into a large hall. Dun noticed the texture of flooring alter under his feet. It was like another texture crossed their path at right angles.

"There's another path here," he said.

"So there is," Myrch said. "But let's be systematic; we can go back that way later."

"Err... Myrch?" Dun said.

"Yes."

"Where is everyone?"

"I don't... I'm not sure."

Dark

Dun thought back to the teeming warren that the Stone-folk lived in. But here there was not a soul about. This place was at least as big as that but the only other voices they'd heard so far were stored and played back to them automatically. And now that felt creepy. They passed under another automatic voice.

"The Machine-folk welcome you. Pass immediately to the customs house. On paying any tithes required, you can be granted movement through the city. Follow the smooth carpet for the customs house. Thank you."

"Shall we?" Padg said.

"Why not?" Dun said.

"Carefully," Myrch said.

The hall was massive and eerie. In complete silence they walked, even their footfalls were muffled by the carpet. Periodically, they heard automated voices piped down to them from above, seeming to recommend goods and services available to them nearby but that was just it. There didn't seem to be anyone around at all to provide anything. The smooth carpet widened out to a round area wide enough to allow all of them to stand abreast.

"Customs Hall," said a voice from above. "Please wait in an orderly and quiet fashion. A customs official will be with you as soon as possible. We thank you for your patience."

"Friendly bunch," Padg said.

"Friendly, but absent," Dun said.

The same held true for the hall here as everywhere else thus far. No folk anywhere. In here Dun thought he could pick up the faintest tinge of distant scent, but it was so faint, he was pretty sure he was imagining it. Willing it into being, as some evidence of anyone would be less creepy than what they faced now.

Chapter Forty-One

"Customs hall," the automated female voice said. "Those with goods for trade please walk the bumpy lane. Visitors walk the striped lane. Those with immunity and returning residents, please walk the smooth lane. Move along."

"Please move along."

"Mithering kind of soul, ain't she?" Padg said.

"I was going to go for firm," Tali said.

"Do we play along?" Dun said.

"I'd say we do," Myrch said, "We haven't got a better search plan yet and playing along avoids setting off any automated systems that might not be so friendly."

"So what are we?" Dun said. "Traders or visitors?"

"Friend or Foe?" Padg said.

"Let's do our best to avoid foe," Myrch said. "Shall we go for trader? It's most like us for now."

Dun felt the carpet texture under his feet. It branched three ways, the left-most being bumpy.

"It's left," he said.

They walked along the bumpy track.

"Trade lane. Please make a sample of your goods ready for inspection and assay. Please move along."

"What shall we say we have to trade?" Dun said.

"What have we got?" Padg said.

"Not a great deal left after our encounter with our metal rat friend," Tali said. "All the rations are shot now; I've thrown the rest of what got wet. I've got some flasks of various stuff left, but I don't want to trade any of that."

"We're not really trading anything though, are we?" Dun said.

"No, but that doesn't account for what might happen if we *say* we want to trade something," Padg said.

"True," Myrch said. "These legacy systems could do anything."

"Customs. Please place any samples on the counter for assessment. Thank you."

They stopped in front of the counter.

"I wonder," Tali said. "Have either of you two got a sack I can put this stuff in?"

"Sure," Dun said. He rustled in his pack. "Here, it's not massive."

'I haven't got all that much left."

There was much clinking and clanging as Tali's remaining equipment was transferred across. Then she draped the tattered backpack on the counter.

"Customs. Please place any samples on the counter for assessment. Thank you."

"That doesn't qualify as goods then," Dun said.

"I'm not sure it even qualifies as a backpack anymore." Tali sighed.

"Hold on, I've got an idea," Myrch said. "Try your knife, Tali."

She unsheathed her knife and placed it carefully on the counter.

"Unauthorized weapon in the customs area. Please stay where you are and officials will be along to help you." A discreet alarm siren sounded too. A low ululating wail.

"Not bloody likely," Padg said.

"Wait," Myrch said.

"Unauthorized weapon in the customs area. Security officials have been dispatched. Please stay where you are."

They waited. One hundred clicks, two hundred. It was easy to keep count with the ubiquitous clock in the background everywhere they went.

Three hundred, Four. There was no security coming. No evidence of them, automated or otherwise. Or any other systems being activated.

"Hmm," Myrch said and lifted the dagger off the counter handing it back to Tali hilt first. The sirens stopped.

"Customs. Please place any samples on the counter for assessment. Thank you."

"Good day for trading knives, then," Padg said.

Tali sighed. "Now what?"

"Don't know..." Myrch said. "Let's work out what should have happened. Dun, carry on along the carpet. I guess there's an out door somewhere."

"Okay," Dun said, walking slowly, feeling for the pattern on the carpet.

"Please present your customs bill to the slot and the doors will open."

"There's a set of doors here and a kind of pillar in front to one side. I think... Yes, that's where the slot is," Dun said.

"So all we need now is a customs bill," Myrch said.

"Do you suppose that's what one of these is?" Padg said.

"Where did you get that?" Tali said.

"Well, if they will leave their posts abandoned and all this stuff lying around," he said.

"Hmm..." Myrch said.

"Do you think we'll need one each to get through?" Dun asked.

"Doesn't matter," Padg said. "I've got loads."

They gathered around the small pillar, and Padg placed the ticket in the hole.

"*Customs. Your goods tithe is ... zero. Please proceed through the doors.*" There was a small hiss as they opened and a cacophony of sounds and smells from the other side.

"Perhaps this is where everyone is?" Dun said.

"Perhaps..." Myrch said.

They walked through the doors into a huge space. Music played and voices talked from every level and direction. This must be a marketplace, but there was something wrong. Lots of folk voices, but Dun's air-sense couldn't pick up that feeling of a space occupied by moving objects. No folk here. And listening carefully, the voices: all insistent but not conversant, more stored voices? Yes, now they all listened. The closest ones they could hear repeated after a short phrase or swift tune. But slightly more alarming than that, there was a smell: still, lingering, complex, because this was a marketplace after all, but waning. There had not been a fresh smell created here for, what? Five cycles, maybe more. Near them, a food stall, with that familiar vent smell, but when Dun moved behind the counter to check, the food on the vent heater was dried up.

"Hey, there's food here," Tali said.

She had found another stall. This one with dried patties of chopped leaf and fungus.

"Be careful," Dun said. "We're not sure how long its been here."

"Nah, tuck in," she said. "This stuff keeps for eons."

They ate rapidly, not realizing how hungry they'd become. Each of them pocketed more of the stuff for later.

"Hey," Dun said from across the market from them. "Got a present for you Tali!"

"Oh right?" she said.

"This stall sells bags," he said amused. "Nothing as useful as your backpack, but still."

"I'll find something," she said and ferreted amongst the stock.

"No looters," Myrch said.

"Sorry?" Dun said.

"This place has been abandoned for what..."

"Ten cycles?" Dun said.

"...give or take, and the things that strike me are no folk, no chaos, no looting."

"They left in an orderly way?" Dun said.

"Or were forced to, yes," Myrch said. "And no one has been here since. It's left like they've only just gone."

"Creepy," Padg said.

"But where did they go?" Tali said.

"More importantly, why?" Dun said.

Dark

Chapter Forty-Two

"The looting... us, I mean," Tali said, "it's peoples' lives..."

"Don't let it bother you," Myrch said.

Dun said, softer, "I've got a feeling it doesn't matter. I don't think they're coming back."

The others didn't dare to ask if it was a foretelling or just a hunch. Dun didn't have the heart to tell them it wasn't, but something about the totality of the Machine-folk absence and Myrch's assured reaction told him all he needed. No special powers necessary.

They carried on, moving from abandoned stall to abandoned stall replenishing their supplies. The stalls were laid out in avenues of careful spokes radiating from some kind of communal area in the center. Except for weapons, they found everything they could have wanted, food, blankets, rope. Tali even found some more potion ingredients and glass flasks. There seemed to be a communal drinking water fountain in the center too and presumably another sound-damping curtain, as the fountain's gentle trickle was all they could hear. Dun thought this would be a lovely meeting place, imagining the murmur and laughter of a people at work. No lingering scent here, the damp mist from the fountain had dispensed with that. They filled some water bags they had found at a plastic goods stall. Dun drank most of his and filled it again. The water was clear and fresh tasting, so unlike other water courses down here. Was it different water? Or did the Machine-folk have the technology to alter it, freshen it in some way? Filter it? Back home at the Bridge, *sip-reeds* were a favorite: fresh young reeds of a type that imparted the fresh-cut plant flavor to the water. Gods, they were so far from there now. What he wouldn't give to be back there. No, far as they were, he wouldn't swap. Least of all now he was so close to finding out one of their goals: What had happened to the Machine-folk?

"Come on," Myrch said "Let's move on. I think we're running out of time."

"For finding the Machine-folk?" Dun said.

"Yeah, that," Myrch said.

"Which way?" Dun said.

From a cursory circuit of their small respite, Dun had discovered each of the routes radiating out—there seemed to be eight—had a different number of stripes on its carpet. It took a while for him to work out the different sensations under his feet, but he worked it out in the end.

"Hmm... left," Myrch said. Not the way they came in, but not the straight route through the cavern.

"Why that way," Padg said. "Out of interest."

"I don't know," Myrch said. "Why not?"

The sensation of leaving their small oasis was strange, they walked out through the "sound curtain" and back into the echoing market hall of competing sounds, chirps and twangs, bells, and voices, following the path with three stripes underfoot.

"Last chance to grab any bargains!" Myrch said.

"We're fine. Thank you," Tali said.

"Suit yourself, might be a while till you're back this way," Myrch said.

Dun couldn't help but mentally check his pack. He and Padg had one sword-spear each left. They'd both found two nice, but short knives, clearly not meant to be weapons, but anything might do in a pinch. They had enough provisions now: new sacks, bedrolls, and water pouches. He walked on after the others with that uneasy feeling that he'd forgotten something but knowing at the same time he hadn't. He shook his head and jogged on to catch the others up.

After the market was a non-descript joining corridor, one or two indents either side implying doors but nothing more interesting. One of the doors yielded a storeroom full of large empty plastic crates on investigation, the other a room with three walls full of gently clicking machines, all whirring and blowing warm air.

Before anyone could step in to investigate, Myrch intervened. "Don't go any farther into there. Who knows what these do."

"What are they?" Dun said.

"My guess," Myrch said, "controllers. They do simple things: maybe operate a door or a fan, could store some words to play back under certain circumstances—that kind of thing."

"Wow," Padg said.

"But don't touch. If they are controllers, we don't want to be turning off the controls to a door we might want to get through, or alerting our presence to anyone who might be here before we're ready to meet them."

Dark

"Feels a little like a room of unsprung traps," Dun said.

"Yeah, that too," Myrch said.

They all backed out and closed the door quietly.

Turning back the way they were headed they felt a distinct, thick breeze ooze warm and lazy toward them. The corridor smelled warm and faintly of sulfur. The smoothness of these corridors continued to impress Dun. What cycles of work had it taken to complete them? Then they walked out into the deepest space they'd ever encountered.

The floor beneath them was perforated in some fashion, metal-smelling, but Dun could feel through it with his air-sense. In many ways, he wished he couldn't. Beneath their feet was a sheer drop, too far for Dun to feel the bottom. Luckily there was a rail in front of him. He grabbed on and held on with both hands and steadied himself. Padg and Tali did the same. The room seemed to be a vast cylinder, as high up as it was deep down. It's far walls detectable to air-sense, maybe two hundred fifty to three hundred strides across, accessible to the other side by way of a bridge in the same translucent metal material they were standing on. The place had the feel of some kind of temple.

"What is..." Dun said.

"I have no idea," Myrch said, cutting him off.

"Impressive though, isn't it?" Padg said.

"That it is," Myrch said.

"Beautiful," Tali said.

The warm air was rising up to them, not a breeze as such, just a continuous convection current. They stood for a while in mute appreciation.

A folk who could do this, Dun thought, *what must they have been able to accomplish*? But that didn't sit easily in his head with the Machine-folk tinkers who'd arrive at the village with interesting trinkets, clever toys and sell them for a few trade strips, which they'd inevitably end up spending on food anyway. It was almost as if...

But Dun's thought faded there. There was a huge click sound and slowly from the depths of the pipe the air started to move faster up toward them. They could smell more of the metally-oily warmth from below and then with the smell came the noise of dozens of fans. Tali leaned over the rail, her face into the warm current.

"Wow!" she shouted over the rising noise. "This is incredible! Come and feel this!"

Padg joined her and leaned in. "Whee-hee! That feeeeellls weird."

As the rush of air was picking up speed Padg could start to feel it ruffle his hair and pull on the sides of his face. Dun tried too, briefly, Myrch was ominously absent. The air was now rushing past them, talking into it was becoming harder.

Myrch shouted from the opposite side of the chamber to the one they'd come in, "Out! Now!"

Dun was already pulling away from the edge of the rail and freed himself. Padg had more trouble, and Dun helped pull him free against the rising vortex of the heating wind. Padg, in turn, had to pull Tali free. Dun, having reached the rail at the wall of the room grabbed hold with one hand and shouted.

"Grab my hand! Padg!'"

Padg did and Dun pulled along the outside rail toward the last noise he'd heard from Myrch. Padg held tight to Tali's hand and heaved her along as Dun pulled him. Dun placed Padg's first hand on the rail.

"Grab the rail and pull Tali!"

Dun, once the three were secure on the rail started, edging along toward where they supposed the door and Myrch to be. Then as they thought the cacophony couldn't get any louder, a harsh honk broke out, swirling around them.

HONK HONK HONK

"Run!" Myrch shouted.

"We can't!" Dun shouted back against the wind.

"You'd better!" Myrch hollered back. "Door's closing!"

Dark

"Gods! Come on!" shouted Dun to the others and pulled hand over hand along the rail, feeling out at each grab in front to be careful of where the rail went and behind to make sure each time that at least Padg was behind him. Padg himself would have to check for Tali. The pulling got harder with each reach.

HONK HONK HONK

"Come on! Come on!"

Myrch's voice at least seemed louder now, although only just in the swirl and pound of the rising vortex. Dun pulled, but Padg had stopped.

"Tali's slipped! Help."

Then Myrch's voice came from the door, "Dun! Grab my hand, now!"

"No! The others!" Dun said.

"Forget th—" but Dun had gone again.

HONK HONK HONK

Dun reached back over Padg to grab Tali's one hand, he couldn't find the other. There was a lot of weight on the hand on the rail but she had a firm grip on it.

"Help.'"

HONK HONK HONK

Myrch's yelled again in a strained voice, "I can't hold this door for... ever"

Dun pulled with all his might on Tali's arm but there was too much weight in the wrong place.

"I'm..." Tali said.

"No, you don't," Dun said. "Hold on!" Then to Padg, he said, "Hold on tight to the hand on the rail, grab her wrist if you can!"

"Not letting go, don't worry!" Padg said.

HONK HONK HONK

"Come... on!" Myrch shouted.

Dun reached past Tali's hand on the rail, grabbed a firm grip, and leaned himself out into the wind. His hand touched Tali. He grabbed a clump of fur and held on for all his might.

"Where's your other hand?" he shouted. "Grab on!"

"Can't!" she said, panting. "Hurt."

HONK HONK HONK

"Kay," he said. "Padg! Go to Myrch! Stop the door."

"Can't," he said, "Tali!"

"Go!" Dun said.

Dun reached around Tali and pulled her close into the rail with all the strength he had.

"How's the arm?" he said in her ear.

"Okay, hand hurt."

"Okay." He hooked her arm over the rail. "Now hold on and I'll push."

HONK HONK HONK

"Dun!" Myrch shouted. "Oh, Padg."

Padg edged past Myrch jammed between the closing metal door and the wall, heaving. He reached over his shoulder and pulled free his last sword-spear and rammed it into the gap. His spear blade under the door, and his butt against the wall. He could hear Dun's voice now.

"Come on, nearly there."

HONK HONK HONK

"Padg!" Dun's voice was really close now. "Grab Tali's hand. Pull!"

He pulled and the sword-spear gave a sickening creak.

"Dun! Get in now! Myrch shouted.

HONK HONK HONK

"Come on!" Dun shouted.

There was the sound of splintering wood.

Then silence.

Dark

Chapter Forty-Three

"Sound off, chipmunks," Myrch said.

"Huh?" Padg said.

"Never mind," Myrch said. "Everyone okay? Dun?"

"Yeah. Tali?"

"Just," said Padg.

"What the hell was that place?" Dun said.

"A massive great vent?" Padg said.

"I don't think you're too far off there," Myrch said.

"Do you think that thing controls all the vents, everywhere?" Tali said.

"Maybe," Myrch said.

"How's your hand," Dun asked Tali.

"Hurts."

"You got anything you can treat it with?" Dun said.

"Yeah, but I can't do some of the grinding and mixing one-handed."

"Anything we can do to help?" Padg said.

"Sure, I need to help me tear up one of those sacks."

"And, Dun, I need some wound-wort. It's in the tiniest jar in the bottom of my bag. No, not that one, here."

"Look, whatever you're going to do, can you hurry it along? We haven't got forever here," Myrch said.

With Dun grinding a pestle and Padg tearing strips, some form of slave and bandage first-aid was administered.

"Thanks," Tali said.

"Go now?" Myrch said.

"Okay, patience," Tali said.

But they moved on.

The corridor out of the opposite side of the vent cylinder was similar in size and air-shape. It smelled less oily, slightly more, musty. Dun recognized the smell of compost before he started picking up traces of it under his feet. They passed over an intersection, where more compost seemed to be adding to their new carpet. Although it was a complete crossroads they passed, the compost only seemed to be in the left-hand passage and underfoot, more and more as they walked. The next crossroads they passed was doorways, not passages. Curious, Tali tried one of the doors. It pushed open easily. As well as a lot more compost, she could smell, mushrooms, or at least where mushrooms had been. And smells of sap bearing plants rotting. The air in the room felt dry. Inside she felt around and found racks of shelves in bays, each one carrying trays of compost, some with mushrooms, some with something dead and decaying. Dun tried the door opposite and, save for a different variety of mushroom, it was the same. They walked on and found room after room on each side. The ones they bothered to check were all the same, dead flora, except for a few mushrooms and air dry as a bone. They counted two, four, six, eight rooms a side.

"All too little too late!" a voice said ahead of them out of nowhere. "Who are you, and what do you want here?"

"We mean no harm!" Myrch said.

"Liar!" the voice screamed. "They have all spoken those words, or words like them, who came here. And now I am the only one left. Do. Not. Lie. To. Me."

And ear-splitting, high-pitched sonic slap crashed across them all, pinning them to the spot. Dun pressed his hands to his ears and clenched everything else. He felt like he was going to be sick. Then it stopped. The ringing of the aural attack reverberated from everything that wasn't fixed down for a few seconds. Then there was silence.

"I am not without my defenses, even now. I have others. Do not test me. Do not lie. I have a device that can tell me if you lie by the amount of stress in your voice. A true marvel of the age. Of the age that was..."

"I'm sorry, who are you?" Myrch said.

"I will ask the questions,' the voice said. "And you will answer."

"It would be easier to answer if we knew your name," Tali said. "Please?"

"You may call me the Sentinel. The last, for all it is worth. Now the truth, please."

Dun answered, "We've come from the Bridge-folk. To find you."

"Not the only reason though, I think."

"No. Once my father, he came this way, I think. He was an explorer; he made maps. I have one with me..."

The voice softened, and said, "Hmm... I think you are safe. Step forward into the steam."

A loud hissing indicated where they were to step. The steam tasted sharp and acidic but smelled sweet at the same time.

"At your feet is a cart. Please place any weapons in it."

"No way," Myrch said.

"Then you may not enter," the Sentinel said, simply.

"I'll wait out here," Myrch said.

"As you wish."

The others placed their weapons in the cart, knives and their last sword-spear. Tali hadn't mixed any more weaponized potions since the encounter with the rat-thing, so she figured she was safe. Once she'd placed her last knife in the odd smooth cart, it began to move ahead of them into the steam.

"Hey!" Tali said.

"Do not be alarmed, follow the cart," the Sentinel said.

They walked on into the steam. The cart trundled on ahead of them. The steam thinned out, and they followed the cart into what their air-sense said was a spherical room, with something in the center, a pillar or something lower.

"Your weapons will be kept safe and returned to you when you leave."

"What about Myrch?" Dun said.

"Your care about him is touching. He will meet you when you leave. But you are not here for him, for all he thinks."

"What do you mean?" Dun said.

"You have questions you would ask of me." It was a statement, not a question.

"Err.." Padg said, "I have one. What exactly are you... you know, sentinel-ing?"

The Sentinel chuckled, a deep-throated, warm sound.

"Come forward, young Bridge-folk. Bring all your questions. I will hopefully give them the answers they deserve. And you still haven't told me your names."

"Dun."

"Padg."

"Tali."

They walked forward, to the middle of the sphere, to what turned out to be a dias with a throne-like seat atop it.

"May I touch your faces?" the Sentinel said.

"Sure," Dun said. The others murmured assent. The fingers were gentle pads, with the paper thin skin of the old. Warm.

"You are all so young, to have to"—he paused mid-sentence—"never mind. You are the last to visit me from the river. I am Sentinel of the systems. It is a burden I have carried long. I hoped I would pass on my burden before now but my people became... Well, at the end, they came to me for answers but could not understand them. Had stopped listening to things they did not want to hear."

"What happened to them?" Dun said.

"All in good time," the Sentinel said. "First you must know the where, before you can know the why. And to do that, you must discover if you can understand at all."

"I'm not sure I understood all that," Padg said.

"Hmm, you might," the Sentinel said. "I hope. Are you ready?"

"Is there some kind of test?" Dun said.

"Of sorts."

"Oh another ritual, hooray," Padg said. "What happens if we fail?"

"Nothing."

"Nothing?"

"No. Nothing, you just go on your way, none the wiser."

"Oh," Padg said.

"Are you ready?"

"I guess so?" Dun said. "You guys feel ready?"

"Sure," Tali said.

"Why not?" Padg said.

"What do we do?" Dun asked.

There was a hissing noise from in front of the dais, and they detected the slight suck of air into some kind of space below them.

"Here," the Sentinel said and handed Dun a knotted rope. "The rope is tethered up here. Descend into the room below. It is like this in shape, although it has but one way in and one way out. Explore what you find within, and then tug on the rope three times when you wish to come back here."

Dun lowered the rope carefully into the hole. "Coming?" he said.

Dark

Chapter Forty-Four

Dun carefully lowered himself down. The sphere below seemed to be offset from the one above, as far as Dun could tell, so he was lowering himself down some distance from the middle of the chamber. Which was a good thing on balance, as the center of the chamber contained a massive something, another smaller sphere? Textured in some way.

"Hurry on down here you two; this is weird," Dun said as his feet touched down.

"What is?" Tali said, having slid down the rope beside him.

"This thing. In the middle of the chamber."

"Let's go and examine," Tali said.

"No, don't wait for me then," Padg said from above them.

"We won't," Tali said.

They edged forward. The structure occupied most of the middle of the sphere. Dun and Tali both reached forward inquisitively to touch its surface. It was some kind of metal, but not cold. Pocked and rough on the outside but not in any regular fashion; huge pocks here, tiny ones there. No seeming logic to it at all.

"You guys okay?" Padg said.

"Come on over," Tali said. "It seems safe."

"Hey, over here," Dun said. He had crept a quarter of the way around the giant object, feeling and testing all the way. "Feel this. The texture just stops here. It's completely smooth."

"Gods, so it is," Tali said. "Its like there's a line that runs from the floor to, well, however far it goes up and beyond that it's smooth. Wait. I've got an idea."

She scuttled around the chamber following the smooth part of the surface.

"Yes!" She scuttled back. "Dun, give me your hand."

He did and she led him around guiding his hand over the surface as she had done before. At exactly halfway around the shape, the rough random texture began again.

"Do you get it? Do you remember anything like that before?" Tali said, excited.

"Err, no? I've never been here before in my life," he said, bemused.

"I didn't ask you if you'd been here. I asked you if you remember anything *like* this? Like this sphere? Like this sphere but smaller?"

And then slowly, understanding.

"The egg!"

It all fell into place, the old song and that strange trinket they'd picked up. They were all one and the same. They were, whatever this thing represented.

"Hey you guys, it moves!" Padg said from the pocked side of the sphere.

"Careful!" Tali said.

"It only moves slow and it seems it only goes one way," he said.

By placing his palms flat on the rough surface there was enough purchase for him to move the sphere. It rotated slowly about its axis. With their hands on the smooth surface on the opposite side, Tali and Dun had a different reaction.

"It's not moving over here," Dun said.

"Isn't it?" Padg said. "It is here. Shall I stop?"

"No, keep going," Tali said. "But slowly."

"Okay."

He exercised more caution and carried on. There was something comforting about the feel of the surface under his fingers. For something so artificial, it felt strange, organic somehow. Lost in reverie he almost didn't stop when the others shouted.

"Ow!"

"Sorry," Padg said. "What's wrong?"

"Your half of the sphere is the only part that's moving," Dun said.

"Eh?"

"The rough bit of the sphere is like a shell; it moves over the surface of the smooth bit," Dun said.

"And it bashed my sprained hand!" Tali said.

"Oops," Padg said, "sorry."

"How far around does it go, do you think?" Dun said.

"Don't know; let's try," Padg said. "Everyone's hands clear?"

"Yes."

"Okay, let's go."

He carried on for another quarter turn then the shell came to a halt with a clunk.

"Oh," Padg said. "That was less exciting than I'd hoped."

"Then wait til you come round here," Tali said.

"Why?" Padg said.

"It's got an inside."

"What?" Dun and Padg said in unison.

"Come over here and feel," Tali said. "The bumpy shell thing was like a cover for an inside."

Dun and Padg crept around the other side of the sphere and joined Tali. She led their hands.

"Here?"

"Good gods," Dun said. "It's so complicated."

Tiny shelves and rills. Holes and boxes. Tiny tubes and spaces. Tali leaned forward; there was a click beneath her feet. There was a hum and then faint noises echoed up from the interior and tiny breezes began to blow from it. Dun wasn't sure, but he could swear that the tiny breezes smelled differently too.

"It's like it's alive," Padg said in awe.

"It is alive," Tali said.

"Eh?" Padg said.

"It is alive. It's us."

"No, still not following," Padg said.

"Oh, don't be *dim,* Padg," Tail said, exasperated. "...sometimes! Dun, you explain it to him."

Dun was still distracted by feeling the massive creation. "Sorry, what did you say?"

"Please explain to your dense friend what this is."

"Oh, yes. Sorry. Well, you know that egg thing we found? And I said it wasn't just an ornament, but it was meant to represent something? Well, I think this is what it was meant to represent. It's almost like the little egg was a message or a reminder to people about this. Maybe they worshipped it or something, I don't know. There's more to it somehow too. The inside here, feel it? It feels like pipes and rooms and corridors. It's got tiny vents blowing. I think it's a kind of map."

"Not very convenient on long journeys," Padg said.

"No, but I think that's what it is," Dun said.

"Gods," Tali said, still lost in exploring the depths of the thing. "It is, it really is."

"That's what we just said," Dun said.

"No, feel *here*." She guided Dun's hand again. "This here. It's the wind tube we've just escaped from. It goes, way along here, and up here, completely straight. And right near it two tiny rooms, one sphere here and one right below it. Amazing."

"It is amazing," Dun said. "Let's try and feel our way back."

And they did. Losing all track of time, they felt the artifact in great detail, finding the land of the Bridge-folk, the Stone-folk, the Lake-siders, the Badlands. The entire route they'd taken. Tiny artifacts of who knows what, tiny pipes, and tubes. Minute fans blowing thin puffs of air. Places that felt like crops, mushrooms, and reeds. Huge strange spans of places they'd never imagined. Then the entirety of the whole thing started to hit them.

"Where we live. It's so small," Dun said.

"But it's not small, is it? We live there," Padg said. "The village is big, the settlement is big, the river is *huge*. Where the Stone-folk live is *massive*."

"But all of it is dwarfed by..."

"Everywhere else?" Padg said.

"There are lands beneath us and lands above us," Tali said.

"And lands above that," Padg said.

"Amazing," Dun said. "I need to add to my map, check details."

"No time for that now," a voice from above said. "There are more things I need to tell you. I will send the rope back down, come up. We need to talk."

"But the map, the... artifact."

"It's called a globe," the Sentinel said.

"The globe then..." Dun said.

"Will have to wait. There isn't time. They may be back sooner than we hope."

"They?" Padg said.

"Come up," the Sentinel said, "and I'll explain everything I can. Please close the globe before you climb up."

The rope knots clanged off the globe as it was tossed down to them. Padg placed his hands on the rough side of the globe once more and slid the cover. There was a click as it went back into place. One by one, they grabbed the rope and climbed. Dun first and Padg last. Back in what Dun could only think of as a throne room; they gathered at the Sentinel's feet. There was a click from the direction of his chair and some kind of noise from behind them indicated the hatch to the globe room had closed.

"It is good you understand the globe," the Sentinel said.

"How could we not?" Tali said.

The Sentinel laughed dryly. "It is surprising the number of folk who ignore the very things they can feel under their hands."

"Where are the rest of the Machine-folk?" Dun said.

"Killed, some rounded up, maybe killed later."

"When?" Padg said.

"Over many cycles. They have slowly plundered the treasures and the knowledge of the Machine-folk."

"Who are *they*?" Tali asked.

"We call them the Over-folk, although who knows what they call themselves."

"It sounds as though you don't know very much about them," Padg said.

"That is true," the Sentinel said sadly. "They come in swift and silent; take what they want and leave."

"Haven't you got guards? Hunters?"

"Yes..." The Sentinel lapsed into a silence that hung deep.

They waited and waited, not sure what to say. Tali spoke first, gently, "What happened?"

He spoke slowly, "It was terrible. We had... officers, they... they used to keep the peace and sort out any minor scuffles. Deal with customs and sort out trader disputes. Not a trained fighting force, or hunters as you would describe them, but good folk, could defend themselves, had access to many strange found objects, some weapons, others usable as weapons. They had fought before, disputes with gangs of river pirates and so on, but this was different. I was called when the first casualties came back, terrible wounds... torn apart. All of them killed, but one of them spoke before he died. Said they were like supernatural beings; knew exactly what everyone was about to do, shot with their terrible weapons, always first and never missed. No one ever even got close enough to smell the enemy. A massacre."

"That's terrible," Tali said.

"Yes," the Sentinel said, "it was. The traders and tinkers took up what weapons we had left and took to trying to defend the rest of us, the women, the children. They hid me away, I did not want to go. I am not glad I did."

"You can't blame yourself," Tali said, hearing the tears in his voice.

"I don't!" he said. "I just wish I could have done, thought of... something."

"How did you hide from them?" Dun said.

"We had one piece of technology that I guess they had never expected; still don't I suppose."

"What is it?" Padg said.

"It is a secret and my only protection. I intend to keep it that way," the Sentinel said.

"I can understand that," Tali said.

After a while of thought, Dun spoke again, "You said we were the first Bridge-folk here for a while. You have met others?"

"One," he said. "Older. Now I think, he sounded a little like you..."

"Father."

"Perhaps. He was an interesting sort. Came here more than once. Always drawing, wanted to map the whole of the Dark."

"A map like this?" Dun said, proffering his scroll where the Sentinel could feel it.

"Just like that, yes. So you are his son."

"Yes, when was he here last?"

"Many, many cycles ago. He was determined to find out if there was more above, pestered me for a long time to be allowed to touch the globe. Once he had, he would not rest until he had found what else there was to be found."

"What became of him?"

"He went on down the pipe, in the direction the Over-folk came from, but he never returned."

"I must find him."

"Why?" the Sentinel said.

"I need to know."

"Do you?"

"Yes, I think."

"Be sure. He said that."

"It would be extremely dangerous too," Padg said.

"Suicidal," the Sentinel said.

Dark

"The folk here can be so beautiful, even though I've never seen them."

Excerpts from <Distress Beacon SN-1853001>.
Found by E.S.V. Vixen Terradate: 26102225.

Dark

Chapter Forty-Five

The Sentinel bustled them out of the chamber with vague portents of approaching doom. Myrch was waiting for them when they came back and had found a quiet office near the river pipe for them to eat and rest in, while they decided what was to be done next.

"So?" Myrch said.

"Well, we've found what became of the Machine-folk now, and the map is more detailed than its ever been. Let's go home," Padg said.

"We still haven't found Dun's father," Tali said.

"Haven't we found out what happened to him though?" Padg said.

"We can't know that," Dun said.

"We know where he went, toward the Over-folk or whatever they're called; he never came back," Padg said.

"Can't we go on a little more? It just feels like there's so much unfinished," Dun said. "If we were the first Bridge-folk to find a new folk and return to tell the tale, they'll be singing songs about us."

"That doesn't really matter to you though, does it?" Padg said.

Dun sighed. "What about the fish? We've don't even have an idea what's happened to them, or the river for that matter."

"I know," Padg said. "I know, I just can't help feeling we're pushing our luck."

"It can't hurt to approach carefully, investigate briefly, and then return home," Myrch said.

"I'm game," Tali said. "Who knows what new reagents I might come home with."

"Padg?" Dun said.

Now it was Padg's turn to sigh. "All right. But I reserve the right to say 'told you so'. What's the plan?"

"Well," Myrch said, "from what you've added to the map we are six or so bends in the pipe from where there seems to be more of 'above.'"

"That was all from memory though," Dun said. "He wouldn't let us back into the globe room once we'd come out."

"It gives us a rough idea though," Myrch said. "Even with a completely accurate map, we'd still be guessing once we got there."

"The whole thing still gives me the creeps," Padg said.

"Well, what about I scout ahead?" Myrch said. "And then find another bolt-hole we can hide in? We can reconnoiter from there."

"You seem a little sure you're going to find one," Padg said.

"There are plenty of side passages and inspection hatches all over here; there's bound to be something," Myrch said.

Before they'd even come to a consensus, Myrch left. The others sat still. Tali silently broke out rations and handed them round, issuing flasks of the water from the Machine-people fountain. It made small comfort.

"Wait," Dun said suddenly. "I've got an idea."

"The whole ideas thing," Padg said, "is becoming old." But Dun had gone too, leaving a whisp of scent.

"Oh great, and then there were two," Padg said.

"Let him go," Tali said. "He at least knows where he's going. Do you?"

For once Padg was speechless.

"Well? You came on this crazy outing because..."

"Because... Well, because..."

"Shall I tell you?" Tali said. "Because you love him, you idiot."

"I still don't want him to go on this crazy suicide mission after the ghost of his father," Padg said, hurt.

"I know, but you'll follow him all the same."

"We both will, won't we?"

"Yeah, but not for the same reasons," she said.

"What's that supposed to mean?"

"Never mind and pass me that water back, idiot."

They waited huddled into a corner, cold and tired, unsure who would return first. Then distant clanking from behind them startled them into action.

"Someone coming," Tali hissed.

"'Kay," Padg said, drawing his knife and pressing himself farther against the bulkhead.

The clanking stopped, and so did any echo or air-sense of what was there. The silence billowed out.

"What the..?" Padg said under his breath.

"I was sure..." Tali said.

"I heard it too," Padg said.

"Shh!"

There was the merest scraping noise and a tiny waft of air. Then again, closer still. And again closer, Padg and Tali tensed, ready.

"Boo!" Dun said.

"How the..." Padg said. "You complete motherless wretch, Dun! You scared the life out of me!"

"Also," Tali said, "how in the hells did you do that?"

"Neat, huh?" Dun said.

"What the hells is it?" Padg said.

'That crazy 'hiding machine' that the Sentinel had," Dun said.

"What? He's given it to you?" Padg said.

"No," Dun said. "Lent it to us more like."

"What does it do?" Tali said.

"Masks your scent, your air-sense, noises, from anyone."

"That's astonishing," Tali said.

"Yep." The grin in Dun's voice was evident.

"How does it work?" Padg said.

"Well, there's this big, floppy, shield thing, and then a cable going to this box thing that he said was some kind of power pack. There's a switch you flick on it and... swoosh, you're gone."

"Neat!" Padg said. "So, err, what are we going to do with it?"

Dark

"Hide, of course. If Myrch has scouted somewhere to go a little farther on, then we go there, use it as a door. Then wait for any activity. If there is none, we move a bit farther on. And so on."

"You know, that actually sounds like a good plan," Tali said.

Dun huffed. His sulk was a short one though as Myrch returned.

"It's a bit farther on than I'd have hoped but three bends farther on there's a pipe that joins the main corridor from the side. There's some kind of hatch at the end of it, but I think we can jam it from our side; it's got plenty of handles on it," Myrch said.

"That sounds perfect," Dun said. "And wait till we tell you about our new toy."

They sploshed back into the pipe, the water ankle deep, although no one knew what kind of noise, if any, they made, as Dun went in front with Myrch and the hiding-machine. The cross-pipe wasn't as far on as Dun feared from Myrch's description and as they settled into it; it was pleasingly just above the level of water in the main pipe. Dun set up the hiding-machine and flicked the switch. From their side of the shield, there was a faint hum.

"What now?" Padg said.

"We wait," Myrch said.

Chapter Forty-Six

Dun woke to Padg's toe in his ribs.

"There's some of them out there now," Padg said.

"What are they up to?" Dun said.

"Just walking past, I think," Padg said. "But by the amount of noise they're making, they're not expecting anyone to be here."

"Or they don't care," Tali said.

"It feels weird that we can hear them, but they can't hear us," Padg said.

"Yeah, but I'm not going out to check," Dun said. "There are about three of them?"

Padg paused. "Yeah. Three. Heavy footed like they've got a weight on."

"What do we do now?" Tali asked.

"We wait til they come back past," Myrch said. "Listen and wait."

"Right," Padg said. "Chuck me another of those mushroom-bread things, Tali; I'm starving."

"Always starving," Tali muttered under her breath as she threw one over.

"Thank you," Padg said cheerily.

"Dun?" she asked. "While I'm here?"

"Not hungry, thanks."

"Fair enough," she said, getting one herself.

They settled into thoughtful munching. Dun huddled by himself at the entrance to the passage.

"Okay?" Tali said.

"Yeah," Dun said.

"You seem tense."

"Yeah," he said and sighed.

"What?"

"It just feels like something is coming to an end."

"Is that a feeling?" she asked. "Or..?"

"No." He half-laughed. "Just a feeling."

"The journey's coming to an end?"

Dark

"No, it's more than that. Means more than that. Something... I don't know. It feels like nothing is going to be the same again."

" 'You never step in the same river twice'," Tali said, quoting an old folk proverb.

"No. No, I don't suppose you do."

Tali let him drift back into whatever reverie he needed to be in and went to sit back down by Padg. She leaned her head against him and drifted to sleep. After what seemed like an age, Dun needed to stand, as best he could in the low passage, and stretch his legs. He walked to and fro for a while, failed to settle, and then gently sat down on the tunnel floor next to Padg and Tali and lay his head down. *At least if he couldn't sleep*, he thought, *he could not sleep in comfort*. Eventually, his eyes closed.

He didn't know how long he'd slept for but shuffling about woke him. Myrch was up to something at the front of the tunnel.

"Damn," Myrch said, just at the edge of Dun's hearing.

"What's up?" Dun said quietly, so as not to wake the others.

Myrch hissed a breath in. "They're back."

"So?" Dun said. "They can't know we're here."

"No. It doesn't matter."

Dun heard the din of the returning feet splashing in the tunnel. This time accompanied by metallic scraping and bickering voices.

"I think our friends have been looting," Myrch said.

"From the Machine-folk?" Dun said.

"No one to stop them now."

"But there must be some automatic systems left?"

"Oh, there are, but the ... Over-folk, are ... persistent."

"What do you know about them?" Dun said, more accusatory than he intended.

Dun thought he wouldn't answer.

"Fractious. Numerous. Superior. Arrogant. Dangerous. But we must go there."

"Must?" Dun said.

"We've come this far."

"Uh?" Dun said.

"You want to know what happened to your father?"

"Err, yeah," Dun said.

"Well, the answer's wherever they've gone. Are you coming? Bring that thing with us."

And quietly, they slipped out of the pipe, leaving Padg and Tali sleeping.

***

They tailed the Over-Folk through the pipe, not a hard thing to do with the noise their quarry made dragging whatever it was they had pillaged through the pipe. Dun and Myrch moved carefully. Dun in front with the shield and Myrch lagging behind and off to one side. Their quarry sploshed and cursed through the water, but then they stopped. Dun and Padg stopped accordingly and waited. After more scuffling and banter between the Over-folk, they briefly quietened down and one voice who seemed to be in charge took control. There was a faint beep noise and then a hiss and metallic creaking. Dun could feel a doorway opening into somewhere else and felt a drift of sweet-smelling air carrying a hum of bustling noise. Then another metallic creak and the noise went, leaving the waft of smell swirling in the wake of the closed door.

"Ready?" Myrch said.

"Guess so," Dun said.

"Let's go check it out then," Myrch said.

Dun pulled the hiding machine and it's weighty power pack along.

"Quick," Myrch hissed. "Lean it up against the wall just here and turn it on. We might need to get under it in a hurry."

Dun did as he was told, although where he was told to put the hiding-machine was way too close to where the door the Over-folk had gone through for comfort. He ducked his head behind the shield, flicked the switch, and the reassuring hum sprang to life. Myrch had begun patting down the wall.

"Door hinges here, edges here. Blast door, too thick to force. Water, where the hell is that coming from? Oh... Now that makes sense," Myrch rambled.

"What?" Dun said.

"There's a culvert at the bottom of this door letting the water out. I think that's where your stream is coming from."

Dun stood from one foot to the other splishing gently in the ankle deep water. "Doesn't seem like very much of it."

"No," Myrch said. Then something came to him. "Aha! Security pad. Let's have a feel for what we're getting ourselves into here. Hmm... No keys—worse luck. Ah, but there is a ... What's this? Ah, okay—a pad. Does it press?"

There was a low bree-ooop noise.

"And that will be our cue to exit. Get behind that shield," Myrch said.

They huddled down behind with a surprising amount of room. There seemed to be an indent in the wall behind them that meant enough room for the two of them without being in close proximity.

"What happened there then?" Dun said.

"I think it's a thumb pad security scanner," Myrch said.

"Okay?"

"It means you put your thumb on the pad and if you're recognized as friendly then the door opens."

"Seems it works then," Dun said.

"Yes," Myrch said, "all too well."

There was a hiss and the grind of the door opening again.

"Knock, knock!" Myrch said.

Dark

Low-level grumbling in the odd Over-folk tongue. Two folk. Dun was starting to think what they spoke wasn't so far from what he understood, but was so heavily accented it made it tricky to follow. He thought he could pick out a few words and the tone gave him more clues. There was definitely a superior again and some kind of underling being harangued into something. Then the door hissed closed again. There was tentative sploshing of what Dun presumed was the misbegotten underling.

"Ooh, I've got an idea," Myrch said slyly.

Dun was too tired to worry about ideas anymore.

"Come to Myrch... a little... closer." And he sprang faster than Dun guessed he could. "Gotcha!"

"Mmmmmpphhhh!" The Overfolk guard struggled but Myrch was clearly much stronger.

"Now, we can do this with you conscious or not, your call."

The noises of struggling stopped.

"Yeah, thought you might feel that way about it," he said in mock friendly tones. "Now, how do you feel about us using you as a door wedge?"

More struggling. "Mmmp!"

"No. Wrong answer. Feel this?" The struggling stopped again. "Yeah, I can tell we're going to get on just fine."

Myrch half walked, half dragged the struggling guard to the door.

"Coming?" he said back over his shoulder to Dun.

Dun heard the beep of the door pad verifying.

"Ding, dong!" Myrch said cheerfully.

The door hissed, and they were met with the chattering of their guard's superior.

"Hi!" Myrch said brightly. "We'd like to interest you in some of... this."

Four short phut sounds barked out and both guards dropped to the ground.

"No?" Myrch said, stepping over the bodies. "Ah well, some other time then."

Dark

Dun stepped through the door and edged past one of the guards, still clinging onto some kind of door lever.

"Hmm," Myrch said, "not the reception I was expecting."

"Sorry?" Dun said.

"Nothing," Myrch said.

The chamber was long, cuboid, and had a channel running through the floor where all the water ran under the door through the culvert. Behind the fallen guards was a small door into a not much bigger room. *A small guard post*, Dun thought. Myrch pushed the guard at the handle off with his foot, squeezed past Dun in the doorway, and began banging about the room. The door slowly creaked, and then hissed shut.

"Ah, I wonder," Myrch said, running his hands over some panels he'd found.

Then an ear-splitting womp, womp, womp noise burst from above Dun's head and battered off the walls in echo.

"Oops," Myrch said.

Dun was about to reply when the sound of approaching feet splashing in the water stopped him short. There was a hasty order barked out, and then twangs and thuds all around as some kind of projectile fire rained in. Dun crouched low in the guard post.

"Hells!" Myrch barked. "Not the reception at all..."

"You were expecting *tea*?" Dun shouted over the sirens and the shooting.

There was a click and returning phutt noises as Myrch returned fire from low round the doorway.

Phutt-phutt-phutt

Ting - twing - twang

"We need to get out of here," Myrch said, voice tight.

"Yeah, no argument here," Dun said.

"Right, give me your hand." Where they touched, something about Myrch's skin felt oddly smooth. "This is a needler. That is the pointy end; it goes toward the bad guys. Finger? Good, that goes in here, careful. Squeeze and go. Okay?"

"I guess?" Dun said, feeling the strange weight of the small metal weapon.

"Good, I need to get to that door handle, cover me."

So Dun ducked his head out of the doorway and aimed toward the noise of firing. Shots ricocheted off the door all around him. He pulled the trigger and heard the familiar phutt noise: once, twice, three times. The incoming fire briefly stopped. Then began again in a hail of needles. Dun felt fire in the top of his arm. He heard Myrch curse and then a creak and the hiss of the door opening. There was a beautifully familiar smell on the other side of it.

"Tali! Padg!" Dun shouted.

"Out of the way!" Myrch shouted, barging through the gap.

"Dun!" Padg yelled from the doorway.

"Leave him," Myrch shouted.

"Hells, will I," Padg shouted.

"On it," Tali yelled. With a quick rustle, she produced a flask and threw it with the familiar tinkle. Then the massive compression blast.

"Dun!" she yelled into the fracas.

"Here!" Dun coughed. Tali reacted quickly to the brief lull in the firing to grab for Dun and pull him out of the doorway. Blood slicked her hands.

"You're hurt," she said.

"Not now," Dun said. "Help me grab the hiding-machine. Feel, here. No, give it to me. Have you got any more compression flasks, Tali?"

"One left," she said.

"Grab it and wait til we hear them following us. Padg?" Dun said.

"Here."

"Is Myrch okay?"

"Hurt pretty bad, I think."

"Okay, lets head back to that side tunnel; there's a bit more room there. Can you help Myrch walk that far, Padg?"

"Yeah, I think so."

"Okay, let's go," Dun said.

They had not rounded the corner far when they heard running feet and a loud battle cry, followed by incoming needle fire.

"Tali!" Dun yelled.

"Away!" Tali yelled, followed by the tinkle-whooomph Dun had been hoping for.

"Run!" Dun shouted.

Hobble was more like it, but hobble they did while the sounds of their pursuers collecting themselves from Tali's blast were still evident. They rounded the last corner, and while Tali and Padg dragged the prone form of Myrch into the tunnel, Dun set up the hiding-machine in the mouth and turned it on. The hum began. He shouldered himself against the wall wincing as he bashed his injured shoulder, but he needed to cock his ear around the screen to hear for sounds of pursuit. Two sets of feet splashed toward them, paused, waited, and then splashed off again where they had come from.

"Dun!" Tali said.

"How's Myrch?" he said.

"Dun, he's... We pulled him... up," she gabbled.

"Is he okay?" Dun said.

"No, I don't think so, but that's not it... his fur... He doesn't have any fur..."

"What?" Dun said. "I don't understand."

"What Tali's trying to say," Padg said, "is he's not folk."

Chapter Forty-Seven

"He's what?" Dun said.

"He's not folk," Padg said.

"I *knew* there was something," Tali said. "No smell; he didn't want us to touch him."

"No fur," Padg said. "Funny hands."

"What is he then?" Dun said.

"He's ... awake." Dun's pained voice was heard through his gritted teeth.

"Oh, sorry," Dun said reflexively.

"Now that... is funn...y," Myrch said, panting.

"What is? Dun said.

"You... app... pol... gising... to... me." He snorted, nearly a laugh, then coughed impressively.

Dun could smell metal on Myrch's breath: blood?

"I don't understand," Dun said.

"I... sold you out."

"What?"

"... to... the Over-folk..."

"You motherless river turd!" Padg said.

"Why?" Tali said.

"There's not time... to explain. If it matters... I'm sorry I had ... to do it..." More coughing.

"Let's just leave the scumbag here," Padg said, incensed.

"No," Tali said, "he can't move."

"I'm not going... any... where."

"Why should we listen to you now?" Padg said.

"He's right," Dun said.

"Because... there are... things... you... need... to... know..."

"Wait, we've moved on from the *you setting us up* already? What in the hells was going on there? What was supposed to happen?"

"The Over-folk... a faction of them. They have my wife... my mate."

"And we should care?" Padg said.

"They are going to kill her."

"Why?" Tali said.

"I don't really know why. There... is... there are factions... a war..."

"But what have I...?" Dun said.

"I sold you... to them..."

"In exchange," Tali said.

"For her," Myrch said.

His breath was coming in wheezes now. Tali let out a slight groan. "No," she said.

"Too late... for that now..." Myrch said.

"Why me?" Dun said.

"Don't... know," Myrch said.

"Where's your mate?" Tali said.

"Don't... know... that," Myrch said, strained.

"I mean the exchange?" she said.

"They... weren't... They broke... She wasn't... It was wrong, it was wrong."

"They didn't come?" Tali said.

"They bloody did," Padg said.

"No," Myrch said. "Not them... wrong."

"Faction?" Dun said.

"Yessss..."

"*Gods*,' Dun said.

There was silence, save for the sound of whistly breathing.

"Dun," Myrch said, quietly.

Dun moved closer to Myrch's alien mouth. Felt the smell of who knew what life-giving fluids leaching away from him.

"I'm here," Dun said.

"I owe you," Myrch said.

"No, you..."

"Shh..." More coughing. "There's not long. They are coming... the Over-folk... the war, their war... it's coming."

"What can we do?" Padg said.

"Nothing!" Myrch said. Then more gently, he continued, "Run... hide?"

"What about fighting?" Padg said.

"You can't... fight them," Myrch said.

"We fought the Stone-folk, the River-folk..."

"Not the same," Myrch said. "They're different. Have ..."

"What?" Dun said.

Myrch exhaled. "Sss... aaa... hh"

"Can you do anything?" Dun said.

"Nothing to do," Tali said, slowly. "He's gone."

***

They carried Myrch's body between them, taking turns, two carrying, two resting. It took them the rest of the cycle to struggle back to the entrance to the Machine-folk that they'd used before. They rested in the first anteroom they could find.

"What do we do with him?" Tali said.

"Leave him outside?" Padg said.

"We can't," Dun said.

"Can't we?" Padg said. "He'd have left us."

"I don't think he would," Dun said, "in the end."

Padg huffed.

"Give me a hand, Tali," Dun said.

Gently, carefully, they brought his body in and laid it down along one wall. Dun crossed the lifeless hands over the silent chest.

"We'll bury him tomorrow," Dun said.

***

Dun woke to the sound of someone scuffling about. He heard Tali over by where Myrch's body lay against the wall. He rose and went over, he laid a hand on her shoulder. She was knelt down with a hand out touching the skin of their late guide.

"He was a bit wrinkly," Tali said. "Around the eyes and mouth. Feel?"

"Yeah," Dun said softly. "Old?"

"Maybe. I wonder what he really was?"

"I think he told us the truth, in the end, a spy and a guide, I guess."

"No, not that. I mean, what kind of creature was he?"

Dark

"Oh, I don't know."

"What do you suppose his mate was like? Did he have cubs somewhere?"

Padg stirred on the far side of the room. Dun made a noncommittal hum noise to Tali.

"Come on, Padg; you're last awake."

He dispatched Padg to search for food while he and Tali broke camp. They had fashioned a kind of bier, out of some found plastic pipes and sheeting to make it easier to carry Myrch. They had little time to appreciate their handiwork as the door crashed open.

"Dun, something's wrong," Padg said, panting. "Wronger,"

"What?"

"The marketplace; it's been wrecked. There was some food still there, but there's not a stall still standing, and there's piles of stuff everywhere. I nearly broke my neck tripping over on the way back."

"Oh gods," Tali said. "The Over-folk?"

"I think so," Padg said. "And..."

"What about the Sentinel?" Dun said.

"I don't know," Padg said.

"We need to find out," Dun said.

They picked their way carefully between the piled debris; it was like a whirlwind had swept up and back through the market hall. Staleness, salt and congealing food. Garbled half chitters and squeaks from the automated voices that remained. Snatches of music repeated endlessly in a brain-damaged symphony.

"Bu... bu... bububub..."

"Shally, shally b..."

"Ratty... ratty... ratatata..."

"Bibbidi-bibbidi-bibbidt..."

"Bu... bbbbbbbb... bbb..."

"Let's go!" Dun shouted over the chaotic noise. "This way!"

They hurried down corridors once familiar, now strange again. Smells of sweat and fear, salt and blood. Blood and tears. They reached the strange room of controllers but didn't stop. Sounds of fizzing came out to meet them as they walked past. They entered into the strange throne room of the Sentinel. Dun knew in his heart what he'd find. All was still in the chamber, but Dun could sense the large shape of the Sentinel in the chair. But no sound. And the smell of blood, one cycle, maybe two old.

"No," Dun said and hurried up the steps to the Sentinel. Tali and Padg flanked him. He reached out a hand and felt the lifeless fur, pitted with scores of fine metal needles, and the cold skin underneath, torn in places. Tali touched him on the other side.

"Be careful," she said. "The needles. They might be poisoned."

"Why?" Padg said. "What had he done?"

"I don't know," Dun said. "But we should find a way to lay them both to rest. Here somewhere."

They decided to make the globe room the final resting place of both Myrch and the Sentinel. They slowly roped down the bodies and laid one gently on each side of the great sphere. They searched the market for things to cover them with and when they had finished, there were two long cairns, built of bags and boxes, poles and wires, and batteries and springs.

Tali sprinkled some sweet-smelling oil over each of the piles.

Dun said a prayer. "To the egg again, we go once more. Inside the shell to wait until the next hatching; into a time of peace."

They climbed slowly back up the ropes and trundled back to the small anteroom by the river pipe. They huddled around what supplies they could find and the opening of a warm vent.

"You know, I've got to go back?" Dun said.

'What?' Padg said.

"Back through that door to the Over-folk. I promised Myrch."

"Seriously? Why? You don't owe him anything!"

Dark

"Hmm, maybe not, but that's not the only reason. We've still not found out what's going on in there, and why the stream's drying up. My father is still in there somewhere and these dreams have been leading me there. I've got to go."

"Then we're coming with you," Padg said.

"Not this time," Dun said. "You need to go back to the Bridge and tell everyone what Myrch told us."

"But he said there's nothing we can do about it," Padg said.

"Yes, but that's no reason not to give them a chance to prepare," Tali said. "Dun's right."

Dun spent two more cycles with them, helping them fashion a cart out of what bits they could find.

"That should sort you out for going home," Dun said. "Take the hiding-machine with you. You're going to need it when you get back, I think. Take Myrch's weapon too; there's still some metal box things in his pack. I think that's what he loaded it with. You'll have to work it out."

"So this is goodbye then," Tali said.

"Yes," Dun said.

"Smell ya," Padg said.

"Soon," Tali said, although none of them believed it.

"Be careful," Padg said.

"Always," Dun said, "you too."

They embraced each other, and then Dun left the pipe. Padg strained to listen until his splishing footsteps had long gone around the corner and out of even keen folk hearing.

"Well?" Tali said.

"What?"

"Shall we get going?"

"Home?"

"I wasn't thinking of home just yet," she said. "We've got some unfinished business to attend to."

"Oh?" Padg said.

"Amber, we're going to get Amber."

"It amazes me how quickly conflict builds up in a given population. I've seen it so many times but it always shakes me. Perhaps it's part of the human condition. Maybe even if you're not human."

Excerpts from <Distress Beacon SN-1853001>. Found by E.S.V. Vixen Terradate: 26102225.

Dark

Chapter Forty-Eight

Dun reached the door of the Over-Folk. He stopped to scratch his leg where the water had been splashing on it. Then he adjusted the straps on his backpack. It was a lot lighter now. Just food, some water, and his knife. The map, clicker beetles, and all their other traveling kit had been left with Padg and Tali. He reached in for his drinking flask and took a long pull on it. He shifted his weight from one foot to the other, sighed, and started to search for the security pad that Myrch had used to get in. Finally finding it, all he could do when he applied his thumb was illicit the low boop noise that seemed to mean "wrong thumb: no entry". He pressed it a few more times and waited.

Dun had prepared himself for a good many eventualities in order to make this trip. *Nobody home* wasn't one of them. He could feel tension turning into a cramp in his calves. He pressed the button a few more times for good measure. There was a hiss and a familiar metallic creaking. The odd smell of the Over-folk wafted out. Along with the noise of a guard with some kind of breathing condition.

"Hi..." Dun said.

"*Wha?*" the guard yelled, a rebuke and not a question.

"Er... I'm..."

"*Rah! Brah raddah.*" The guard leaned out and poked Dun in the chest with his finger. "*Buh!*"

And the door creaked closed again, leaving a dumbfounded Dun on the threshold. This was not how he was expecting this to go. His shoulders slumped. He returned to his flask, took another swing from it, wiped the drips from his mouth with the back of his hand, and resumed beeping the pad. One of his baby siblings knew this game all too well. Back in their nest, it consisted of her poking Dun in the ribs til she got her own way. Dun considered himself quite patient, but she seemed to have a boundless ability to outwait him, long outlasting his ability to ignore her. Who knew one day he would be channeling his baby sister Ban to get any further. She would be pleased and probably giggle about it.

Dun sighed and buzzed again.

More hissing and creaking, and the, the wheezy guard said, ay his breaking point, "*Whaaaaaa?*"

Dun pushed past. "I'm Dun. You wanted me; I'm here!"

It was the guard's turn to be dumbfounded.

"Well?" Dun said. "Take me to your leader... or whatever."

Instead, the guard rounded on Dun and struck him on the side of the head with something long and heavy. Dun's head woozed. He tried to hold himself up, but his knees went out from under him, and he fell face down into the thin water at his feet.

***

He woke to an unpleasant ripping sound and a more unpleasant sensation of something sticky binding his hands behind his back. As his dizziness started to clear, he realized there was more of the stuff around his waist and someone was trying to get him to his feet. The side of his head throbbed like all hells and inside his head felt sharp and spiky. He could taste blood in his mouth.

"Up!" the guard said, doing the sticking.

It was someone other than the wheezy door guard, and this one at least spoke in a way Dun could understand. Come to think of it, now Dun's ears had stopped ringing, he realized that he couldn't hear the wheezy guard at all. He was still at the guard post behind the door though. Perhaps there'd been a shift change. Dun didn't fancy another bash like the last one, so he got his joints in order and slowly stood.

"Move!" the guard said.

Dun shuffled off. The guard poked him in the back any time he stumbled. The bay containing the guard post and door were quickly closed off into a narrow corridor with smooth metal-sounding walls. Their footfalls echoed harshly. Or maybe that was just the inside of Dun's head; he couldn't be entirely sure.

"Where are we going?" That earned him another poke. At least what he was getting poked with was blunt.

Dun could hear noise in the distance. The corridor they were in had a definite downward slant to it, and it was starting to feel damp underfoot and he could touch the walls on either side. A waft of air brought awful smells toward him. A melange of the worst things he could imagine: vomit, body waste, fear. Some fresh, some old. Those smells weren't just what had happened here, they were here, whatever this place was.

Another poke in the back from the guard. "Move!"

The smell got stronger as Dun got poked farther down the slope, and he was sure he could hear low moaning. This was not at all going how he'd imagined. Although, what had he imagined, really? Go to a new place in the Dark that no one seems to have returned from, except maybe Myrch, and what? Say "*I've been having these dreams...*" He felt stupid, alone, and now scared. There was a half-hearted scream from ahead of him; it was the sound of anguish from someone who was worn down and exhausted. The moaning was distinct, or at least all around him. Lots of voices, like some kind of damned choir.

"Stop!" the guard barked.

Dun stopped. The guard hit him anyway. Dun didn't give him the satisfaction of any noise. The guard seemed to be doing something on the wall ahead with his free hand. The other gripped the top of Dun's arm, his spatulate fingers digging into him uncomfortably. There was a beep and the guard pulled Dun forward again. Odd there was no door to accompany the beep sound. It was certainly an identical beep to the front door one.

"Here!"

The guard pushed Dun into an opening: a small room. He could smell someone else. Behind something in the way, as far as his air-sense could tell. A low desk?

"Uhh?" the *desk-sitting* Over-Folk said.

"New," Dun's guard said.

"Uhh," the sitting guard said. "Arm."

"Arm!" Dun's guard said.

When Dun didn't respond, the guard yanked Dun's arm forward and slammed it on the table. The sitting guard stood, grabbed Dun's wrist and then Dun felt a stab of pain in his lower arm.

"Ow!" he said.

Something had broken his skin, and he could feel pressure under the surface. Had they put something in him? He felt a chill down his spine. He hoped it was just fear.

"Quiet!" his guard said and hit him with the stick again on the back of his legs.

He buckled as far as the grip on his upper arm would let him. When the guard pushed him again he almost fell.

"Get up!" the guard yelled.

"New prisoners row," the desk guard said.

"Move," his guard said.

He was pushed out of the far side of the small room into a wide corridor that seemed to have the mouths of lots of other corridors facing them. Moaning issued from most of them. They moved toward the corridor where the moaning was loudest. There was sobbing too. He was pushed on and started to hear distinct sounds. The nearest moan became a person. Before he had a chance to process that, there was another beep, the metal creaking of a gate opening, and then Dun was thrown into a small room with a wall at the back, on which he hit his head. It wasn't all that far away. Dun sat up and rubbed his head. He felt along the back wall and around the cell. Bars on three sides. He reached the gate again where the guard was and was rewarded with a kick in the chest.

The gate clanged shut. 'Quiet!' the guard yelled.

Of the many things this place was, quiet was not any.

Dark

Chapter Forty-Nine

Something metal clanged across the floor of Dun's cell, waking him with a start. He sat huddled in the corner of the cell. It was cold and damp in the cell complex. A smell rose from where the metal thing had come to rest. Dun suspected an attempt at food of some description. It was hard to tell when the smell from the rest of the complex overwhelmed everything else, including his appetite. Dun groaned.

"Hey, you gonna eat that? Because if you don't..." Dun's next door cellmate said.

"No," Dun said. "You want it?"

"No, but I'm just warning you. They feed you once a span. You get mighty hungry."

"I can't eat," Dun said. "I think I might be sick."

"Suit yourself. You don't want it? Shove it over near the bars over here, and I'll reach through."

Dun did as he was asked. "What's your name?"

"Fen," his opposite number said through a mouthful of food.

"Dun."

"No, not yet."

"No, I'm Dun."

"But you've not started; I've got yours."

Dun sighed. "I'm called Dun. Dun is my name."

"Ooooh! Sorry," Fen said.

"Doesn't matter."

Dun let his newfound friend eat. The sound of scrabbling on the metal plate stopped.

"Hey, how long have you been in here?"

"Me?" Fen said. "Not long. Twenty spans, maybe?"

"Where are you from?"

"River-folk."

"Ah, I thought I recognized the accent. You're a long way out of your way for a River-folk, aren't you?"

"Might say the same about you for a Bridge-folk," Fen replied.

"Good point. Good ears too."

"Kept me in work as a guard."

"Guard?"

"Yeah."

"Sorry," Dun said. 'Too nosy."

"For around here? Yeah. Lemme give you some advice in return for dinner, and then we's straight, okay?"

"Okay."

"Keep your head down. That way you get hurt less. Don't hear nothin'. Don't smell nothin'. Most of all don't say nothin'."

"Get hurt?"

"They interrogate people here," Fen said.

"Oh."

"Mostly folk they think are hiding something, or might be spies, they're obsessed with spies. Don't know who's spying on them, or who'd be bothered, really. They're all mad."

"They?"

"You *are* nosy. It's gonna get you into trouble. Just sayin'."

"Probably."

"They are the Fiefdom. That's what they call themselves or this place anyways, but they've got lots of tribes like us."

"Are they, you know..."

"Like us? Dunno, they smell funny if that's what you're asking. I've never really got close enough to feel one that wasn't punching me."

"Hmm... It's just that I've been spending a lot of time around someone who... Well... wasn't."

"Wasn't punching you?" Fen said.

"No wasn't folk."

"Oh, you mean like this lot?"

"No, I don't think so, these lot, Over-folk or whatever, they're a bit taller and a bit skinnier, but they're still basically folk. Myrch was something ... different."

"I don't follow."

"Well, no fur, a smell like nothing I've ever come across before, really tall, he owned lots of weird tech."

"Gods, don't talk to me about tech. These lot are obsessed by it."

"Oh?"

"Yeah, it's everywhere..."

A loud clanging rattle echoed down the cellblock as something hard, a stick maybe, was run along the bars. Loud-clunking feet followed the noise: three, four guards?

"Quiet down in there, prisoners! You!"

The feet stopped outside Dun's cell. He froze, holding his breath. The shouting guard clattered around with keys in the lock but it was the door to Fen's cell that opened.

"Did you miss me?" Fen said.

"Quiet!"

There was a sharp crack and the faint smell of singed fur. Dun could hear Fen hiss a breath in, too proud to let out a shout. The guards scuffled briefly with Fen, there was another crack, Fen cried out, and then Dun could hear them drag him out of the cell and on down the corridor. A door somewhere at the end banged shut. Dun breathed out slowly, his heart hammering. Ten clicks, twenty, then thirty.

Fen's piercing shriek rent the air. Dun clamped his hands over his ears and squashed himself as far into the corner of the cell as he could go. The bars and the cold stone of the wall pressed into opposite sides of his face. That felt comforting somehow. He kept his hands clamped to his head but only managed to dull the sounds. He felt tears streaming down his face and running down his arms. When did that start?

"No, no, no, no, no, no," he said to the wall of the cell, although there was no one to hear him. "No, no, no, no, no, no." The rhythm of the words was calming. "No, no, no, no, no, no."

Then the screaming stopped.

Dark

The door opened at the end of the corridor. Two of the guards marched out, back toward his way, and then past Dun's cell. Then silence again. The two guards marched back with someone else, soft sounding feet in tow. They went back down to the room. Dun heard distant discussion and some raised voice sounds, none of which was intelligible from so far away. The door to the room slammed again and the soft-footed Feifdom person stomped back down the corridor muttering under his breath, past Dun's cell and off.

No one else came out of the room for a long time. Eventually, Dun heard the door creak open gently, and a guard, hardly clumping at all, progressed back down past Dun's cell. Dun presumed he was back off to the guard post that everyone seemed to pass on their way in. Fen did not return that cycle. Or the next. The meals came and went. The third one Dun was hungry enough to eat. It was dry and tasted of plaster and bitter plants. When he wasn't eating, Dun slept and wept.

He dreamed again, in that vivid way of foretelling, but all he could hear was hissing, like his head had sand pouring in one ear and out the other. There were no emotions at all. He could smell nothing, or everything at once he wasn't sure. A bit like that feeling when you smell something so strong; it stuns your senses for a bit. Except there was no smell to precede it. And his skin felt sensitive at every point as if he was being held in a snug suit. Not pain, but like being touched everywhere at once.

He woke up with a gasp. The door of his cell rattled. He'd didn't hear the feet of the guards. Now he was awake he could smell them though. The guard captain, the one called Batcha, that had the fine line in shouting was rattling keys at his cell grill.

"Wakey, wakey. The people in the office at the end want to talk to you."

"I need to pee."

"Hurry. Thirty clicks and I'm dragging you there peeing or not."

Dun didn't need telling twice. He knew he was in a fix and didn't need to make things any worse for himself. Play safe and ride it out. Wait for an opportunity.

Dun gulped. The trickling noise of the gully and it's drain faded away. "Finished."

"Okay, move."

To avoid more poking and whatever else came with the sticks the guards were so fond of hitting everyone with, Dun moved quickly. They progressed down the corridor to the end, Dun alongside Batcha and two guards clumping along behind them. The procession stopped at the door. Batcha banged on it with his stick.

"Enter," came a silky voice from the other side of the door.

"Prisoner for interrogation."

"Good, bring them in."

Batcha poked Dun to a place in front of the interrogator.

"Good. Thank you, Batcha. I will call if I need you."

Dun waited patiently. The room was large and cuboid. It contained some kind of desk between him and the interrogator. There was scratching of some kind of stylus and the faint sound of a regular clicking, weirdly not an organic sound like a clicker-beetle, more like some kind of clicking machine. Everything smelled similar to a kind of plant Tali used for cleaning. What did she call it? Antiseptic.

Two hundred clicks went by. Then four hundred. Six. Dun's calves were starting to ache. Some instinct told him not to speak, so he stood in silence, breathing slowly and as quietly as he could manage. He shifted his weight from one foot to the other. Then back. Still, he waited.

"You may go. Guard!"

Dark

The door opened and grabbed Dun firmly by the arm. Dun turned back to the doorway, but his feet stumbled on the way out. The guard waited til he'd collected himself, renewed his grip in Dun's arm, and led him back down the corridor to his cell. How long he'd been in there; he'd lost count. Dun sat down on the floor. There was a flump of something landing gently behind him before the cell gate clanged shut. It smelled organic and stale. Dun reached out. It was some kind of woven blanket.

"Thank you," Dun said, bewildered.

But the guard was gone. What on earth had happened there? Was that meant to be an interrogation? Was he getting some kind of special treatment? Fen hadn't come off so easy. More importantly, these people had no idea who he was, did they? So if Myrch's advice was to be trusted there were a number of factions, and this wasn't the one that wanted him. Was that a good thing or not? Dun wasn't sure and all the speculation was giving him a headache.

He lay on his side on the blanket and wrapped the rest of it around him. It was thin but better than nothing. He tried again to collect his thoughts, but drifted off to sleep, straight back into the creepy sand dream he'd had last cycle.

Chapter Fifty

Two cycles of being summoned to the interrogator, being stood for varying lengths of time and being dismissed was starting to freak Dun out a little. He knew there was some kind of game being played here, and it was being slowly ratcheted up. He didn't know what the rules were, but he guessed that was part of the game too. He was now being summoned two or three times in a cycle at random times. It was only a matter of time until they started waking him up to interrogate him. It seemed the logical next step.

Dun also had a new neighbor; brought in last cycle. Barely conscious but Dun could tell it was an Over-folk and a female at that from her scent. As if in answer to Dun thinking about her, she groaned faintly.

"You okay?" Dun said.

No answer. He went to the opposite side of his cell and reached through the bars. He felt the prone form to work out which way up she was. She lay supine, spine against the bars. He changed position to find a pulse: slow, heavy, and her neck was cold, although matted with fur. Was that dried blood? She sighed slowly. Dun smoothed her fur gently and removed his hand. What was this place, and what the hells was going on out there?

The slightly limping guard that brought the food bowls struggled out of the guard's office at the near end of the corridor. Why they didn't have some kind of wheeled trolley thing to help the poor chap out was bemusing to Dun. Callousness? Carelessness? The usual procedure seemed to be the guard taking two battered metal plates at a time, sometimes three and flinging them contemptuously across the floors of the cells through a small slot in each grill at floor level. The plate dinked across the floor of his neighbor's cell and thudded into her.

Dark

Dun sighed, ignoring the sound of his own plate arriving and reached over to brush food from the fur of the limp form through the bars. Breakfast/lunch today seemed to be wetter in consistency and smelled of something sweet. Dun still wasn't hungry. But he knew he needed to keep his strength up somehow. Water got brought intermittently involving a bucket and some kind of scoop, which didn't properly fit through the bars. There was inevitably a performance involving slurping and dribbling, which Dun thought would have been funnier if it was only him. Hearing some of his other counterparts farther down the corridor trying to sip through bruised and broken lips made him want to cry. The scarcity of the water made him behave otherwise. The bucket run usually followed the food, the only time they could be certain of it. Dun suddenly thought, his new counterpart had had nothing to drink for at least one and a half cycles. Judging by her state, maybe more. He reached his foot behind him to check where his bowl was, and then hooked his foot around it to drag it across the floor toward him. Maybe he could help out here.

He forced the sorry excuse for food down him and gulped hard to prevent reflux. If he could finish it before the guard came back with the bucket, he might be able to keep some for his sleeping oppo. He swallowed down the last mouthful as he heard the limping steps on their way back to the guard post. Sure enough, the door banged open again with an accompanying splosh of water on to the floor; the guard always opened the door bucket first. Since no one was between the two of them and the guard post the guard arrived at Dun's neighbor first with a clang-clang of the metal spoon on the bars. When there was no response from inside the cell. The guard scooped water up anyway and sloshed it in. There was a wet splat as it hit the floor and the prone form. *Why would you do that*, thought Dun?

The guard clanged on Dun's bars.
"Here," Dun said. "offering up the plate."
"Suit yourself," the guard said.

Dun caught most of it, the larger challenge being getting the flattish plate down to the floor without spilling any. He knelt down in the damp pool that had spread between the cells and waited for the guard to go. To move any earlier would certainly invite unwelcome attention. The guard clanged off up the corridor as far as the interrogator's office, and then as far back as their cells, past them and back into the guard post. Dun waited a hundred clicks or so to make sure he had gone. Then he gently prodded his neighbor through the bars. She groaned.

"Hey, you okay?" Dun said gently.

Another groan.

"Can you move?"

"Uhh."

"I can help you try to move. You need to drink something. Can you turn your head?"

"Uhh."

"Here, let me help."

Slowly and gently, Dun turned her head from facing away from him to a little closer to vertical. Or at least an angle Dun felt comfortable pouring water into her mouth without the risk of choking. He wet his finger and went to wet her lips.

"Here, try this first."

"Mmm."

Slowly by wetting his finger and applying it to her mouth, he managed to get half a plateful of water into her.

"More..."

He helped her roll her head over more toward the bars. Then he poured a handful of what water was left from the plate into his hand. From there he dribbled it into her mouth.

"Th...anks."

"Welcome. You want the rest? There's not much more."

"S... ure."

She panted heavily then lay down again.

"What's your name?" Dun said.

But she had drifted back off to sleep. At least the noises she was making now were more restful.

"Mazzy."

"Sorry?" Dun said.

"My name. It's Mazzy."

"Oh, hello, I'm Dun."

"Is there ... any more water?"

"Yeah, I saved you some; the guard came by while you were asleep."

"Thanks."

"There's a bit more than there was last time, I made a dent in the plate. They're pretty bendy. I hope it doesn't leak."

"Thanks," she said again, amusement in her voice.

"What?" Dun said.

"You're funny."

"I saved some food too. If you feel up to it."

"I guess," she said.

Dun passed some food through the bars that he'd kept wrapped up in a strip of the blanket.

"How did you wind up here?" he asked as she ate.

"Oh I shouldn't... can't..." she whispered. "They'll hear."

"Are you Over-folk?"

"What?"

"Over-folk. Sorry, I'm from a long way away, from Bridge-folk; it's what we call you."

"Oh." She laughed. "We call ourselves Duchy."

"You're quite like us though."

"I guess," she said. "We talk the same."

"Your face is the same."

"How do you... oh."

"I had to feed you water... and check you were okay. Sorry."

"Oh, that's okay. I don't mind." She stopped talking to chew. "Gods, what do they put in this stuff?"

"I know, today's is... chewy."

The door at the guards end of the corridor opened. Batcha, by the smell, and another two guards.

"Here we go again," Dun said.

"Where?" Mazzy said.

"Oh, interrogation time." At the noise she made, Dun said, "Oh, don't worry; it's more surreal than harmful."

Then the guards stopped at Mazzy's cell, unlocked it, and led her out.

"No, no, no, no, nooo!" Dun said. "She's only just got here."

He clung to the bars between the cells and tried to grab Mazzy's hand. He was rewarded for his efforts by a poke with the stick, but this time when it touched him there was a *crack* and a sudden knifing jolt. He could smell singed fur; this time his own.

"Aahhh!"

"No fraternizing among prisoners!" Batcha said, almost cheerfully.

They dragged Mazzy down the corridor, the door at the far end opened, and then closed. And the screaming began.

***

Dun had the sand dream again only this time it was accompanied by a piercing high-pitched squeak. He woke up panting. When he had calmed down and began to breathe slowly once more he could hear sobbing from the cell next to him.

'You okay?' he said.

Mazzy was silent. Dun reached out through the bars to find out if she was okay. As he touched her, she flinched away.

'I'm sorry,' he said quietly.

The rest of the corridor was quieter than usual. The sounds of snoring and nightmares were somehow dimmer. Dun sat awake in vigil for a while, but as he heard Mazzy's breaths lengthen, he too drifted off.

***

When the keys rattled in the door of his cell, he expected the guard captain and another trip to the inquisitor. Instead, as he came around he heard a hissed conversation at his cell door.

"Hurry up, the gas won't work forever."

"There are a lot of keys."

"Well, eliminate a few of them, or we'll be behind them."

"Shush and let me concentrate. Go check on the guards."

Two voices, similar to the guards, so Over-folk then. One male, one female. Dun heard steps plodding back to the guard post, unshot steps, so, not a guard. The rattling at his cell door continued.

"Come on," the male voice said.

The footsteps came back. The female said, "Nah, they're still dead out."

"Good," the male said, rattling keys. "Just check the other end of the corridor is still locked."

Of she trundled in the other direction. While she was away, her colleague made some progress.

"Gotcha!"

There was a loud, satisfying click.

"Come on out then," the male voice said, the first time it had addressed him directly.

"Me?" Dun said.

"Yes, you," the voice said. "Who else?"

"Well, her next door for a start."

"What are you on about?"

"If you want me," Dun said. "You need to bring her too."

"What?"

"You heard. If you want me, bring her too."

"Why the hell should we try and get everyone killed for that? Do you know her?"

"No," Dun said, "just met."

"Then no."

"If you want me to come with you and not scream the place down for the guards, get her out."

"Okay my tetchy friend, come out yourself, and we'll find out what we can do."

Dun came out and they set about finding another key that might free Mazzy. When they had, Dun helped her to her feet and gave her a shoulder to lean on.

"Who the hells are you? Not the guards for sure," Dun said.

"I'm Tam, that's Bel," the male said.

"Enough time for jolly hellos later," Bel said. "I think I can hear the guards stirring."

"Let's move!" Tam said cheerily.

He led them toward the guard post at as much of a trot as the dragging of a nearly unconscious Mazzy would allow. Tam leaned under Mazzy's other arm to help, and Bel went in front. She kicked open the guard room door and barged in. The guard captain's hazy voice came up from the floor.

"Whaaa...? Hey! You! Stop!"

"Oh, no you don't," Bel said and there was a crunch as she kicked out.

The guard captain slumped back to the floor with a groan. Bel advanced but had to stop to open the door to get out. A loud booming alarm started to sound from beyond the doorway. From the way it was echoing it seemed like there was an enormous space out there.

"Whoops, time to leave," Tam said. "Right, outside quickly."

Tam shuffled Dun and Mazzy through the door into a massive cavernous space with some kind of raised causeway that seemed to trail off into the distance.

"Stop where you are!" came a distant distorted voice from the other end of the causeway.

"Not likely!" Tam said.

"Time for plan B." Bel seemed to be fiddling with something down by her feet at the edge of the huge space they were in. "I'll take the girl, you take the Bumpkin."

Dark

Chapter Fifty-One

"The who?" Dun said.

"Bumpkins," Tam said.

"Is that what you call us?"

"Yeah? What do you call you?"

"Bridge-folk."

"Less politics," Bel yelled, "more sports! Jump!"

Bel had found a ledge just below the causeway. The alarm/siren was getting louder.

"Stop where you are and surrender to the authorities!"

"My hairy ass, will I," Bel said and then hissed, "Pass the girl down here, quick."

Dun and Tam struggled with Mazzy's limp form but managed to post her down to Bel. Then they heard loud crack-whoof noises, followed by odd splatty impacts on the causeway behind them.

"Stun rounds," Tam said. "Time to leave."

They pushed off from the edge of the causeway and fell the short drop to the ledge. Dun's world spun as the mass of open air pressed against his air-sense. This place was massive and the causeway was in midair. Bel elbowed Dun in the ribs, unshouldering some kind of weapon.

"Scuse me," Bel said. "Cover the causeway, Tam. There's a love."

Tam pulled some kind of weapon from a pocket and returned fire over the edge of the causeway. Bel had cocked whatever her weapon was. There was a sharp twang and the whirring of a reel unwinding. Then a distant clunk.

"Bingo! Damn, I'm good," Bel said. "Buy me a few clicks to get a decent spar to clamp this to, Tam."

"Aye!" Tam said.

Then after a short grunt from Tam, something flew toward the sirens whistling, and then made a crump noise. The sirens stopped.

"Good shot," Bel said.

"Thanks."

"Okay, all clipped on here. Time to go. I'll go first and check the line. You follow on and show the Bumpkin what he's doing. Shame to get him killed now we've found him."

Bel had erected some kind of a wire just at head height that headed out over the drop. She clicked something metallic sounding onto it, jumped over the edge, and whizzed down the line into the distance.

"Right," Tam said. "You put your hands in here. Hold on tight. Make sure everything you don't want to lose is strapped on."

Dun heard the same metallic click and whatever his hands were strapped in went taught.

"Hold tight!" Tam said again and pushed.

Dun realized he'd forgotten to ask what in the hells was going to stop him once he reached the other end, but then he built up speed and forgot everything as the wind rushed past him and his air-sense was a blur. Traveling forward as fast as he'd ever gone while having nothing beneath his feet was terrifying and exhilarating. Dun would have whooped if he'd had the air to do it with. Then his air-sense started picking something up, something large, level and looming up at an alarming rate. Another causeway? And he could hear a voice over the rush of the wind.

"Feet up!" Bel shouted.

He had just enough about him to do that as he whirred into the bottom of the line, colliding first with something that slowed him and threw his feet in the air, and then colliding with Bel as she caught him.

"I gotcha, fella. Pretty good for a first-timer."

Dun was going to say thanks, but he felt like he'd left his breath behind on the previous causeway. He heard the wire burr and twang as Tam descended, with the most weight of all carrying Mazzy, however, he was managing that.

"Grab a hold of that wire you're stood on, Bumpkin; that's our brake line. We'll both need to pull on it to slow them down with all that weight on. Come on; pull. The extra weight was your idea."

Dun pulled but said, "The extra weight's called Mazzy."

"You can introduce me if she survives."

The whirring on the wire grew higher-pitched and louder and then took on an odd resonance.

"Okay, incoming. Stay sharp, Bumpkin!"

"Quiiiiiiiiiick!" Tam yelled as he came in.

The wire whipped as they landed. Dun was yanked in the shoulder, but he and Bel took the weight. Tam fell to his knees. The wire was still buzzing.

"Quick! Get me loose. Cops."

"Cops?" Bel said.

"On the wire!" Tam said.

"Gotcha," Bel said and Dun heard the familiar sound of a knife being drawn, except the metal of this one seemed to sing.

Then, he yelled, "Duck!"

A quick swish slashed through the air, an almighty metal twang and the distant sound of screaming.

"Good," Bel said. "Shall we go? On the bike, everyone; we should all fit."

Tam poked him forward. His knees bumped something metal.

"Swing your leg over." Tam tapped him on the appropriate leg and helped him on.

He was sat precariously astride whatever a "bike" was.

"Now hold on around my waist!" Bel shouted.

Dun did as he was told. Tam struggled Mazzy on behind them and grabbed the back himself. Then without warning, there was a squee noise, a slight smell of something chemical, burning, and they shot off. Dun leaving his guts behind for the second time in a cycle. At least this time there was ground beneath his feet. Sort of. The bike sped on. Dun could feel the shapes of other causeways with his air-sense, twined and intertwined all in midair. Maybe with more bikes on them. Then he felt a huge wall ahead of them, rushing up to meet them, very, very fast. Just as Dun thought the adrenaline pounding was going to make his heart leap out of his chest, his air-sense squashed in on him: a tunnel. The noise of the bike dinging loud off the walls. Mechanical, motor whirring and rip of wheels on a concrete surface. Then out into the open again, briefly, and back into another tunnel.

"Now for the clever bit!" Bel yelled over the noise.

She tweaked some control in front of her. Dun could feel her shift slightly in her seat. The bike let out two loud peeps in succession.

"Hang tight! Lean right!" Bel yelled.

And the bike swung around to another screech and rubbery smell. Dun clung on to some part of Bel's jacket as he got whipped around. Then the bike whooshed off again, this time down a very narrow tunnel indeed. Dun's air-sense told him not to lean at this point or he might rip something off. Then the bike came out into a large metal room. They sped across this too, to the far side. Where a room just big enough to hold the bike opened toward them. Bel slowed the contraption, shifting again and came to rest just inside the smaller room.

"Close the gate, Tam."

A metallic squeaking, then a clang. "Done!"

"Ta! Down we go."

She made the bike peep twice again and after a loud clunk and a lurch, the floor started very slowly to fall. Third time in a cycle. Dun was amazed he hadn't lost his lunch, especially considering what his lunch had been. They fell, exceedingly slow for about a thousand clicks, or rather the floor they were stood on did. Then they landed with a firm bump.

"Gate please, Tam."

More rattling. The bike moved backward out of the tiny room.

"Okay, not far now," Bel said.

They screeched around a final bend; the bike peeped again and Dun felt a door lifting up with his air-sense. The bike drove in. There was a click of a weapon cocking, then a harsh voice.

"Password!"

"Hi, honeys! We're home!" Bel said.

Dark

*"They often sing together, these 'Folk'.
But sometimes, there is a strange song, sung
by one male on his own. A strange keening,
mournful. Everyone else stays stock still and
listens. It's crazy but it feels like a hymn
to the past, something left behind."*

Excerpts from <Distress Beacon SN-1853001>.
Found by E.S.V. Vixen Terradate: 26102225.

Dark

Chapter Fifty-Two

Dun could feel a large room full of clutter: crates, machines, and who knew what. The door closed behind them with a quiet hiss. Then bustle broke out all over, had people been keeping quiet when the door was open?

"Medic!" Bel shouted.

"Welcome to the Community," Tam said.

Folk rushed everywhere. A small team arrived with some kind of medical kit and took Mazzy away to some other room to treat her. Another group swarmed around Tam and Bel removing equipment and taking things away.

"Right," Bel said, "food and debriefing. In that order, I think?"

"Canteen, it is," Tam said.

They led the way through the throng of folk and Dun was starting to form an opinion of the Overfolk. Taller than him, although skinnier. Sweeter smelling, often in subtly different ways; underlying a male and female smell, different but similar to the ones he recognized. The people at least seemed to be cheerful from first impressions. That at least they had in common with the Bridge-folk.

They reached the canteen. Dun thought he'd heard bustle before. No, this was bustle. The folk here were shouting, laughing hysterically, bartering, and bantering. It seemed like very little actual eating was going on.

"Lunch seems to be miso," Tam said.

"Could be worse," Bel said.

"Yep, could be rat again."

They joined the edge of another throng of people, and Dun was presented with a plastic mug of something watery but wholesome smelling and some kind of soft and beautiful smelling warm round thing. Once they had sat in curious molded plastic chairs around a raised table, Tam explained it was hubbous and was for dipping in the thin broth. It tasted fantastic, sweet and savory at the same time and a beautiful texture that melted in the mouth. The soup was pretty good too, salty and a bit fishy smelling, but not fish. It was the best thing he'd eaten for a cycle. Bel arrived with a handful of more plastic beakers containing flat tasting but clean water.

"Feelin' a little better?" Bel said.

"Mmph," Dun said.

"Good. Your friend's gone to sickbay, not sure how she'll do. She seemed pretty rough to me," Bel said.

"Never know though, and she's in the best place," Tam chipped in.

"Right, get the rest of that down you. We need to get you debriefed."

Dun didn't really like the sinister sound of that, but these people had rescued him, and they seemed okay. Besides he had so many questions. He had to know the answers to some of them. Why had he been led here? What was going on in this world of crazy folk, cells and torturers, factions and fights? He gulped down the hubbous with the remainder of the soup and felt better than he had for cycles.

Some kind of whoop-whoop alarm went off, drifting into the canteen from the landing bay that they had all come in through.

"What's that?" Dun said.

"Door opening alarm," Tam said. "Means everyone knows the doors opening so's they know to be quiet."

"Why?"

"Because that's what happens in a secret base?" Bel said.

"Oh."

"So be quiet now."

Dark

There was some kind of movement to the landing bay from some of the canteen residents. Some kind of outgoing party? For what reason he was a little afraid to ask after being cut off quite so abruptly. Seemed like Bel could be a bit spiky when it suited her.

Tam tugged gently on Dun's arm and led him back out of the canteen. He could hear more vehicles revving up in the landing bay. He recognized the sound of bikes and some kind of larger bike-like thing. Quite an outing then, wherever they were off to. They turned in the corridor away from the noise and past a quiet room with a faint smell of antiseptic, and then another room that smelled of wood with two of the community arguing over something. Then they passed a room with the smells of cooking coming from it. Some kind of stewing meat? It smelled fantastic whatever it was. They certainly ate well here.

From behind them, the sounds of bikes and folk faded and a different siren, and a longer horn sounded. It echoed through the corridors.

"All clear," Tam said. "Come on."

Tam led them to a long wide room that had a big shape that Dun could sense, in the middle of the room, another table? They were fond of those here. Dun was led to a plastic chair; they seemed fond of those too.

"Sit," Tam said in a friendly tone.

It seemed that they'd lost Bel on their journey there. It seemed that Tam was aware of that too.

"She'll be along in a minute," Tam said. "She's gone to get someone else, I think. I'll get us some water."

He left through the door they'd come in through, and Dun could hear his voice in the kitchen, joking with someone. He returned with some kind of receptacle and some more cups. Water sloshed onto the table as he put it down.

"Oops."

"You probably want to mop that up," Bel said from the doorway.

"Just going to," Tam said with a hint of testiness.

There was someone else with Bel in the doorway. They both came in and sat.

"Hi," the new someone said.

"Sorry," Bel said. "This is Stef, our technician. Stef, this is the Bu... oh, I never did get your name."

"Dun," he said.

"Right, Dun... Stef, you get the idea."

"Hi," Dun said.

"Hi," Stef said back. She had a patient tone.

Tam came back in and set to squeaking the water up off the table.

"Okay, sit down Tam," Bel said.

"Make your mind up."

"We need to orientate..."

"Dun."

"Dun here quickly, so he can start being of use. Okay," she said, warming to her theme. "This is how it works. You're not being interrogated, but the more stuff you tell us the more it will help us and probably you too. To show our good faith, we'll do this on a turn by turn basis. And you can even go first."

"Okay," said Dun. "First, who did you rescue me from?"

"Good question. They are called the Duchy. A nastier bunch of folk you'll never want to meet. We're the Community, and we're... Well, a guess you'd say we're at war with them," Bel said.

"I was starting to work that out, what with the torturing and all."

"Yes. Okay. Now. Why are you here?"

"Oh, I had a foretelling, that I was supposed to come here. I'm a shaman. Well, a trainee shaman anyway."

"Ah," Stef said.

"Yeah," Bel said.

"I think," Tam said, "we have something you need to know about."

Chapter Fifty-Three

They led Dun farther on down the corridor to another door. This one seemed to have some kind of security pad on it from the clicking and beeping that ensued. The door opened with a final cheerful beep. The room on the inside was bizarre. There seemed to be one wall made entirely of something so smooth and featureless that it reflected every tiny noise. The rest of the room was some kind of precisely textured metal. An odd deep kind of texture that seemed to damp down any noise. Truly strange. In the center of the room was a chair. Dun was getting used to the sense of foreboding from that setup.

"So," Bel said, "let us explain."

"Better still," Stef said, "let us demonstrate."

"Okay..." Dun said.

"It's all perfectly safe," Bel said.

"Who's going in the chair?" Tam said.

"Me, I guess," Bel said, "since Stef needs to operate."

"Sit on down then," Stef said. "We'll get you all wired up."

And she set about with whatever it was needed doing to the apparatus, humming cheerfully as she went.

"What do I need to do?" Dun said nervously.

"Nothing," Bel said breezily. "You just stay there. Someone might find you a chair though."

"I'll get one from the collecting room," Tam said and disappeared toward the smooth wall. It seemed to have a door in it that opened outward when pressed.

Stef continued buzzing about Bel until she reached some stage of satisfaction, signified by a click of her tongue and a humming noise. Tam returned from the smooth wall, carrying a chair. He placed it on the floor with a clunk.

"Sit down?" Tam said.

Dark

"I'll stand, thanks," Dun said.

"I'd advise you sit," Bel said. Not a threat, but what?

"Okay," Dun said and sat.

"Ready?" Bel said.

"I guess," Dun said.

"Wasn't asking you," Bel said.

"Yeah, ready here," Stef said.

"Good," Bel said. "Charge her up!"

A low hum throbbed around the room, and Dun thought it began to get warmer. The hum reached a steady tone and resonance.

"Okay, select pink noise program."

"Yeah!" Stef yelled.

"Transmit."

Dun felt like his head was about to split open. The sandy hissing from his dreams was back and as loud as it had ever been. But he wasn't asleep. Was he?

"Stop!" Bel yelled.

The noise and feelings and smells and tastes stopped.

"I don't underst..."

"Transmit," Bel said.

***

Dun screamed, unprepared this time, the sensory input felt like blows coming from all sides at once.

"Enough!" This time it was Dun yelling.

"Okay!" Bel shouted and the sensations stopped at once.

Tears streamed down Dun's face. "What in all the hells was that?"

"You know already," Bel said.

"What does it remind you of?" Tam said, a little more kindly.

"Of ... for... foretelling."

"Is that what you call it?" Bel said.

"But... What... Why?" Dun said.

"It's called projection," Stef said, joining them. "Here."

She gave him an odd object, some kind of a helmet festooned with wires.

"What is it?" Dun said.

"It does the... foretelling?" Stef said.

"How? I... don't understand."

"It transmits thoughts," Bel said.

"But how?"

"Well, the truth of it is we don't really understand how exactly," Bel said.

"It amplifies thoughts to a point they can be sent out," Tam said.

"The amplifiers we understand, the transmitting and receiving, less so," Stef said.

"How... I..."

"Foretelling... It doesn't exist, Dun," Tam said gently.

"But it does... I... hear it."

"Well, yes you do," Stef said.

"But it's not you telling the future. It's us," Bel said.

"But there have been shamans for eons."

"No doubt there have," Bel said.

"But how long have you—"

"Been projecting? Three or four eons," Bel said.

"We only came into possession of the equipment four or five eons ago," Stef said. 'It took a while to get it set up. And then longer to find folk that could work it."

"Don't you work it?" Dun said.

"Well, yeah," Stef said. "But that's not what I mean."

"Listen," Tam said. "Do you need time for this to sink in? We can do more of this later."

"But the debriefing?" Bel said.

"Can wait," Tam said. "I think Dun needs to rest."

"He can use my bunk for a bit if he wants," Stef said. "Until you find him somewhere. I won't be in it for a bit; I'll be doing lates here. There's tweaking to do."

"That'd be great," Tam said. "You want to take him, Stef? I think he might be sick of hearing us two for a bit?"

"Sure. Come on you."

***

They walked back toward the landing bay in silence. There was another corridor opposite; it seemed to be where they were heading. There were lots of identical door depressions in the sides of the corridor. They stopped early.

"I'm here," she said. "Need to be near the action when folks break stuff."

"Mmm."

"Sit down. Bed there." She led his hand to it and gently kept it there. "It'll be okay."

"Yeah."

She moved to go.

"I thought I was special," Dun said quietly.

She stopped. Walked back, sat, and let out a breath. "You are though, kind of."

"Oh, good, that makes me feel the opposite of special."

"No, that's not what I meant. I mean, not everyone can receive projections. It takes us ages to achieve resonance."

"What are you talking about?"

"The projector; it's kind of a communicator, really, but you've got to tune it in. You find someone who can transmit, play things through them, and then fiddle with the settings until you find someone who can pick the signals up. Then that comes back on the sensors as resonance; it's how you know you've found someone. How we knew we'd found you. You're rarer than you think."

"So all those noises, feelings, senses?"

"All came from us. We projected them all."

"Even the premonitions of the crazy metal rat-thing?"

"Oh, that was my idea to give you a heads-up. Some Community spies found out the Duchy had sent it, so I hacked into their sensor grid, and, well, you know the rest."

"Oh."

"Talking of rest," she said. "You should get some. I'll come get you when it's shift change. You can talk about it more then if you want."

"Thanks," Dun said and curled up on the bunk.

Dark

Chapter Fifty-Four

There was a gentle hand on Dun's shoulder, but he still woke bolt upright.

"Hey, take it easy there, fella," Stef said. "You should probably get yourself down to the canteen while there's still any food left!"

"Okay. And thanks," Dun said.

"You're welcome," she said with a smile in her voice. "Always pleased to help out a Bumpkin."

"Hey!" Dun said.

"I used to be one, you know."

"What?"

"Used to live, you know, way down deep like you."

"Did you? Where from?"

"I used to be Machine-folk."

"Why did you move?"

"Long story, another time."

"Ok..."

"Promise. Now go! Leave me to sleep and go eat."

Dun left. The bay seemed to be filled with Community. What would they be, militia? They were carrying out some kind of drill. There was lots of clunking and clicking and swearing and shouting by some kind of sergeant at arms. Dun kept to the back of the landing bay, passed a door in the back wall, and moved around to the door that would take him to the canteen.

Dark

The smells from there seemed to include the fantastic hubbous from the day before except this time it was warm! Dun thought he might drown in his own saliva before he got there. There was some resinous dark-tasting, bitter drink being handed out in the plastic beakers from the day before. Some kind of spread, sweet to the point of sickliness accompanied the hubbous. He followed the sounds of a particularly noisy table and sat. It transpired that the rowdy crew on the table had returned from a raid while Dun was sleeping. They seemed to have stolen or *liberated* some medical supplies and explosives amongst other things and taken a ground car to bring it back in. Dun wasn't sure what most of it meant but it seemed to be good news to the Community folk.

Coming around a little, Dun realized that one of the voices in the conversation was Tam. Whether he had been out on the raid or not wasn't clear, but when he had noticed that Dun had filled the unoccupied chair he stopped.

"Hey, you lot," Tam said. "This is Dun. He came up from Down-Below yesterday."

There were loud choruses of hellos and introductions too many for Dun to take in. When the hubbub had died down Tam spoke again, but quietly to Dun. "When you've had something to eat, shall we go and finish the rest of that debrief?"

"Sure," Dun said.

They reassembled in the same room as before, and Bel was summoned. Dun and Tam waited for her and talked.

"Is Bel your Alpha then?" Dun said.

"My what now?"

"King? Chief?"

"Oh." Tam laughed. "No, we don't have those."

"Eh?" Dun said. "Well, who organized that raid then?"

"We choose leaders for particular jobs and aptitudes, and we change them on a regular basis. It saves anyone getting too carried away."

"Oh."

"Doesn't that happen where you come from? Bridge-folk, right?"

"Oh. We change leaders but its usually a big thing. We choose a new Alpha if the old one isn't leading well anymore."

"What happens if one gets too self-important?"

"Oh, they can be challenged."

"Voted out you mean?" Tam said.

"No, more like a series of ritual combats."

"Wow," Tam said.

Bel arrived, trailing the scent of another cup of whatever Dun had been drinking.

"That sounds a pretty elaborate set up you Bridge-folk have got down there," Bel said.

"It works for us," Dun said.

She sat and shuffled some papers she seemed to have brought. Creaking back on the plastic chair and tapping some kind of plastic sounding stylus on the table.

"Okay, where did we get to yesterday?" she said, more to herself than anyone else. "Are you feeling a little better by the way?"

"Yes, thank you."

"Good. Do you understand what happened yesterday?"

"A little more now, yes, I think. The projector thing shoots sensations out everywhere and you have to find someone that's picking them up. Then you can kind of communicate with them."

"That's about the size of it," Bel said.

"How long have you been doing it for?"

"Two, three eons, maybe?"

"Why?" Dun asked.

"We need recruits," Bel said.

"What for?" Dun said.

"There's a war on," Tam said.

"But why from our world, not your own?"

We don't know why, but the projector seems to work best with your people, not ours. It's quite a hit and miss process. First, you've got to find someone, and then you've got to send the right kind of message," Tam said.

Dark

"And finally you've got to hope they don't think they've gone mad and keep it all to themselves, although that doesn't always preclude people coming here," Bel said.

"So the need to come and explore up here, that was all sent from you?" Dun said.

"Pretty much yes," Bel said. "You wouldn't make very good recruits if you went anywhere else, now would you?"

Dun had a terrible chilling feeling run through him. His father had just upped and left, no shaman he was, but perhaps he had been getting the signals just the same but never mentioned them. The whole mapping extravaganza, just cover to make him look better?

"So there must be a massive number of folk you project to who just never get here?"

"Wastage," Bel said. "It's one of our biggest problems."

"What happens to them?"

"Some, as I said, go mad and never arrive," Bel said. "Many fall into the hands of the Duchy or the Bureau."

"Like me?"

"Yes, and they're a suspicious bunch. They know we're recruiting, have done for a while, but then don't know how. We want to try and keep it that way."

"My father, Abdun, disappeared on a mapping mission up this way," Dun said.

"I don't know him, I'm sorry," Bel said.

"So he became *wastage* then?" Dun said.

"I said I was sorry."

"Yes, you did. Why are you fighting?"

"Ah yes, I'm glad you've brought us on to that. It makes things easier to explain the right way around. We all used to live in a relatively peaceful society until a section of us started believing more in the privileges of office than the treatment of the people."

"Okay," Dun said.

"The remains of that society is the Bureau, and they hold jealously onto the records of our society and yours, but don't want to share. A resistance movement formed to try and escape that formed from some sections of the peacekeeping officers, but it quickly got out of hand when a little power became available to people too long powerless. We broke off from that faction believing that we could organize a little better and a little more fairly than that which we were trying to usurp. It works mostly."

"Why do you need to be telling me all this?"

"We are rather hoping you'll stay," Bel said.

"That gives me the impression I haven't much choice."

"No," Tam said a little too cheerily. "Of course you've got a choice."

"In which case let me think on it," Dun said.

"Err, okay," Bel said.

Clearly, she was used to getting all of her own way more often. True to his word though, Dun went off to think. He went by the canteen and found himself a beaker of water from one of the catering folk. He took it and found a crate to perch on at the back of the landing bay. His back supported by the wall facing the outer door he felt oddly calm. He found the bustle of this place where everyone knew there own small part in what they were doing, peaceful. He began to think of all the things he thought he'd come here for: because he was a shaman, because he was looking for his father, because he wanted an adventure. Was there anything left? Maybe there was. Maybe there was one thing.

A familiar scent tweaked his nose.

"Hi," Stef said. "Room on that box?"

"Sure."

"You gonna stay?" she said.

"Maybe," Dun said.

She left a companionable silence between them. Eventually Dun broke it. "The drains here, do they all empty into the sluice that we came in over?" Dun asked.

"Weird question. I guess so. I'm not the best one to ask."

"Oh, who is?"

"Nev. He looks after the drains. Want me to introduce you?"

"Why not," Dun said. Slowly, for the first time in this whole adventure, he felt like he could be the agent of something, maybe.

They found Nev in the canteen where it became apparent quite quickly even without Stef's introduction that he looked after the drains. The smell didn't seem to bother Stef any, and Dun found it reassuring: no matter people's differences in technology or outlook their drains smelled the same.

"So, Nev," Stef said. "My crazy friend Dun here has a bizarre interest in drains."

"Nothing bizarre about drains," Nev said. "The intestines of a civilization. You can tell a lot about a people by their drains. What do you want to know?"

"The drain that runs out under the door that goes back home to, what do you call it? Down under? Deep down?"

"Sluice," Nev said.

"Eh?" Dun said.

"Not a drain as such," Nev said.

"Oh?"

"No. A drain is foul water, that water going out is fresh."

"Ah," Dun said. "Who controls it?"

"Now?" Nev said, "Duchy, I reckon."

"Brilliant," Dun said.

"Is it?" Stef said.

"Yeah, it might be," Dun said and marched back to the office to find Bel.

Chapter Fifty-Five

Dun crashed through the door of the office, so it banged against the wall and sat himself down. The meeting in the office abruptly ended.

"Hello?" Bel said.

"I said I was going to think," Dun said.

"Okay," Bel said.

"I've thought," Dun said. "First I've got some more questions."

"Okay," Bel said.

"Myrch," he said.

"Yeeess?" she said.

"He traded me with you?"

"Kind of..." she said.

"You're holding his mate... wife?" Dun said.

"No," Bel said, on the back foot now. "Wait. Right, folks meeting adjourned," she said to the others in the room.

As they filed out, she said, "Tam, not you."

"Okay," he said.

"Right," Dun said. "So you haven't got Myrch's wife?"

"No..." Bel said.

"Did he know that?"

"Not exactly..."

"Wow, you really are a piece of work, aren't you?"

"Hey!"

"You know he died trying to get me to you?"

"No... I'm sorry."

"Not though, are you?"

"I liked him," she said.

"Gods help the poor folk you don't like," Dun said. "Who's got her: his wife, I mean?"

"The Duchy."

"Okay. Right, if you want me to help you, I want you to help me first."

"What?" Bel said. "I don't make deals."

"Sure you do," Dun said. "You owe Myrch, you owe me."

"I don't owe you anything. We busted you out of prison," Bel said.

"Where I wouldn't have been if you hadn't used your crazy mind-machine on me. I'd rather you'd left me there. At least I knew what the torturers were up to. You want me, you trade."

"Trade what?"

"A mission," Dun said.

"I don't understand."

"Yeah you do, you do this stuff all the time. Sabotage, hit and run, all that kind of stuff."

"I'm listening," Bel said.

"There's a control gate on the water out of the Duchy. Control of that water is starving my people. I want that gate gone."

"Gone how?" Bel said.

"I don't know. You're bright folks. You work it out. It's my price. Do that and I'll serve you in the best way I can for a cycle."

"Hmm," Bel said.

"We could," Tam said, "I mean, it's possible."

"Okay, let's meet up and vote on it," Bel said.

She left the room, muttering.

"I thought she took that rather well," Tam said.

They heard clanging and Bel's shouted tones echoing up and down the corridors announcing the meeting in the landing bay.

"We'd better go down there since you called the meeting!" Tam said.

"I guess we better had," Dun said.

***

They could hear the crowd before they got there. The bustle sounded like fifty percent excitement at the gathering, thirty percent disgruntlement at being interrupted, and the remainder, grumpy apathy. Stef met them at the door.

"This *your* plan then, Dun?" Stef said.

"Yeah, kind of," Dun said.

"Nice." She laughed. "This should be interesting."

Once everyone was in, the clanging noise started again, from over by the dock doors.

"Order, friends, order!" Bel shouted over the din.

The din slowly died down to a murmur. Bel waited but that was as quiet as it was ever going to get. She cleared her throat.

Bel spoke, "Okay, friends, Community-folks. Here's what we need to decide. Young Dun here has a crazy fool plan that he wants us all to join in on."

"Point of order, Chair!" someone shouted from the crowd.

"Yes," Bel said tiredly. "What is it, Dory?"

"With respect, you're condemning his plan before we've heard it," Dory said.

"Hear hear!" another voice shouted.

"And," Dory went on, "we're behaving in a rather unconstitutional manner. Surely the motion should be proposed and so on before we discuss it and vote on it?"

"Right."

Murmurs from the crowd rose up. Bel sighed and carried on. "All right, Order! Who's going to propose this motion?"

"Me?" Dun said.

"No," Bel said, "You can't, you're not Community."

"I will!" came Stef's voice from out of the crowd.

"Okay. Seconder?"

There was a slightly longer silence.

Tam spoke, "I'll second him."

Bel hissed breath out.

"Let him speak!" Dory shouted.

"Okay," Bel said. "Take the stand."

The stand turned out to be an upturned packing crate wedged in front of the door. Dun clambered up onto it and turned toward the expectant murmur.

"Err... Hi, I'm Dun. Thank you for hearing me. I'm a long way from home. My people, I guess, the Under-folk you call them, live a long way away from you. In real walking distance but also in culture. But we are relations, cousins even. You called me here with your projector machine, and I came. Now I'm here, I need your help."

"How?" someone yelled out.

"The Duchy have control of the water that goes to my people. They have been reducing the flow slowly and are starting to cut it off. If that happens, no fish. No fish, no food. I want you to help me get that valve turned back on again."

"What's in it for us?" a new voice from the back.

"Honestly?" Dun said. "Not much, except the gratitude of the Bridge-folk. And I guess everyone else who uses the river."

"And the chance to strike a blow to the Duchy!" a woman shouted below where Dun stood.

"Yes, Dasha!" someone else nearby said.

"It sounds dangerous to me," Dory said.

"I think it will be," Dun said.

"Make it all volunteers only then," Stef said. "I'm in."

A few more murmurs of agreement.

"Okay," Bel said, "so the proposal is that we let Dun, who is not Community, help arrange a mission to strike at the water outlet from the Duchy and that it should be volunteers only? Is that correct."

"Yes,"

"Let's move to a vote then," she said. "All those in favor shout yes."

A loud shout rang out.

"All those against shout no."

One or two shouts.

"Motion carried. Volunteers for the mission in the briefing room straight away," Bel said.

She turned to Dun. "Well little, Dun. You have your wish. I hope it goes how you plan it, and I hope you plan it well. We can't afford to lose anyone."

"Aren't you coming?" he asked.

Chapter Fifty-One

"No," she said. "And neither are you. You're going to wind up chair of this little excursion."

"You don't trust me," he said.

"No, oddly I do," she said. "You're young and naive, but I think you are trustworthy. Let's hope that's enough to stop you getting anyone killed."

Dun waited patiently in the briefing room. Tam had already said he would volunteer and had brought some water and cups. They waited. The door creaked.

"Hey," Stef said. "Don't think I'd miss all the fun, do ya? Oh, and Dasha will be along in a moment with some of her cohorts."

"Have you been canvassing?" Dun said.

"Maybe," Stef said with a smirk in her voice. "To be honest though, Dash doesn't need much persuading to a scrap."

"Hmm..." Dun said.

"So you got a plan?" Stef said.

"Not really," Dun said. "I don't know the place as well as you folk. I was hoping I might be able to use some local knowledge and we could formulate one."

"I think I may be able to help there," Nev said from the doorway.

"Oh, hi, Nev," Stef said. "Come and sit down."

"Dasha's behind me," he said.

And she was, with three more folk that she didn't introduce. They followed her in sullen silence.

"We begin now?" Dasha said.

"I think that's probably everyone," Dun said. "So as I kind of said before, we want to open the door that lets the water out to the Under-folk."

"It's a sluice," Nev said.

"Thanks! Sluice. That's why I need the local knowledge!" Dun said. "So how might we open it?"

"Well," Nev said, "we could find the plans of the sewer system and... locate the valve, then..."

Dark

"Pah!" Dasha said. "Know how we should open it?"

Everyone in the room knew Dasha well enough to recognize a rhetorical question when one was asked. Dun was too scared to reply.

"Permanently! We should go with picks and smash it."

"Okay... good suggestion. Anything more practical?" Tam said gingerly.

"It is an excellent suggestion!" Dasha said. There were grunts of assent from her cohort. The first sounds they had made.

"Yes," Nev said, "but while we are busy smashing, along come the Duchy militia and pick us off like rats."

There was a brief pause, underscored by muttering from Dasha's camp.

"Hmm..." Stef said. "I might be able to improve the smashing plan."

"Go on," Dun said.

"Well... I've just recently got my storeroom filled with explosives from our pillaging comrades."

There was sniggering in the ranks.

"They might be put to good use?" Stef said.

"Do you know how to time them?" Tam said.

"Yes!" Stef said in hurt tones.

"How might we deliver them?" he said.

"Dunno," Stef said. "Hadn't got that far."

"Where does the sluice water run on this side?" Dun said.

"I've got a map of it somewhere," Nev said, got up from his chair and crashed out of the room.

"Always keen when someone takes interest in his drains," Stef said.

More sniggering.

"What are you thinking then, Dun?" Tam asked.

"Have we got a boat?" he said.

"Don't use 'em much around here," Stef said.

"Could we knock one together?" Dun said. "Only needs to be some kind of flat-bottomed raft."

"Won't be a problem," Stef said.

"These explosives, could they go off by a *where* and not a when?" Dun said.

"I suppose," Stef said.

"Then can we sail the boat all the way to the sluice and..."

"Boom," Dasha said.

"Yeah," Dun said, "boom."

"Okay," Tam said. "I reckon if Stef and I spend the rest of the cycle building and collecting gear, and Nev goes over the plans with Dun and Dasha so we can work out which way to attack from. Meet back here before sleep-cycle to check on progress?"

"Sure."

"Great."

"Later."

By the next meal break, Dun had established that there was a plausible route for the boat to take. There seemed to be a vent shaft above the causeways they'd escaped through, and Dasha said she had access to a glide-car that could get them there. It seemed the tech crew knew what they were doing raft building, and Stef could concentrate on explosives and detonators after meal break. After a good-natured meal and a reasonable amount of banter, the company broke up again in order to pile into their allocated tasks.

Dun had an itching feeling under his scalp about the whole thing while he was eating. It was only once he had finished and they got back to the conference room and they restarted that he began to realize what he had been bothered about.

"So we are done now?" Dasha said.

"Hmm... I'm not sure," Dun said.

"Why?" said Dasha. "We have a boat, we have a bomb, we have a shaft, we have a glide-car. What more do we need?"

"My problem is... Well, once the boat reaches the bottom of the shaft, how far does it need to go to reach the sluice, Nev?"

"One hundred fifty maybe a hundred sixty strides," he said. Dun liked Nev a lot. In an uncertain world, Nev was within a small frame of reference, completely certain.

"You understand my issue?" Dun said.

"No, elucidate," Dasha said.

"Well, for a thousand or so strides, the bobbing boat swishes along to its target. And then how do we make sure no one fishes it out of the water? If that happens, then it just doesn't go off."

"Easy," Dasha said. "We booby trap the boat and boom!"

"Yeah," Dun said, "but we don't really complete the mission, do we?"

"We cause chaos and disruption! Sounds good."

Dun sighed. "Look, if you want me to command this mission, you need to understand we're aiming to complete it, not just to wreak random havoc."

"Why not random havoc?" Dasha said.

"Because then the Duchy will not think that you are anything to contend with, and they will move to crush you. If you are organized, hit strategic targets hard, aim to reduce casualties, you are increasing the Duchy's fear of you and removing the sympathy they'd get from you killing innocent people."

"No guards are innocent," Dasha said.

"Aren't they?" Dun said.

"I don't think so, no."

"Well, we do it my way, or no way."

Dasha humphed.

"Besides," Dun said, "there's no fight here. Doesn't that bore you?"

Silence.

"Well," Dun said, "my thought is that we need is a distraction."

"Ah!" Dasha said.

"If we were to attack somewhere else when the boat touched down, then it's passage would be smoothed," Dun said.

"Where?" Dasha said.

Dark

"I don't know," Dun said. "Where does the watercourse pass, Nev?"

"Cellblock?" Nev said.

"Perfect!" Dun said.

So they added flesh to the bones of the plan. It seemed that the easiest thing was to lower some folk down the shaft first to check the boat and ensure it was going to sail right. That party had to include Stef to provide final checks. Then the party from the top doing the lowering. A party doing the distracting in the cell block, surely the noisiest and most dangerous part of the mission, as it would attract the attention of the militia if it worked. Dun figured this was where he should be since it was all his idea in the first place. It would be impossible to keep Dasha from this bit, although it seemed like her own faction followers would be spread thin if each party was to be guarded properly. Organizing a mission was starting to give Dun a headache. At that point, Tam came in with fresh hot drinks and some kind of salty tasting fresh wraps. He touched Dun's shoulder.

"You okay?" he said.

"Yeah, thanks," Dun said, and then to his party, he said, "Break time, folks. Five hundred clicks or so. Don't go too far"

"Going well?" Tam said.

"Yeah, I think so, just sorting who's going to go where and when."

"Always a tricky bit," Tam said.

"We need to split our forces and have a distraction," Dun said once the room had emptied.

"Sounds sensible," Tam said.

"I was going to go with them."

"That sounds less sensible."

"Oh?" Dun said.

"Well," Tam said, "with the best will ever. Who's going to communicate your mission, and it is *your* mission, if you're dead? No water, no fish, and no one here really cares."

"Your point?"

"Woah," Tam said, "get you, suicide mission guy. You want to bring as many people back as you can and get your mission completed. If it's worth completing, then you do it from the recording room."

"Recording room?"

"Where we monitor and record the inputs of all the Duchy sensors, and we can receive sound from all of our agents and transmit to them too. Coordinate, if you will."

"Okay, I think," Dun said. "Although we're still perfecting our distraction."

"What else is down that neck of the pipe then?" Tam said.

"The cells for one," Dun said.

"Job done then, surely?" Tam said. "We organize a jailbreak."

"Are they not used to you guys sneaking folk out of there all the time?" Dun said.

"Oh, sure," Tam said, "Not exactly used to it. Mostly, they hate it, but we still get away with it!"

"So they're going to fall for that?"

"No, we'll have to use different tactics."

The door opened.

"Blow them up!" Dasha said.

"Boom..." everybody said.

Chapter Fifty-Seven

The last meeting that span was a sober affair; checking and rechecking that everyone had covered all the bases. Dasha's plan for the explosive jailbreak seemed too crazy to be true, but the idea of checking who was inside first with a small force of armed folk, and then blowing away the outside walls of the jail seemed like it had too many useful side effects to not be carried out anyway. Dun sighed and concurred. The whole planning process had too much damn exploding in it for him to be entirely happy with it. After all, he'd spent a lot of time with Tali. Gods, what he wouldn't give for her advice right now.

The boat part of the plan was a quite ramshackle affair, but Dun, having spent most of his youth in ramshackle aquatic craft, was quite at home with that. Having had a go of the raft in a test tank, a boat was too grand a term for it really. Still Dun was relatively happy with it. The team provided as muscle by Dasha seemed to have some kind of flair for raft assembly.

Dark

That left the crux of the operation: the explosives. Stef had done a fine job designing the mechanism by which an adapted spear at the front of the craft would trigger an explosion, only when a prior "arm" signal had been given to a small radio control strapped to the front of the raft. Again a demo of this in the test tank was given with a loud beep instead of the explosion. A large round of applause broke the nervous tension when the test worked perfectly. Stef had also rigged a number of packets of explosive to detonators and explosives with a short-timed trigger that had ten clicks worth of beeping then a sizable explosion. This provided the biggest round of applause of the demo, even though the test explosion was rigged using a weighted package right at the bottom of the tank. It satisfyingly "whoomphed" and lifted so much water that everyone in the demo party went back to the canteen wet.

The time for the raid was arranged: straight after sleep-cycle. They all retired to the canteen and some vine-fizz was broken out and everyone drank heartily. Dun's head was starting to swim, not just with the effects of the fizz.

"Hey, good work in there today," Stef said from his elbow.

"Same to you," he said.

"Engineer," she said, "it's what we do."

"Very clever though, and while supervising Dasha's lot at the same time."

"They didn't turn out too bad once I'd shouted at them a few times to stop them fighting," she said.

"Fighting seems to be what they do best," Dun said.

"Ain't that a good job?" Stef said.

"Suppose so," Dun said.

The party was becoming rowdier. Dun worried about how much sleep everyone was going to get.

"Wanna go to bed?" Stef said.

"You still using that mind reading thing?" Dun said.

"No!" Stef said, mock offended. "Engineer's honor. Come on."

"But if we both go back at once, where will we sleep? There's only one bunk."

"For someone who might make a quite good leader, you can be awfully dim." She laughed and grabbed his hand.

Dun was led through the back of the crowd who were building up for a rousing chorus of something extremely rude. They went back through the door to the barracks corridor and the couple of doors down to Stef's room. She kicked the door open and, still holding Dun's hand, swung him in, toed the door shut, and gently deposited him against the bed. She pushed. He fell.

"Hey, wait!" he said as she climbed onto the bed astride him.

"Wait, what?" she said dreamily.

"If we... What about... Aren't you worried about pups?"

She laughed heartily. He liked her laugh, full-throated, sincere.

"Ain't you old fashioned? We've got stuff to prevent that now."

"But we hardly know each other..."

"You really do make me laugh, you know. We aren't getting mated. Just, you know, doing it. If you want to." She sounded unsure for the first time.

"No, I want to. I really want to, but it's—you're different."

"And you're sweet. Living here, it's all a bit "anything goes", especially the night before a raid."

"Don't people have mates then?" Dun said.

"Sure they do, sometimes. Bringing up pups, sometimes. Sometimes just because. But we don't have to; pups are brought up by everyone anyway. We have to have lots of parents, y'know, in case."

Dun scratched his knee, reaching between Stef's legs.

"Gerrof! That tickles."

And she fell on him, tickling him back, and then nuzzling him. The warmth of her body and her scent made Dun feel the happiest he had since he'd left the Bridge.

***

They woke curled around each other and warm. Dun was scared to move, scared to break the moment. He felt warm breath against his neck, and her heart beating against his spine. Gods, she smelled good. Then there was the rough rasp of an alarm going off. Stef reached out an arm, batted whatever piece of tech had made the horrible noise and beat it into silence.

She turned over and kissed Dun briefly on the nose.

"You're up, kid. Good luck," she said.

"You too."

"Go!" she said. "Get outta here. I'll be there over breakfast and briefing."

He left. He walked the corridors hearing the bustle that, this time, he had created. He found himself at the canteen, not entirely remembering the trip that got him there. He collected things to eat and something hot and bitter to drink. He was pretty sure they were the same things he had yesterday. He ate silently.

A bell clanged from the doorway and Tam's voice followed it. "Briefing room in five hundred clicks for anyone who's going on the sluice mission!"

Dun thought he'd better be in there first and made his way to the doorway. Stef squeezed past him and pinched his bum on the way past.

"Hey, you, sorry I'm late. Stuff to sort! I'll grab a drink and be straight in."

"I miss you."

Excerpts from <Distress Beacon SN-1853001>.
Found by E.S.V Vixen Terradate: 26102225

Dark

Chapter Fifty-Eight

The meeting came to order quickly. To Dun, the group felt nervous, no banter or joking. Focused concentration. Tam took the chair. It felt like Dun had lost control of this already. In many ways he was glad. He lowered his nose into the steaming cup sitting before him on the table and let the plan that he was already very familiar with flow over him, as narrated by Tam. The only news to Dun was that Tam had insisted on each team having code names. This was all a bit bizarre sounding to Dun, but he figured the locals knew best. The raft team were called Fish, the team flying the glide-car, Bee, and the jailbreak team, Rat. The base team were called Nest. There were few additions to the plan. Team Rat had purloined more explosive from Stef and tied it into neat bundles with a ten click fuse. Dasha had claimed this was because the Rat party had the most dangerous job. Dun figured her to say that, whatever mission she was offered.

Team Rat needed to leave first as they had the most of the traveling to do to be in the passage closest to the cells when Team Fish arrived with the raft. Everyone else crowded into the packed communications room for Tam to test out the radio links.

"Nest to Rat, Nest to Rat, do you receive, over?" Tam said in a tone of voice that implied that he'd done this a thousand times before.

There was a pause, fifty clicks or so Dun thought, and then the reply came from a loudspeaker over Tam's head.

"Rat to Nest, you're coming through nice and crisp," Dasha said. "We are on schedule here with no hold ups, over."

"Nice to hear that, Dasha. Good luck. Nest, out."

"Does a signal always take that long?" Dun said to Tam.

Dark

"No," he said, "it's instant, but sometimes folk take a while to find the right button to reply if they've not used the kit for a while."

"Oh!" Dun said and giggled.

"Dasha's lucky if she can find it at all while she's busy ordering everyone about," Nev said from the doorway. It raised a flurry of sniggers.

"What happens now?" Dun said.

"Bee and Fish teams get ready in the launch bay, and we go get a hot drink and something to eat while we wait for Team Rat to reach checkpoint one," Tam said. "You coming?"

"Will they take long?" Dun asked.

"All being well, no. Quarter span or so? No point us all waiting around here though. We'll leave one radio tech to listen while we stand down for a bit."

So stand down they did. Dun grabbed a quick drink and then went to loiter in the launch bay, but soon realized with the craziness going on in there, that he would only be in the way. He retreated to the control room where at least he could hear what was going on. When he arrived the radio tech switched on the overhead speaker again. Dun imagined some kind of headset was used for the rest of the time.

"Team Bee, radio check, over." Nev's voice came through the speaker.

"Nest hearing you clearly, Bee, over," the radio tech replied.

"And, Team Fish radio check, please, Nest," It was Stef's voice. Dun's heart leaped.

"Nest to Fish, hearing you fine. Remember to call over please, over."

"Sorree," Stef said. "Over."

"Smart-ass," the radio-tech said under his breath.

Then there was static over the radio, and then silence. Dun shifted his weight from foot to foot, drained the rest of his drink, and was just about to take his cup back when the radio crackled into life again.

"Rat at check-point one, request confirmation, over."

"Nest receiving, Rat. Stand-by, over" Then over his shoulder to Dun, he said, "Can you go and haul Tam out of the canteen? Quickly, please."

"Sure," Dun said, already on his way.

Tam was in the doorway of the canteen, so they nearly collided.

"Rat at point one," Dun said.

"Thanks," Tam said.

Back at the control room, the radio tech said, "Good, you're here, Tam. Team Rat at checkpoint one requesting confirmation of mission."

"Tell them they're good to go," Tam said.

"Nest to Rat, you are clear to proceed to check-point two, over."

"Rat here, proceeding to two, thanks, over."

Tam took control of the console and spoke, "This is Nest to Teams Bee and Fish, final checks, departure in two hundred clicks. Bay technicians, standby doors. Militia to your posts for *doors open*, please."

Adrenaline started flooding through Dun's system even though he wasn't going anywhere himself. He wished he was. Going and doing seemed much easier than controlling and waiting.

"One hundred clicks..."

"Fifty clicks..."

"Fish to Nest, final checks are done we're good to go... over."

"Bee to Nest, final checks done, also good, over."

Tam said, "Militia stand ready. Doors go."

The familiar whooping alarm of the doors being raised echoed down the corridor from the bay along with a rattling noise of the doors grinding into action and the noise of engines warming up.

"Doors clear, Nest, over."

"Thank you, doors. Bee and Fish you are clear to leave. Gods luck. Over."

"Thank you, fellas, team Fish and Bee are airborne... and we are clear of the doors. Speak to you at checkpoint three. Over."

"Doors close, please, over."

More whooping and rattling, a final clang, and then silence.

"Doors and militia stand down, please, over."

"Doors, over."

"Militia, over."

"And that's us done for now,' Tam said. 'Back to standby and back to the canteen. Coming?"

"Sure," Dun said.

They trundled back and collected a snack bowl of salted dried mushrooms and had water, flavored slightly, but Dun was too tired to tell with what.

"Is it always like that?" Dun asked.

"Like what?" Tam said.

"The missions, raids, whatever they are. Are they always that tense?"

"When you know people on the missions, it's worse. The constant fear you might lose them, and there's not a great deal we can do from up here if we do."

"How do you cope?" Dun said.

"We take it in turns to be mission control, and we look after each other during and after. There's always someone to talk to."

"That's gotta help."

"Sometimes. Other times it just takes a while," Tam said. "It's half a span 'til everyone reaches their next checkpoint. Why don't you cram in some bunk time."

"Good idea," Dun said, although he doubted he'd sleep.

Chapter Fifty-Nine

Dun surprised himself by having slept at least a little. He was still in Stef's bunk. This on account of the fact that she didn't need it right now and therefore no one had to bother themselves to allocate him a new one. When a passing militia-folk knocked on the door on the way past to tell him food was up in the canteen for wake span, he couldn't wait to get there. He hardly tasted the food, gulped down a drink so fast it burned his throat and dashed across to the control room. Tam was already there.

"Hi," Tam said as Dun entered. "Sleep well?"

"Okay. Thanks."

"Good. Ready for an update?"

"Sure."

"Okay. Rat team are at checkpoint two. They're standing by for a signal. Bee Team are having a little trouble with a jammed hatch to the down-pipe that will get them down to the river we need. Stef's busted out some tools to try and help them get in."

"Where'd she get the tools?" Dun said.

"Stef always takes tools," Tam said, matter of factly.

"How long ago did you hear from them?" Dun said.

"Not long, couple of thou clicks, maybe. Stef said she'd be back when she'd cracked it."

"Good. Rat Team have a good trip?"

"No problems," Tam said. "They sent a scout into the prison block for a check through, and although there are one or two maintenance staff, there are no prisoners there to liberate at the moment."

"Oh, that rather puts our liberation distraction plan to the sword, doesn't it?"

"Well, Dash said she'd think of something distracting. Although if I know Dasha, it'll wind up being destructive. Still, we can't argue about finesse at this point now, can we?"

"No, I suppose not," Dun said. "What now?"

"Wait," Tam said.

Dun could smell familiar bitter hot drink fumes, but coming in some volume from the corner of the control room. There was faint bubbling and hissing too now. Dun listened carefully.

"Oh yeah," Tam said. "I had the catering roster put a drink station in the corner of the control room. Figured we'd be here for the long haul. Just don't hover over the consoles when you've got one, okay?"

Despite Dun's aching throat from the last cup, he plodded over to the drink station and felt around to pour himself another one. More to do something with his hands than anything.

The speakers crackled to life. "Bee to Nest, Bee to Nest."

"Nest receiving Bee, send your message, over."

"We are clear to descend the down-pipe, Nest, the door is open," Nev's said over the static.

"Good work, Team Bee!" Tam said.

"Technically, it was Team Fish," Nev's said over the speaker.

"We won't split hairs. Well done, all. Proceed to checkpoint four. Gods' luck."

Tam fiddled with the console in front of him briefly and then turned to Dun.

"They need to sort themselves before they ping us back; there'll be a reasonable amount of sorting the raft and the winch."

"What happens while the winching is taking place?" Dun said.

"Hopefully nothing," Tam said. "But it's when everyone's at their most vulnerable. While the winch is running Team Bee can't move, and they're stuck in position at the top of the shaft. There's a whole team of militia on board, armed to the teeth. They should keep any risk down to a minimum."

"Hopefully," Dun said grimly.

"As you say..." Tam said and left the chair he was sat on for the corner containing the drink equipment.

There was a crackle of static from the loudspeaker and everyone jumped. No communication followed. Tam walked back to the drink station and pulled on the spout. Only air hissed out. He cursed under his breath.

"Where the hells is the catering rota? Come on!"

Someone behind them sighed and then sidled out of the door. Dun could hear cooling fans from Tam's console kick in. Tam went back over, clicked a few controls, and then huffed into a chair at the console, tapping something on the surface in front of him. A few more folk shuffled into the control room and sidled along the back wall.

Another hiss from the speaker. "Bee to Nest, Fish is ready to go. Do we have clearance, over?"

"Thanks, Bee!" Tam said. "You're clear to proceed!"

"Received and understood, Nest. Proceeding to positions for phase two, over."

"Great!" Tam said. "Okay, Nest to Rat standby at phase two positions and wait on my order."

There was a brief pause.

Static. "Rat receiving," Dasha said. "Standing by, over."

There were now intermittent noises over the speakers of the winch from Team Bee. And brief snatches of talkback between Team Bee and Team Fish. Tam adjusted something at the controls and the interference became less.

"Team Bee to Nest."

"Send your message, Bee."

"Half winch line paid out. Five hundred strides left, over."

"Thanks, Bee, proceed, over."

"That thing works fast," Dun said.

"Sure does," Tam said. "Okay, now for our distraction. Nest to Rat."

"Rat receiving, Nest, go ahead."

"Team Rat, phase two go. Repeat, phase two go!"

Dark

"You got it," Dasha said. Then she added, "Over."

There was more brief exchange from the other end, and then a massive boom, followed by sounds of whatever had blown up, coming down again.

"Boom," Dun said.

"Now, let's find out what happens," Tam said.

The noise from the speakers now became more urgent and had shouts from voices that Dun didn't recognize.

"Duchy have arrived," Tam said.

Then came sounds of weapons fire.

"I'm hoping that's Team Rat," Tam said.

"Can't you tell?" Dun said.

"No, not really. It all gets a bit chaotic at this point."

"Oh," Dun said.

More weapons fire. Someone shouted in pain. Then a loud chorus of yells and the level of noise rose considerably. Dun noticed an ache in his hands, then realized he'd been clenching the edge of his chair for, how long? 500 clicks or so?

"I reckon they've found each other now," Tam said. "Come on... Where are you?"

"Fish to Nest," Stef's voice came over the speaker. "Fish touched down, proceeding with phase two, over."

"Received, Fish. Team Rat is on phase two now. Gods' luck."

"Thanks, Nest!" she said brightly. Dun released his grip on the chair.

More weapons fire, and then a huge shout and a cheer, certainly featuring the voice of Dasha. More fracas followed and another brief explosion. There were more cheers, and then a new burst of weapons fire.

"Rat to Nest! All done here. No one to rescue, small amount of resistance. Eliminated. And we wrecked that silly torture office, over."

More weapons fire and some shouts were heard.

"Gods," Tam said. "That shooting's coming from Fish. Damn."

"No," Dun said.

"Nest to Rat," Tam said. "Fish has come under fire up the tunnel. Anything Team Rat can to to help out? Over."

"On our way, Nest. Hold tight Team Fish. Over."

The weapons fire became more intense. Dun was sure he heard a shout from Stef. There was certainly more desperation to the sounds as well as an increase in volume. Dun hoped the rescuing Rat Team weren't too far away.

"Stop pacing and sit down, Dun!" Tam said.

"Sorry."

There was a change in noises; something new, a deep thudding, followed by splashes and crashes. A hiss broke through the speakers.

"Under heavy ... ungh... They've got ... kind of... heavy slug firer... Damn, we're gonna be in shreds if we don't get back-up... Gods!"

A huge splintering noise and a splash rent the speakers.

"Rat to Fish, we're nearing your position."

"Fish to Rat, can you hurry the hell up, or there'll be no one here to save!"

More splashes, swearing, and cries of pain. Dun felt like he needed to cover his ears.

"Rat to Fish, we've got you. Let's find out what we can do about those heavy guns," Dasha said.

Lighter weapons fire joined the orchestra of destruction hammering through the speakers, and then a crazed whooping cry and an explosion.

"Boooooom!" Dasha shouted over the radio, her voice distorted.

The heavy gun did not sound again and the battle descended into sporadic light weapons fire. When the melee died down, Tam stopped hopping from foot to foot and ran back to the console.

"Teams Fish and Rat, this is Nest, report!"

Dark

"Team Rat here, Nest. We have isolated the resistance pockets for the time being. The heavy gun installation has been neutralized. We have sustained losses but nothing we can't cope with."

"How many of your team are there left, Rat?" Tam said.

"Two, but we'll be fine to help cover," Dasha said.

"Team Fish, report," Tam said.

"Hey, Nest," Stef said and coughed. "We took some hits on the raft with all that heavy slug-fire. We need to off-load the raft. I'm pretty sure it'll only take the charge and one folk onboard at once."

"Can you float it and let the timer take it?" Tam said.

"Well... the thing is"—she stopped for another coughing fit—"that's the worst of it. The whole electrics package is shot to hell. Took a direct hit. Half a stride farther up the raft, and we'd have all gone up."

"What do we do now if the timer's wrecked?" Dun said.

The control room was starting to fill up with the rest of the tribe. Even Bel had come in. Everyone seemed to know something and was holding their tongue behind their teeth.

"What?" Dun said. "What happens now? Tell me."

"Tam?" Stef's voice came from the speaker. "Is that Dun? Put him on."

Someone pushed Dun forward, and Tam gently guided him to a high stool in front of the console. As he sat, his feet left the floor. Tam placed a metal band on his head that covered his ears with a curved arm that reached in front of his face. Immediately he could hear in great detail all the goings on in the tunnel at the Duchy's entrance. He could almost smell the debris in the water. He could hear Stef's breathing, heavy and very close up.

"Hey," he said.

"Hey, yourself. Tam, mute those control room speakers, can't you?"

"Sure," Tam said and reached past Dun to flick a switch. The noises over their heads above the console cut out.

"Better," she said and broke into coughing again.

"You okay?" Dun said.

"No, not really," she said.

"Are you..."

"Shush. And listen. That raft's got a bomb on it, and its timer is all broke up. I can set it off manually, and I'm the only one who can."

"But..."

"Shush already," she said half wince, half laugh, "Dun, I'm not going to make it back either way."

"We c...could abandon the mission," Dun said. "Get you some help."

"We've got it all down here, Dun. There may not be another chance to do this. Remember how many lives you told us this would save? That hasn't changed."

"But I don't want ..."

"No, I don't want either kid... but there you go."

"Stef?"

"Uh-huh."

"I... um, I err."

"I know, kid."

More coughing, then she spat. "Hey, Dun?"

"Yeah?"

"It was fun, right?"

"Yeah..."

"Yeah. Put Tam back on."

Dun turned in the seat, but all of the control room had emptied.

"Tam!"

He came back from the doorway and flicked the switch over again and the hiss returned over their heads.

"I've not got much... time here, Tam. Let's do this," Stef said.

'Sure?" Tam said.

"Mmm-hmm," Stef said.

"Okay. You got any of your team left, Stef?"

"Negative, Tam. We lost Nev and the two vent-techs in that last exchange. Just me, Dash, and her other fella."

Tam made some kind of noise in his throat. "Okay, Dasha, am I right in remembering that where you are there's a walkway either side of the sluice channel?"

"That is correct."

"Okay," Tam said. "Rat Team split up. One of you on either side of the sluice and cover the raft. Keep complete silence unless you hear anything or you're engaged by the enemy."

"Received," Dasha said.

"Gods' luck," Tam said.

The next thousand clicks were the slowest Dun had ever experienced in his life. The entire control room waited in silence. Over the speakers was an occasional faint splish of a paddle. No one breathed. A massive explosion took the speakers to their limit, and then they just cut out. Tam tapped some controls and the relay cut in again in time to hear tonnes and tonnes of stonework falling back to earth and a sound that brought so many emotions to Dun at once that he froze: gushing. Gallons and gallons of water gushing in great gouts. Even over the noises of falling debris, he could hear it pouring billowing out of the ruptured machinery made to contain it.

Dun fell to his knees and heard his own voice echoing around the control room, laughing. Laughing so hard he couldn't stop. So hard the tears ran down his face.

Chapter Sixty

Dun didn't emerge from Stef's room for five whole spans. The nervous folk from the catering rota who were tasked with sending him food sometimes heard talking, sometimes crying. More often than not they heard nothing and never did he respond to their calls or eat any of the food they brought. The remainder of the Rat Team returned muted, but intact. They had even had the foresight to get the floater working again and collected that. Various parties of folk in various numbers were sent to try and talk to Dun. After span three they stopped trying except for food.

Finally, at the end of span five after the catering team had left the usual tray of food and water, on their way back to the galley they heard the door to the room open, and then shut. Later they found the tray empty in the corridor.

The following span, the team got there to find the door already open and Dun not inside.

In the conference room, Tam and Bel were deep in conversation with Dasha and several other folk from various disciplines. As Dun entered, the room went silent.

"Okay," he said. "Tell me about your war."

THE END

Dark

Next... Darker

Can Dun help stop a War? The problem is, he started it.

Dun didn't want to be a hero and the war has cost him dearly: his friends, his innocence. Maybe his mind.

Now he's a fully-fledged Shaman, Dun's mind is a receiver for those who can transmit, but what will he do when starts getting messages from someone who's dead.

Dun's new powers might allow his Underfolk, victory. But he must quiet the demons inside his head, and find his oldest friends Tali and Padg if they stand a chance of defeating the merciless Rowle of the Cat-People. And she is about to release demons of her own.

Read on for a taste or buy now!
paularvidson.co.uk/find-books

Chapter One

Padg and Tali huddled in their den above the main market of the Stone-folk behind the *hiding shield* that they'd found before they parted company with Dun. It had taken great care and time to find such a good hiding place, but after Padg's insistence they not rush in and do some reconnaissance first he felt obliged to find somewhere good. It was an odd, tall, and thin metal room in the wall between the grand entrance to the Stone-halls. It smelled like rust. All the action from the market floor could be heard from high up metal grills in one side of the room and the main river was accessed by a hatch via a flooded water pipe on the opposite side. Padg thought they were impossible to surprise.

"I'm wet and tired," Padg said. "Is this the bit where we get to go home?"

"No, this is the bit where I murder you for whining, and your lifeless corpse floats back to Bridgetown. Now shut up, I'm counting," Tali said.

They had fashioned a listening horn from some thin sheet metal Padg had found. By tweaking its direction it was possible to pick up a reasonable amount of sound from all around the central cavern and some of the passages. Tali listened to interactions at the main entrance as the Stone-guard filtered goods and folk in. It was all mostly in and not a lot of that. The guards outnumbered the civilians two to one. And it was the same everywhere. Curfews had been imposed after Work-cycle. Identification tattoos had become mandatory and were examined at a ridiculous number of checkpoints. Although people still tried to go about their business, no female folk were allowed out without special dispensation. It was eerily quiet, the main noises being new bells rung every cycle to command people to action or to bed and announcements of new edicts from criers. The only thing not curtailed by these new happenings was the regular services of the Tinkralas. Though their hideout backed on to a temple, so they were immersed in the goings on by proximity, if nothing else. Most of their spying had to be done outside of the services as the noisy Tinkrala worship drowned out everything else.

"I'm glad, you know," Padg said.
"What?"
"Glad. To be here. Really."
"Oh good."
"Despite everything, you know?"
"Yeah."
"You know, with, you."
"Oh."
"It's... I'm... I like it."
"Yeah," Tali said. "Yeah, me too. What the hell is that?"
"Pardon?"

Dark

"That chanting? Far side of the market—listen."

When Padg strained, using their bespoke listening horn, he could make out the half chant/half shout just at the edge of his hearing. It came from right over the far side of the massive market hall. Maybe down one of the passages off there even. A repetitive shout.

"What are they saying?" Tali asked.

"No—I think. It sounds like they are saying no. Over and over."

"Sounds female? The voices..."

"Yeah, almost all."

"I wonder if that's where we'll find Amber?"

Since their stakeout to plan a rescue for their Stone-folk friend who'd done so much to help them, they hadn't heard hide nor hair of Amber. Padg, whose sense of smell was the keenest, and as a half decent hunter, hadn't detected so much as a lingering whiff. In the time it took them to return from parting company with Dun, it was like Amber had been spirited away.

"We need a plan to get in there," Tali said.

"Guess so," Padg said. "How?"

"Disguise?"

"O...kay. As what?"

"Mmm...traders?"

"Would have to be River-folk."

"Why?"

"Don't be dense—plan ahead. Can't be Bridge-folk; 'cos—uh, we're at war. Can't be Machine-folk; 'cos they're all dead. Can't carry off being Stone-folk; they'd smell a rat straight away. Would have to be River-folk."

"Think you can carry that off?" Tali asked.

"Whoa there! That 'we' turned into a 'you' quick enough."

"Single trader, easier to hide? Got to be you or me, leaves one of us as backup if anything goes wrong."

"Okay, not instilling me with confidence."

"Come on, Padg. We need to know more to have a chance of rescuing Amber."

"That was your crazy plan, as I remember."

"And you'd leave her to rot in a Stone-folk cell, would you? Or worse."

"Okay! Okay! I'll go."

"My hero."

The next span was punctuated by planning, sleeping, and practicing a decent River-folk accent. From the supplies she had left and the food they had, Tali thought she could compose a half-decent scent. They decided that a scout out of who was where would be advisable first.

"I reckon Dun would like us to add to the map," Padg said.

"Not if it's in your handwriting."

"Harsh."

"Hmm."

Tali repurposed Padg's traveling clothes, much to his dismay, carefully making some fabric cross-gartering for leggings and a makeshift cloak that the River-folk all wore. She finished the ensemble by making a jingling necklace of used flask tops and things she'd collected along the way.

"Bang goes my stealthy approach," Padg said.

"You're a River-folk. You don't give a splosh about stealth. Cocky, remember? Thought you wouldn't have a problem with that bit."

"I used to like you."

"I'm sure my fragile ego can cope. Now, give me your best River-folk."

"Arrrrrrhhh."

"Nice. Gods help us."

A loud clanging of handbells broke the conversation. Then a pause and then the same again. A sudden clamor of noise followed, almost as if someone had thrown a switch and turned the market on.

"Pipe's waiting, River-boy," Tali said.

"Better get at it then," Padg said.

"Hey"—she came toward him—"you really stink."

They embraced then, Padg still holding on, and said, "That's high praise from an Alchemist,"

"Go," Tali said. "You want to get in, in the first rush. Less scrutiny,"

"Yeah, I should."

"Good lu—"

"Won't need it," Padg said.

He climbed through the pipe hatch and was gone. Tali listened hunched at the grill facing the market, listening for signs of him passing through the checkpoint.

Dark

Buy Darker now!

paularvidson.co.uk/find-books

paularvidson.co.uk/find-books

Dark

Newsletter

Join my newsletter for free reads and news about new releases.
paularvidson.co.uk/find-books

SIGN UP TO MY MAILING LIST, INTO THE DARK

AT WWW.PAULARVIDSON.CO.UK/FIND-BOOKS
AND GET A FREE COPY OF

PAUL L ARVIDSON

DARKISH

A VOLUME OF SHORT STORIES SET IN THE DARK UNIVERSE,
FEATURING 'TELLER MAS SCENT DETECTIVE'

Dark

Thank you

You know by now how many people are involved in this, even in a crazy keep it all in-house thing like ours! Top of the list my amazing wife Cheryl, *really* without whom. She's responsible for layout and putting up with me. Then the kids, who inspire me and make me proud every day. To the editorial genius at Write Divas and especially Lauren Schmelz – thank you! To all the fantastic people who've inspired me to think I can: James Yarker and all the beautiful people at Stans Cafe Theatre, Paul Magrs, F. D. Lee, Chella Ramanan and all the folks at Taunton Writers Anon, especially Martine Ashe.

To the people who kept me going in the process: Little Bridge House Hospice, Swan UK, Claire Goodman, Musgrove Park Compass Team, Tina Hill-Art, Team Nenna, Emma Corless (and all the other Ainscough-Halliwell-Corlesses), Ali Bibby.

And to you, for reading it and sharing it, thank you.

Printed in Poland
by Amazon Fulfillment
Poland Sp. z o.o., Wrocław